CHRISTMAS IN MARSEILLE

PETER CHILD

Benbow Publications

© Copyright 2004 by Peter Child

Peter Child has asserted his right under the Copyright, Designs and Patents Act, 1988 to be identified as the author of this work.

All rights reserved. No part of this publication may be reproduced, stored in a retrieval system, or transmitted in any form or by any means, electronic, mechanical photocopying, recording or otherwise without the prior permission of the copyright owner.

Published in 2004 by Benbow Publications
Willow Springs, Cranfield, Bedford, MK43 0DS

British Library
Cataloguing in Publication Data.

ISBN : 0-9540910-3-5

Printed by Lightning Source UK Limited,
6 Precedent Drive, Rooksley,
Milton Keynes, MK13 8PR

First Edition

THE MICHEL RONAY TRILOGY

MARSEILLE TAXI

AUGUST IN GRAMBOIS

CHRISTMAS IN MARSEILLE

OTHER TITLES BY THE AUTHOR

VEHICLE PAINTER'S NOTES

VEHICLE FINE FINISHING

VEHICLE FABRICATIONS IN G.R.P.

NOTES FOR GOOD DRIVERS

Characters and events portrayed in this book are fictional.

ACKNOWLEDGEMENTS

Once again, I wish to gratefully acknowledge the help and assistance given to me by Sue Gresham, who edited and set out the book, and Wendy Tobitt for the splendid cover presentation. Without these talented and patient ladies this book would not have been possible.

Peter Child

INTRODUCTION

Marseille, second only to Paris in size and the premier French Port, is a bustling, lively city with millions of its population always hurrying around in search of a good income, good food and plenty of sex. At Christmas time, everyone seems to hurry that little bit faster and the taxi drivers do their very best to accommodate the demand at the correctly inflated Christmas rates. Michel Ronay, well known as a taxi driver and respected by the police, gangsters, prostitutes, gays and his mistresses, does all he can to serve the good citizens of Marseille in their quest to get around the overcrowded city at the best possible profit. Sadly, however, people and events beyond his control often plummet him into an abyss from which, so often, there seems little hope of escape. Luckily, he has his second wife, Monique to rely on for support, as well as her son, Frederik, her Mother, her two aunts, her cousin Henri and his wife from Le Touquet; all of whom are coming to stay at Christmas……..and Michel wishes that they were not!

CHAPTER 1

Monday 15th December

It is always very cold in Marseille at Christmas time. The Mistral blows down from the Alps and grips the city like a frozen iron hand and it surprises visitors to see the change from the blistering summer heat to the icy clear atmosphere. Many people assume the South of France is always hot.

Michel Ronay was wrapped in his short suede coat over the top of the thick jumper that Monique had bought after they returned from their August holiday in Grambois. It had been an unsettling month, several of Michel's mistresses had become a little too demanding and the fire had not helped. The accidental shooting of Cyril Gerrard, a plain clothes Gendarme, in the back of Michel's taxi whilst they were following Claude Salvator, a high profile gangster and drug smuggler, also dampened the holiday. Still, such is life, and from September until now, the fortnight before Christmas, the taxi business had been good and Michel had made plenty of money. As it was strictly a cash business he declared only half to the tax authorities, he always felt that was the right balance to be fair to both parties. He retained large amounts of cash in his safe deposit box lodged with the Banque du Sumaris just off the Bourse. He was a regular visitor to the strong room and always recognised and greeted by the bank staff.

Much had happened since August and it looked like events might well come to a head over Christmas, this concerned Michel as it was a very busy time and there were endless opportunities to make extra money over and above the income he had as a taxi driver. He did not wish to be deflected from those opportunities by demanding mistresses, wounded Gendarmes, gangsters or the myriad of friends and acquaintances. Michel had a deep sense of unease as he left his flat in Montelivet, crossed over the road to his garage and started up his white Mercedes taxi. It was a cold bright morning and the diesel engine spun over on the starter a little longer than usual before it clattered into life.

He drove down to le Vieux Port and parked in his station. He bought a paper and some cigarettes from the nearby kiosk and settled back in the Mercedes to glance at the headlines and relax for a moment before the day began.

He had just turned the first page when a tap on his window made him look up. René, his best friend, smiled in at him. He wound down his window.

"René"

"Ça va, Michel?"

"Bon."

"Are you in the Christmas spirit yet?" demanded René.

"Non, mon ami, not with my problems."

"Michel, you're the luckiest man I know and you have no problems, other than those you make for yourself!"

"Me?"

"Oui."

"Make problems for myself?"

"Oui."

"René, you haven't been listening to what I've been telling you since August."

"Yes I have."

"Was the fire at Grambois my fault?"

"Well, er, no I suppose not."

"Was I responsible for shooting that idiot Gerrard in the back of this taxi?"

"Well, no, I …."

"And what about Salvator, was it me who let the bastard escape?"

"No."

"Correct, everything that has happened to me has been the fault of other people and they've involved me in their problems."

René nodded, he realised that Michel had a valid point. His friend did seem to have more than his fair share of serious adventures.

"Because silly Gerrard and his bunch failed to arrest Salvator, I reckon that I'm on top of his hit list and where ever he is I expect he's planning my untimely end this very minute."

"Do you think you'll live to see Christmas?" asked René seriously.

"I hope so!"

"So do I" replied René gravely.

Suddenly a fare arrived in the form of a middle aged man in a grey suit carrying a briefcase.

He climbed into the back of the Mercedes and slammed the door very hard so the car vibrated. 'Why do some people do that?' wondered Michel as he enquired "Monsieur?"

"La Plaine, driver."

"Oui, Monsieur."

Michel started up, waved to René and swung out of the rank and into la Canebiére, the main boulevard up from le Vieux Port.

La Plaine is a large square near the top of la Canebiére where the Arabs have a bustling market. Everything imaginable can be bought there after a short period of barter and although much of the merchandise is either poor quality or of uncertain ownership, good bargains could be had.

As the Mercedes progressed up la Canebiére, Michel ventured some conversation "Christmas shopping, Monsieur?"

The was a pause and the man stared at the interior mirror where their eyes met.

"Non" he replied with the clear message that polite and enquiring conversation was not an option.

The journey continued in silence and Michel turned his thoughts towards plans for the day. He had to see Josette tonight to discuss her move into the flat that she had rented for them to live in as soon as Michel left Monique, his second wife. He was glad that Josette was leaving Claude Salvator's flat where she had lived ever since she came to Marseille. He wished to distance himself from this gangster and was certain that Salvator held him totally responsible for the arrest of his father, Edward, at Bandol last August. As far as Michel was concerned, Salvator was right, he had informed Gerrard and the trap was set but Claude escaped and that would almost certainly lead to Michel's murder unless he could hide somewhere. Perhaps he could stay with Aunt Alexis at her villa in Orange. Salvator could not know about that. Michel felt a little better.

He swung the taxi off la Canebiére and into the side street full of badly parked cars that led onto La Plaine. He stopped as close as he could in the crowd and the man paid his fare and got out. He slammed the door harder this time and Michel's ears hummed for a moment.

As he was reversing slowly he became aware of someone tapping on his window and heard a voice he recognised.

"Michel, Michel..."

He stopped the taxi and turned to see the smiling face of Sayid, his Arab friend, with whom he did business. Their relationship had worked well for many years despite the fact that they only ever seemed to break even on all their deals.

"Are you going back to le Vieux Port?" enquired Sayid.

"Oui, jump in."

Sayid joined him in the front of the Mercedes "do you know who that man is?" he enquired.

"What man?"

"The fare you just dropped."

"No, should I know him?"

"I think he's something to do with Trading Standards."

"Oh, great, now all your friends up here will think I've brought him to spy on them!"

"Possibly, but I'll have a word on your behalf."

"Thanks."

"Now then, I've got some things that will interest you, Michel."

"No more Romanian sandals I hope, I've still got loads in Grambois that I haven't sold yet."

"No, quality Christmas cards, boxed and ready to sell."

"How much?"

"I'm not telling you until after you've seen them, they're that good. I also have some T-shirts and jeans"

"I'm not interested in that sort of thing."

"Wait until you've seen them."

"So it's home to your flat then is it?"

"If you want to see the best bargains this year."

Michel smiled as he drove down la Canebiére to le Vieux Port. 'Best bargains this year' he thought 'just like the Romanian sandals with the left shoe bigger than the right and in some cases, the other way round'. He smiled again when he remembered the lovely women on 'Lucrecia', Tony's yacht, naked and stumbling about in the sandals, breasts and bottoms wobbling. He sweated a little. Michel turned off at le Vieux Port and made his way into the Arab Quarter and pulled up outside Sayid's flat with its cracked plaster walls and faded green shutters. He followed Sayid into the dim interior and closed the door. Sayid produced a red box from a large brown cardboard packing case in the corner and presented it to Michel with a flourish.

"There, what do you think of those then?" he enquired.

Michel opened the box and took out a Christmas card which had an elegant Dickensian winter scene of a stagecoach up to its axles in snow on the front and inside read *'NAPPY CHRISTMAS'*

"What's nappy Christmas?" he asked.

"It's English" replied Sayid.

"Well it should be in French, Joyeux Noël."

"English is the in thing this year, it's all the rage and very sophisticated" replied Sayid.

"But this is wrong; it should say 'Happy Christmas'."

"No, that's how the English speak; they say 'have a nappy Christmas' it's printed like they speak."

"It looks like a printing error to me" replied Michel.

"Look, I can let you have these for ten Francs a box, they're a gift, look at the quality of the pictures, I mean, they're masterpieces."

"Alright" said Michel, "I'll take ten boxes and I'll see what I can do."

"Sell them for thirty Francs a box."

"I'll try."

"So that's a hundred Francs" said Sayid as he handed over ten red boxes to Michel

"You must almost be a millionaire" replied Michel as he handed over a hundred Franc note.

"Let me show you the jeans" said Sayid hastily.

"Not at the moment, I haven't got time, later perhaps."

"OK."

Michel left his friend and drove back to his station by le Vieux Port and contemplated the day ahead. He had so much to do and so little time to do it in and in the meantime had to fit in his fare paying passengers. He opened his window and lit a cigarette. No sooner had he drawn the first puff when a smartly dressed woman approached and climbed into the back of the Mercedes.

"Madame?" he enquired as he threw his cigarette into the road with a little irritation.

"The Hospital de Timone" she said firmly.

"Oui, Madame."

As Michel swung the Mercedes round he glanced into the rear view mirror at his passenger. She looked severe and showed no compassion in her features. Obviously a senior matron or a Doctor dealing with accidents all day long, certainly someone used to pain on a daily basis. Michel smiled at the mirror in the hope he could raise some response. It was to no avail. The traffic was quite heavy and it took longer than expected to reach the main entrance of the distinguished hospital. Michel drew up outside and the woman paid her fare without speaking. Michel could not resist saying something to lighten the encounter.

"Have a good day healing" he said with a grin.

The woman grimaced and slammed the door harder than the previous passenger. Michel shuddered and drove off thinking that he hoped he didn't have an accident. Being nursed by the grim faced one would be worse than the accident itself.

He returned to the station and parked behind René's taxi. René, seeing him draw up, slipped out of his Renault and came back to talk. Michel wound down his window and lit a cigarette as René asked "come round for drinks tonight?"

"OK, what time?"

"Early, about six, Yvonne would like to see you."

"OK, but I haven't got time for naughty fun."

"That's OK, Yvonne's not expecting any, she knows how busy we are."

Michel nodded; it was good that Yvonne, René's statuesque wife and Michel's mistress, was so understanding. It made their combined relationships so much easier. Michel wished that all the other women in his life had the same attitude.

A fare came up and climbed into the back of René's taxi.

"See you at six" he called as he slipped behind the wheel and drove off up la Canebiére. Michel waved his hand and then moved forward into the space left by René.

He drew heavily on his cigarette and turned his thoughts to Josette. She was the very special woman in his life. She was very beautiful, loving and gentle. He planned to marry her after his divorce from Monique. He had agreed to Josette finding and renting a flat in Marseille so that they could be together, quietly and privately, until his divorce came through. This might be some time in coming as he had not actually started proceedings, although he had told Monique, whilst they were holidaying in Grambois, of his intentions. She had told him not to be so silly and pointed out that if he remained married he was in line for a substantial inheritance. At the time that seemed like a good idea, on top of that once he married Josette he would have to stop his liaisons with all his other mistresses, who were tolerated by Monique. However, business had been good since the beginning of September and he had plenty of money in his safe deposit box, and Josette was so sweet. Monique could keep her Mother's money and her two dotty Aunt s money and……his thoughts were interrupted by someone opening the rear passenger door and slipping into the back of the Mercedes.

Michel glanced into the rear view mirror as a voice he knew so well said "bonjour, Michel." It was Cyril Gerrard, the wounded plain clothes Gendarme. Michel's heart sank.

"Bonjour, Cyril, where to?"

"Drive up to the Corniche and out to Cassis."

"You're going all the way to Cassis?"

"Possibly."

"On expenses?"

"Oui."

"Has the chief agreed it?"

"Never mind what the Chief agrees, you just drive will you, remember we mustn't be seen together."

"Am I still undercover then?" asked Michel as he swung out and round towards the exit of le Vieux Port.

"But of course" replied Gerrard.

"But I thought that after Claude Salvator escaped your Police stake out at Bandol and you shot yourself in this very taxi, my undercover work was over."

"Once you are selected for this important work, you are never free" said Gerrard with emotion.

"Mon Dieu" mumbled Michel under his breath and then asked "have you fully recovered from shooting yourself?"

"Oui, and it was an accident, if you hadn't driven down the pothole in the road, my gun wouldn't have gone off" said Gerrard firmly.

"Possibly."

"And we might have caught Claude."

"Possibly" repeated Michel.

They drove on in silence, as they swung up onto the Corniche Gerrard said "stop at the first available lay by."

"Expenses run out already?" asked Michel. Gerrard just grimaced at Michel as their eyes met in the rear view mirror.

Michel pulled up in an area marked out with large stones and well off the road. He switched off the engine and waited for Gerrard to begin.

"We think Salvator went to England after he got away from us."

"Really" said Michel.

"We think he's staying with the Englishman and his daughter."

Michel remembered the daughter; she was a tall and very elegant blonde. He had seen her several times in the company of the Salvator family.

"Why are you telling me all this?" asked Michel.

"Because we think he may contact you."

"Me!" exclaimed Michel.

"Oui."

"Why me?"

"Because you became part of his operation and he thinks you're possibly his only safe contact in Marseille, providing he doesn't know of course, that it was your information that set up the trap at Bandol."

"That's just perfect" said Michel and went on "I expect he'll kill me in any case!"

"Possibly, but we'll cross that bridge when we come to it."

"What?" queried Michel in a worried tone.

"I want you to tell me immediately if Salvator contacts you and make sure you get his phone number in England so I can inform our British chums at Scotland Yard and they will track him down and arrest him" said Gerrard confidently.

"This is all very well, Cyril...."

"Don't call me Cyril when I'm on duty" interrupted the Gendarme.

"Right then, Monsieur Gerrard, it's all very well you making all these plans for me but I've got a very busy life to lead." Michel had hardly finished speaking when the unmistakable clatter of a deaux chevaux approaching invaded their senses. The horrific, grey, corrugated, flimsy, noisy and very French vehicle pulled up alongside the Mercedes. Without looking Michel knew it was Jean Gambetta, long time family friend who ran a dark hole of a garage in the Rue de Verdun just off Rue du Camas in Marseille.

"Bonjour, Michel" said Jean as he approached the taxi and Gerrard groaned.

"Bonjour, Jean" replied Michel to the beaming old Frenchman who spotted Gerrard trying to make himself invisible.

"And bonjour to you too, Monsieur Gerrard, I didn't see you hiding in the back there."

"Bonjour, Gambetta" replied Gerrard with a hiss.

"Haven't broken down have you, Michel?" queried Jean.

"Non" replied Michel.

"Oh, bon, you must be having one of your private chats that nobody is supposed to know about."

"Possibly" said Michel.

"Ideal place to stop if you didn't want to be seen together, here by the Cassis road, the busiest coast route out of Marseille."

"Haven't you got any work to do back at that garage of yours?" asked Gerrard.

"Plenty, I was just out collecting spares when I saw the taxi and I thought Michel has either broken down or he's got a woman with him, I'd forgotten about you, Monsieur Gerrard"

"We are on police business, Gambetta, so perhaps you would kindly resume your journey" said Gerrard.

"Of course, Monsieur."

"Au revoir, Jean" said Michel.

"Call me if you need me" said Gambetta as he returned to his deaux chevaux before clattering off towards Marseille.

"We'd better get back" said Gerrard. Michel started up the Mercedes and drove swiftly back to le Vieux Port where Gerrard paid the fare and disappeared into the crowd.

Michel made his way straight to Ricky's bar in the Rue Bonneterie, double parked the taxi and went in for a quick, calming drink.

"Ça va, Michel" said Jacques the barman.

"Ça va, Jacques, a brandy s'il vous plaît."

"Mon Dieu, a brandy, problems Michel?"

"Too many to contemplate, everything in my life is a catastrophe" Michel replied.

"Nothing new there then" replied Jacques as he placed the brandy on the bar.

"Thank God you understand" said Michel as he lifted the glass to his lips and poured the golden liquid into his mouth and swallowed.

"Antone is over there, go and talk to him and I'll bring you another brandy."

"Merci, Jacques" replied Michel

He made his way to the back of the bar where Antone sat in a creaking wicker chair reading a newspaper. The great man was dressed in his usual crumpled white suit and his silver topped cane lay propped up against the adjacent chair with his large white planter's hat almost covering the seat. Antone put down his paper as Michel approached.

"Ça va, Michel?"

"Ça va, Antone."

"You look harassed Michel, what's wrong?"

Antone was a great listener and Michel told him in detail the events of the morning. When he had finished, Antone gave his advice and he knew that Michel would follow it without any deviation. The great man was not only very wealthy but had all the right contacts at the highest level. His closest friend was the bi-sexual Chief of Police, with whom he spent a lot of time during the summer on the nudist beach in Cassis, at nights they would frequent the local clubs used by young, virile men. Antone could fix anything and everyone liked him, Jacques, the barman, adored him and was his faithful live-in lover.

The great man hated the Salvators' and their evil activities with a passion and would do anything to bring about their imprisonment. He had been extremely angry when Edward Salvator had been released from custody pending his trial set for January.

Michel stayed at Ricky's in conversation with Antone for longer than he had planned and was just about to leave when Josette walked in.

"Oh, ma petite" said Michel as he left Antone to greet his love.

"Michel" she whispered as they headed for the bar and a beaming Jacques. Michel had another brandy and ordered white wine for the beautiful Josette. Her eyes sparkled and she constantly smiled at Michel as he became silly and romantic in their conversation. The lovers arranged to meet there at eight and then go to La Galleot, their favourite restaurant overlooking le Vieux Port. In the background noise of the bar, now crowded with lunchtime drinkers, Michel could hear the telephone ringing. He hardly glanced at Jacques as he answered it and then was transfixed as the barman turned and said "it's for you, Michel."

The hair on the back of his neck quivered. It had to be Claude Salvator. Michel glanced at Josette as he slipped off the bar stool and went behind the counter. He shook slightly as he took the phone from Jacques.

"Hello."

"Michel?" enquired the voice of Salvator voice.

"Oui."

"It's Claude Salvator here."

"Ah, bonjour Monsieur, bonjour" replied Michel shakily.

"Bonjour, Michel, how are you?"

"Fine thank you, Monsieur, and yourself?"

"As well as can be expected under the circumstances" replied Salvator in a dark and slightly threatening tone.

"Quite" said Michel nervously.

"Now then, Michel, I want you to go and see my father."

Michel gulped.

"Your father" he repeated.

"Oui, and I want you to give him a message."

"Oui, Monsieur."

"Tell him not to worry, everything has been fixed from London."

"Oui, Monsieur."

"Have you got that, Michel?"

"Oui, Monsieur, and how is London?"

"Same as always, overcrowded, raining and full of foreigners."

"Oh, bon, do you want me to ring you back after I've given the message to your father?"

"Oui, I'll give you the number."

"Just let me get a pen, Monsieur" replied Michel as he scrabbled to find a pen.

"Ready, Monsieur."

Salvator gave him the number and asked Michel to repeat it. They then said their goodbyes and hung up. Michel felt relieved and returned to the other side of the bar where he joined his Fiancé. They had one more drink to steady their nerves and left Ricky's bar. They kissed goodbye and then Josette wandered off to do some shopping whilst Michel set off unsteadily in the Mercedes to his flat in Montelivet. He thought it would be safer to phone Gerrard from there and he needed a lot of black coffee before he could start taking fares again. In fact, he thought it better that he stopped work for the day.

As Michel staggered through the front door Monique demanded "why are you back so early?"

"I've had a bad experience; Claude Salvator phoned me from London."

"Mon Dieu."

"Oui, a very upsetting moment."

"Luckily you were in Ricky's then to take the call and then have a drink or two to steady your nerves."

"How do you know I was in Ricky's?"

"Oh, Michel" she replied and raised her eyes to the ceiling and then added "I'll put the coffee on."

Michel phoned Gerrard and gave him all the information.

"Well done, Michel, I'll contact my British chums and they'll pick him up. You've nothing to fear now." Michel felt uncertain about that.

"Make sure you give the message to his father, we must keep the situation normal."

"OK, Gerrard, I'll go this evening."

"Bon chance, mon ami" said Gerrard and he hung up. Monique appeared with a steaming cup of black, sweet coffee which Michel then sipped gently.

"Now then" she said as she sat in the armchair opposite her husband "there have been a few changes to the Christmas arrangements." Michel groaned inwardly at that.

"Mama is coming tomorrow."

"What?"

"Aunt Alexis is bringing her, so you won't have to go and get her."

"But tomorrow is the sixteenth, I'd much rather go and get her on the twenty second as we arranged" wailed Michel.

"Well, they're coming tomorrow."

"Mon Dieu" mumbled Michel.

"Don't complain, they're all getting older and we must make the most of them whilst they are still with us."

The thought of Mama and Aunt Alexis for six extra days over the holiday was almost too much.

"When is Aunt Hélène coming?" he ventured, fear gripping his throat.

"Not until the eighteenth."

"She wasn't due until the twenty second" Michel complained.

"I know, but Henri and Jackie are coming down from Le Touquet for Christmas, and we all want to see them."

"Mon Dieu, not your dopey cousin and his ugly wife as well."

"Oui, and he's not dopey, he's a very clever man whose made more money than you have."

"He's dopey."

"He's not."

"His wife is ugly."

"This is true; but she has a kind heart."

"Mon Dieu" mumbled Michel who was now sober as a judge. He continued to sip his coffee.

"Where are they all going to sleep?" he suddenly enquired.

"Mama and Alexis in the spare room as usual and Hélène on the floor in here."

"And Henri and Jackie?"

"I've arranged with Madame Rochas downstairs that they'll sleep in her spare room."

"Mon Dieu, what a circus" said Michel gloomily.

"I don't know why you're so anti my family" she complained.

"Well there's so many of them, and look how they behave, Alexis is always drunk and constantly argues with Hélène and Mama cries all the time."

"That's not true."

"You just watch this Christmas and see if I'm not right."

"We'll see."

"And only God knows how dopey Henri and his ugly wife are going to behave."

"They are quiet and reserved people" countered Monique.

"We'll see" replied Michel as he sipped his coffee and felt better by the minute. It was at that moment that Monique dropped the bombshell.

"And I've told them all that we plan to go up to Grambois after Christmas and stay there until the new year."

"What?" shrieked Michel.

"I've told them all that we're going to Grambois after Christmas."

"Oh, no, oh, no, no, no way am I carting all that lot up to Grambois and suffering until next year."

"Come on Michel, it will be better than staying cooped up here in the flat, besides I've told Madame Rochas that we'll all be leaving the day after Boxing day."

Michel was now as sober as two judges as the enormity of Monique's commitment struck him forcibly. He had to put up with the whole family at his quiet villa, a haven of peace in the countryside of Provence.

"You'll have to make an excuse, tell them anything, tell them I'm involved with the police and expect to be arrested, tell them anything you like but make them all understand there's no going to Grambois!"

"I'm not doing that, we are all going to Grambois and that's that" she said and she got up and went into the kitchen. Michel wanted to cry and he felt even more determined to divorce Monique and marry Josette.

At that moment Frederik, Michel's stepson, came in and Michel heard him talking to his Mother in the kitchen. A few moments later he came into the living room and observed his glum step father.

"Dad."

"Oui, Frederik."

"Is it alright if Angelique stays with us for Christmas?"

Michel looked at his step son, smiled and replied "why not, your Mother has invited half of Marseille so one more won't make any difference."

"Thanks, Dad, I knew you'd say it was OK." Angelique was the daughter of Nicole, one of Michel's mistresses who lived at Grambois. Everyone was pleased that Frederik was going out with Angelique as, after catching him naked with another boy in their bedroom, they thought he might be gay. Michel did not care as long as Frederik was happy, but Mama and the Aunt's were very concerned.

Michel and Monique did not speak again until it was time for him to leave and visit René and Yvonne.

"I'll see you later" he said as he made his way to the front door of the flat.

"Bye" she mumbled.

As he walked to the taxi he went through the evenings arrangements. After drinks with René and Yvonne he would go on to Ricky's to meet Josette and then a quick dash to Salvator's house with the message from his son and then dinner at La Galleot and back to Josette's flat for a slow, deeply moving and romantic sexual experience. He thought that he might not come home.

The traffic was a little more boisterous than usual and it took longer than anticipated before Michel turned into the Rue du Camas and parked as close as he could to number 116. It was cold and he shivered as he rang the sonnette. Yvonne answered and he was soon inside his best friend's flat. Yvonne poured him a petite brandy at his request as he settled into a comfortable arm chair.

"I've heard from Claude Salvator today" said Michel solemnly.

"What!" exclaimed René whilst Yvonne murmured "mon Dieu!"

"He phoned me from London."

"London?"

"Oui, he's hiding there with that Englishman and his daughter, remember we saw them altogether in the restaurant at Le Cavalier?"

"Ah, oui, the tall blonde and a grey haired man" replied René.

"What did Salvator want?" asked Yvonne, her breasts heaving.

"He gave me a message for his father, I've got to tell him that everything has been taken care of from London."

"Mon Dieu" said René.

"I'm going to see the old man tonight" said Michel.

"Be careful, ma petite" said Yvonne.

"I'll be OK, Claude gave me his phone number in London and I've told Gerrard who is going to contact the police and they'll arrest him."

"Oui, just like his father and he's out and waiting for his trial, it'll be the same with Claude and he'll know who gave his number to the police!" exclaimed René.

"Mon Dieu" mumbled Michel and he paled slightly. His refuge at Aunt Alexi's villa at Orange came into focus. He might be there sooner than he had planned. The friends fell silent for a while as they contemplated the difficulties ahead for Michel. Yvonne broke the silence and said "we're looking forward to Christmas."

"Bon" replied Michel.

"We're going to have a little dinner party, just for us, I'm going to dress up as a Christmas fairy and you two are going to have me on the table between courses, how about that?" she said with a smile.

"Perfect" replied Michel, knowing that Yvonne's cuisine was as delicious as her statuesque body.

"We look forward to it" said René.

"When?" asked Michel.

"This Saturday OK with you?" asked Yvonne.

"Oui, just perfect" replied Michel.

"Come about eight" said Yvonne "and I'll be all ready for you."

"And what are you doing for Christmas?" asked René.

"I can barely think about it. Monique's arranged for her Mother and Alexis to come tomorrow, Hélène on Thursday and then on top of all that, her dopey cousin Henri and his wife Jackie are coming from Le Touquet!"

"Mon Dieu, where are they all going to sleep?" enquired Yvonne.

"All round the flat and downstairs with Madame Rochas."

"Mon Dieu!" exclaimed René.

"Then, believe it or not, Frederik has invited Angelique, don't ask me where she's going to sleep, and then to cap it all, Monique has invited them all up to Grambois after Christmas!"

"This is a catastrophe" said René.

"I'm glad you see it my way" replied Michel.

"And with Salvator after you, well….." but before Yvonne could finish Michel interrupted her saying "I could be dead by the new year!"

"Don't say that, ma petite" said Yvonne.

"Well" said Michel glumly.

"Let me get you another brandy" said his voluptuous Mistress.

"Merci."

It was almost eight o'clock when Michel left Yvonne and René and made his way to Ricky's bar. Jacques poured him a brandy whilst he waited for Josette. The bar was quieter than usual for a Monday evening and Michel guessed this was the lull before the storm of Christmas drinkers. He began to dread the thought of Christmas and a wave of despair swept over him and began to draw him down into a dark abyss. Then suddenly the light of his life stood next to him.

"Josette, ma petite" he said as he kissed her.

"Michel." She looked lovely as usual in a neat, fitted red coat with fur collar and cuffs and matching Cossack hat almost covering her brow and enhancing her sparkling eyes, which glowed with love for the man in her life. How ever could Michel fail to love her and eventually marry her? He felt sure no matter what, that he was looking at the next Madame Ronay.

"It's cold out tonight, ma petite" she said and she touched his cheek with her little cold nose. Michel kissed it and asked "What will you have?"

"White wine, darling."

"Jacques, s'il vous plaît." The barman nodded and poured the wine. They drank a toast to each other and kissed again.

"I have one little job to do tonight before we go to dinner."

"Oui, what is it?"

"I have to give a message to Edward Salvator."

Josette's face froze in horror.

"Oh, no, mon Dieu, I thought you were out of all that" she cried.

"I am, ma petite, I am, but have to see him tonight, it won't take long, I promise."

"You promise?"

"I do."

"OK then" she smiled and Michel kissed her gently on the lips.

Half an hour later Michel pulled up outside Edward Salvator's flat at 12, Rue Charbonniere.

"Stay here ma petite, I promise I'll be quick."

Josette kissed him and replied "hurry darling."

He rang the sonnette and Salvator answered.

"Oui?"

"Monsieur Salvator?"

"Who is it?"

"Michel Ronay."

"Who?"

"Michel Ronay, the taxi driver."

"I don't want a taxi."

"I know you don't."

"Why are you calling me then?"

"I have a message from Claude."

There was a silence and then Salvator said "you'd better come in." The heavy door clicked and Michel entered the spacious hallway and made his way up to the first floor flat. The door opened and Salvador waved him in. Michel followed the gangster into the living room which was as spacious as it was luxuriously furnished. Madame Salvator sat in a large chair by the ornate fireplace. She nodded at Michel as her husband said "this is Ronay, the taxi driver."

"Madame."

"Be seated" said Madame with a wave of her hand, her diamond rings sparkling as they caught the light.

'Who says crime doesn't pay' thought Michel as he perched nervously on the edge of the settee.

"You have a message from Claude?" asked Salvator.

"Oui, Monsieur, he phoned me today and asked me to tell you that everything has been taken care of from London."

"Is that all he said?"

"Oui, Monsieur."

"Didn't he ask how I was?" asked Madame.

"Non, Madame, that's all he said."

"He's been a great disappointment, that boy" she mumbled.

"Never mind" said Salvator and continued "thank you Ronay, you can go now and make sure that you don't tell the police that

Claude has spoken to you."

Michel gulped and replied "certainly not, Monsieur."

Madame reached for her handkerchief as Michel stood up to leave and murmured "Madame."

He was soon back in the Mercedes with Josette and they hurried away to La Galleot at le Vieux Port. He felt relieved as he entered the restaurant with Josette and was greeted by the ever smiling Madame Charnay

"A discreet table for two?" enquired Madame Charnay.

"Not necessary, Madame, I now have only friends in Marseille" replied Michel. Madame smiled and with a little nod led the way to a table for two in the window which allowed the lovers to gaze out across le Vieux Port at the myriad of moored yachts bobbing gently at anchor.

They spent time looking at the menu punctuated only by smiles and gazing into each others eyes. Michel whispered "I love you, ma petite."

Josette replied "I know and I love you too."

"I could eat you."

"You can later" she replied with a smile.

Michel wriggled in his seat at that and then consulted the menu once more.

"I feel like celebrating tonight" he said.

"Why, ma petite?" she asked.

"I think everything is going to work out well for us."

"Bon, and I have some exciting news" she smiled.

"What is it, cherie?" he asked his eyes wide with anticipation.

"I have signed the lease on a flat for us!" she exclaimed.

Michel was stunned and said "but you never told me."

"I know it's a surprise."

"It certainly is" he replied.

"It was a surprise for me too, the agent rang me this morning and said it had just come on the market and after those others we looked at all fell through, well I just jumped at it."

"Bon" replied Michel with lukewarm enthusiasm realising that his commitment to Josette had just taken a giant leap forward.

"I've been to see it and it's perfect for us, so I signed the lease and paid three months rent in advance."

"Bon" he said mechanically.

"It's partly furnished, but we need a new bed and a comfortable settee."

"Oui" replied Michel and then after a pause, asked "what's the address?"

"115, Rue du Camas" she replied pertly.

It shook Michel to the core and he shivered, of all the flats in Marseille, she had to pick the one opposite to where René and Yvonne lived. How could she do this to him? They would see him coming and going and Yvonne would never approve and Josette would see him when he visited his second best mistress. It was a catastrophe!

"Are you ready to order?" Madame Charnay enquired.

Michel quickly gathered his senses but felt that his appetite had deserted him.

"Another moment, Madame" he blurted out. Madame nodded and moved away.

"Are you alright, ma petite?" enquired Josette.

"Oui" he smiled.

"You look a little pale."

"I'm just overcome with emotion, my darling, it's such good news" he lied.

"I was sure it was the right thing, besides the sooner I'm out of Salvator's flat the better."

"Oui, ma petite, I agree."

"I knew you'd be happy, now let's order."

They both started with salad Niçoise followed by scampi Provençal for Josette and a Tournedos Rossini for him as he thought he needed some meat for strength. A light Cassis rosé was ideal for the meal and Michel's state of mind. There was no getting out of this dilemma. Fancy the silly girl leasing a flat without telling him and then paying three months rent in advance? Surely one month would have been sufficient? She will be after some money next.

"Will you be able to let me have some money, ma petite?" she asked between sips of wine.

"Of course, of course, I'll get some cash tomorrow for you, don't worry about a thing" he replied with a smile.

"You're wonderful, Michel, I just know we are going to be so happy" she smiled.

He gazed into her lovely face and had to admit to himself that he really did love her.

Their conversation ranged through decorating the new flat to guests at the proposed wedding 'some time next year' as Michel put it. He was anxious to keep the arrangements as loose as possible. The commitment of the flat was enough for one day he reasoned.

They finished the meal with pear belle Hélène and another bottle of Cassis wine. Michel paid the bill to the ever smiling Madame Charnay and the lovers returned to Josette's flat in the Rue Benoit Malon.

Michel disliked the fact that the flat was owned by the Salvators' but was comforted by the thought that Claude was probably under arrest in London and that Josette would be moving out within days. He was relaxed as he followed her into the spacious living room.

"Brandy, ma petite?" she enquired as he slumped down onto the settee.

"Oui" he replied, certain in his own mind that he was not going home to Montelivet tonight. She handed him his drink and cuddled up to him, clutching her own. They kissed gently between sips of brandy, saying nothing.

"Are you staying?" she asked when her glass was empty.

"Of course."

"That's good."

With that she untangled herself from his arms and rose a little unsteadily to her feet. Michel was admiring her lovely form as she unbuttoned the white dress she was wearing and let it fall to the floor. Her skimpy underwear was red. Her brassiere was of the lightest lace imaginable and transparent, her stockings were held up by red garters with an embroidered rose on each and her thong had a lovely red rose which was situated in the middle of her black pubic hair.

"I think I'm ready for bed" she said with a smile.

"Wow, so am I" replied Michel.

He followed her into the bedroom where they were soon naked under the sheets. They made love for an eternity until Michel could no longer hold back. Josette screamed out in ecstasy as Michel lifted her body and drove himself up into his beloved again and again until they were both exhausted. They then fell into that deepest sleep that lovers' experience, unconscious to the world.

CHAPTER 2

Tuesday 16th December

Monique was not amused by the fact that Michel had not come home the previous night and with the impending arrival of her Mother and Aunt Alexis her mood was somewhat volatile as her husband stumbled through the front door.

"I won't ask where you were last night or what you were doing, but I can guess, and if you ever stay out without 'phoning me….."

"Don't nag me, I've had a terrible time" he interrupted.

"Liar!"

"I've been dealing with Salvator and….."

"Did you sleep with him?" she demanded.

"Non!"

"I bet you didn't, and I don't care who you slept with, I just need to know you're not dead yet!"

"OK, OK…"

"I mean it Michel."

"Oui, ma petite, I promise…."

"Don't do it again."

There was a pause and then she said in a calm voice "I'll get you some coffee whilst you shave, you look awful."

Michel nodded and struggled off to the bathroom.

An hour later he was at his station of le Vieux Port, clean shaven and feeling refreshed. He bought a paper from the kiosk, sat in the Mercedes with the window open and read the sports page whilst drawing hard on his first cigarette of the day. It was cold but bright and he hoped the day ahead would be a little less frantic than yesterday. He remembered that Mama and Alexis were arriving around lunchtime and he put that unpleasant thought to the back of his mind for the moment.

Marseille Football Club had lost their match last Saturday and the paper's sports page was still pouring over the details and trying hard to fix the blame on someone but the fact was that Marseille had not been at their best. Such is life and Michel shrugged his shoulders and wandered onto another page where he noticed a photograph of Lascelles, a local politician with ambition, attending a charity function with his wife. Michel smirked a little, remembering how he had introduced Lascelles to the two pretty little prostitutes at Aix and how the politician had come to grief each time he had met the girls. A voice he knew suddenly invaded his senses.

"Bonjour Michel."

He looked up to see none other than Lascelles.

"Monsieur Lascelles" he smiled "bonjour, I was just reading about you in the paper."

"Ah, oui, charity you know."

"Oui, it's good to know that you care."

"Oui, now Michel…."

"Jump in, Monsieur, we can talk on the way…."

"Michel, I don't want to go anywhere, I just want you to arrange for me to see the girls at Aix before Christmas."

"Certainly, Monsieur, I can do that."

"Bon, my wife and I are going to Paris for the holiday but she goes tomorrow lunchtime and I will follow on the next day, a political meeting you understand and I have to attend."

"Of course, Monsieur."

"Now if you can arrange it for me to see the girls tomorrow night that will be fine."

"Bon, Monsieur, will that be after your meeting?"

Lascelles blushed and stammered "after, oui, after."

"What time do you want picking up from your flat?"

"Eight o'clock would be about right, I should be free by then" he replied sweating a little.

"I will arrange everything, Monsieur, leave it to me."

"Bon, Michel, I'll see you tomorrow then" and with that he was gone just as René pulled up behind Michel in his Renault.

"I recognised him, isn't he that politician, what's his name?" asked René as he joined his friend.

"Lascelles."

"That's him, what did he want?"

"I make personal arrangements for him."

"Oh, yeah, like what?"

"I know these two girls in Aix, they are lovely young things who perform necessary duties for professional men" replied Michel with a grin.

"I hope you don't indulge, Yvonne wouldn't like it, you know how she is"

"Oui, of course."

"She has strict rules, you can only have her and Monique, two women are enough for any man, one wife and one mistress."

"Quite" replied Michel.

"And save yourself for Saturday, Yvonne's getting really worked up and I can promise you she's going to need us more than once each between courses."

Michel warmed at the thought of Yvonne on the dining room table with her lovely legs spread for him and René amongst the mountain of food that she would have prepared. There is something very sexy about food and carnal activity.

"You can rely on me" replied Michel.

"Bon."

"Now I must go and make arrangements for Lascelles" said Michel as he started the Mercedes.

"Au revoir."

René waved as Michel drove off and double parked outside Ricky's.

"Bonjour, Michel" said Jacques as Michel approached the bar.

"Bonjour, Jacques, a Pernod, s'il vous plaît, and can I use your phone?"

"Oui"

Michel phoned the girls in Aix, spoke to Maria and made the arrangements for Lascelles.

"I hope he's going to be alright this time" she said with feeling remembering the debacle with the moules and his broken ankle the first time he visited them.

"Oui, I've just seen him and he looks fine" replied Michel.

"OK, honey, we'll see you about nine tomorrow night" said Maria.

"Oui" replied Michel.

He returned to his bar stool and sipped his Pernod in peace. It was almost mid morning, he hadn't had a fare yet and he had to go to the bank sometime for cash for Josette. Finishing his drink he left the bar and drove back to his station.

René had gone and the rank was empty. Michel had just switched off the engine when a tall rather poorly dressed man with unkempt hair carrying a large briefcase approached.

"Bonjour, driver."

"Bonjour, Monsieur, where to?"

"I want to go to Aix, the University, can you take me?"

"Oui, of course, Monsieur, please get in" said a delighted Michel. This was a stroke of luck, a good earner and he quickly thought he could go on to Grambois and see Sophia and check the house was alright before the hordes of relatives descended after Christmas. There is a God after all and as his late Mother had always told him 'turn everything to your advantage'.

The passenger slipped into the Mercedes and Michel swung the big car round into la Canebiére and made his way up the broad thoroughfare away from le Vieux Port towards the autoroute that would take him to Aix en Provence and the University.

"Are you going to lecture there, Monsieur?"

"Why, oui, how did you guess?" asked the passenger.

"I think I can tell when I see a distinguished person like yourself, who is obviously a professor, probably of mathematics or applied physics" said Michel with authority. He was remembering his maths teacher at school, who was always unkempt and looked as if he had been dragged through a hedge backwards.

"Quite remarkable" replied the Professor "quite remarkable, I lecture on several science subjects and I'm surprised you could tell that, have we met before?"

"Oh, non, Monsieur Professor, I just know these things, I'm a keen observer of my fellow man you understand."

"Oui, completely, I must say you are very perceptive indeed."

Michel allowed himself to swell a little with pride just as the old Citroen that he was overtaking changed direction with no signal and although Michel braked violently the Citroen caught the front wing of the Mercedes.

"Merde! Merde! Merde!" shouted Michel as the Professor's glasses came flying through to the front of the Mercedes followed by the Professor and his briefcase.

The Mercedes screeched to a halt whilst the Citroen hobbled to the side of the road. Michel got out ready to kill and approached the Citroen prepared to do serious harm to the driver until she turned her pale frightened face towards him. She was about twenty years old and stunningly beautiful. He calmed instantly.

"Are you alright, Mademoiselle?" he purred.

"I think so, Monsieur, I'm so sorry, it was all my fault, I just didn't see you there."

"Alright, Mademoiselle, don't upset yourself, it's only a little bump."

"I'm so sorry, I've only just passed my test and I'm not very good, oh, I wish I was dead!"

"Now, now, these things happen, it was an accident, jump out and let's look at the damage together."

"Oh, Monsieur, you're so kind" she sobbed and she began to cry.

"Come along now" purred Michel.

"My Mother will kill me, it's her car."

"No she won't, I'll talk to her, don't worry" replied Michel in his best soothing voice.

He opened the driver's door and the girl stepped out. She was tall and slim with lovely firm breasts, a small waist and long, long legs.

"Now let's look at the damage together" he said.

They inspected the rather large dent on the rear wing of the Citroen and the quite minor scrape on the front wing of the mighty Mercedes.

"I have a close friend in the auto repair business and I know he can fix our cars at a very reasonable price so we won't have to go through our insurance companies" said Michel as Gambetta entered his mind.

"Monsieur, however can I thank you?"

"It's my pleasure and duty to help any mademoiselle in distress" he replied with a smile.

"I never knew that men like you existed" she whispered.

"There's just one or two of us about in Marseille and one in Paris I believe" he said gently.

"Oh, Monsieur."

"May I have your name and address, please?"

"Oui, I'm Annette Devaux and I live at 23, Boulevard Fabrici off Rue Saint Pierre."

"I know it." said Michel "I'm Michel Ronay and I live at Montelivet, here's my card."

She took his card and said "thank you so much, Monsieur Ronay...."

"Call me Michel, please."

"Oh, Michel, thank you."

"I will be in touch after I've made all the arrangements, so don't worry and tell your Mother not to worry either, it can all be easily fixed."

"Michel, you're so kind."

"Are you alright to drive home?"

"Oui, I think so."

"Bon." He then opened the door for her to slip in behind the wheel. She started the engine and smiled at him as she pulled away into the traffic. He waved, sighed and returned to the Mercedes where he found the Professor still scrabbling under the front seat for his glasses.

"Are you alright, Professor?"

"I can't find my glasses and I can't see a thing without them."

"You sit back whilst I look for them." With relief the Professor returned to the rear seat as Michel dived under the front seat. He quickly retrieved them and returned the spectacles to the relieved Professor.

"We will now continue to Aix, Professor."

"Bon, I hope that the damage is only minor."

"A slight dent and very easily repaired" replied Michel.

The journey continued at some speed with Michel's mind in overdrive. He wondered if he could get to see the delicious Mademoiselle Devaux and her Mother this afternoon or would he have to wait until tomorrow?

They reached the outskirts of Aix quite quickly but took a little time finding the right entrance at the University for the Professor. At last they arrived and the academic paid his fare, gave Michel a generous tip and disappeared into the building.

Michel raced the Mercedes up to Grambois. It was lunchtime when he arrived and he went to his villa first. He and Monique had only been back for a couple of weekends since August and the place smelt a bit musty but Michel put that down to the fire. He inspected the house and everything seemed in order. He closed the front door and double locked it. After a quick walk round the garden he made his way down the drive and then up the narrow road to the square. As he passed through on his way to Sophia's house he glanced over at the shop owned by Jean Paul Manton and his wife Eleanor, with whom he had a long and rewarding sexual relationship which was usually conducted on the table in the store room. The shop was closed for lunch. He walked through the arch and along to Sophia's house where he rang the sonnette.

"Hello" she answered.

"Sophia, it's me, Michel."

"Oh, Michel, cherie!" he could hear the excitement in her voice, "come in, come in quickly, but only if you're prepared to stay and fuck me." She always got straight to the point and Michel appreciated that in a woman.

"Of course."

"Bon." The door clicked and he entered the warm house. He climbed the stairs to her studio come living room and was welcomed by the artist. She grabbed him and kissed him passionately.

"My darling I've only seen you once since August."

"Twice" corrected Michel.

"It seems like only once" she replied.

"I know, ma petite."

"I can't exist on such a little amount of lust" she complained.

"I understand, ma petite."

"I'm getting older and need much, much more."

"I understand."

"Well do something about it, I'm an artist in my thirties, almost dead, I need revitalising regularly and hard, I need it for my inspiration. Ask any artist they need love, lust, perversions and hard sex to give the energy, the spark to ignite their true being so they can express themselves on canvas and be truly great."

"Bollocks" said Michel.

"I know, I'm just so randy and need to fuck you."

"A drink first?" he asked.

"Of course, Pernod?"

"Please" he replied as he sat in rather than on the huge leather settee where they often made love. He looked at Sophia and admired her figure, accentuated by the tight black dress buttoned down the front which was very short and allowed a substantial amount of suntanned thigh to show. It was her passion to remain naked all summer whilst she painted and she used to cause some annoyance to the women in the village when she worked outside on her balcony. The men didn't mind and soon everyone got used to it and after all, they reasoned, she is an artist. As a consequence she was deeply and evenly tanned all over.

She handed Michel his Pernod and asked "what do you think of my latest creation?"

Michel looked at the half finished painting on her easel.

"It's powerful and significant" he replied, struggling a little as he squinted at the two large blobs of radiant yellow and orange.

"I know that, ma petite, but does it carry the message?" she asked.

"Too obscure at the moment but I'm sure it will come through when you have finished it."

"I agree" she replied.

"It needs more detail" said Michel feeling more certain of his constructive criticism.

"Michel, I can always rely on you for sensible comment."

"Always, ma petite."

"Now, what are you doing for Christmas?" she demanded.

"Stuck in the flat at Montelivet with the whole family plus cousin Henri and his wife from Le Touquet until Boxing Day and then, God help me, we're all coming here."

"Ah, bon!" she exclaimed and went on "that means you can see to me every day."

"I may not be up to it, ma petite."

"Nonsense, you'll be rested and ready to go."

"I will have eaten and drunk too much to be any good."

"Well cut down a little, that's easy."

"I'll try."

"Bon, hurry up now and finish your drink, I need you now."

She was so direct, so demanding, Michel liked that. He swallowed the last drop of Pernod and had hardly put his glass down when she lunged forward, flung her arms around his neck and kissed him passionately, forcing her tongue into his mouth whilst pressing her firm breasts against him. She pushed so hard that he found it difficult to breathe. At last he managed to break away gasping.

"Come on, Michel, I'm very hungry!" she exclaimed as she started to unzip his trousers. He unbuttoned her dress and was delighted to find that she was only wearing very flimsy lace panties underneath. They tore at each other until they were both naked. She seized his erect penis in her mouth for an instant before letting it go and laying back on the settee with her legs open.

"Come on, Michel, no time to waste!" He fell on top of her, kissing passionately as she guided him into her moist body. They rode with a steady rhythm with her gentle moans of pleasure becoming louder as time went on. At last she reached her moment of ecstasy and clawed at his back as he thrust ever harder into her writhing suntanned form. He felt no pain until after he had climaxed into her soft and yielding body.

"What have you done to me?" he gasped.

"Fucked you."

"I mean to my back?"

"Let me see" she replied as Michel withdrew from her and sat up.

"Oh, mon Dieu, you have a few scratches, ma petite, I'm sorry but I told you that I was very hungry."

"Be careful, this is the only body I've got."

"I know, ma petite, I will be careful in future, but don't leave me so long next time and I won't be so hungry!"

He kissed her for a while longer before getting dressed and as he was about to leave he asked "what's it supposed to be?"

"What?"

"The painting, of course."

"Michel, you disappoint me, can't you tell?"

"Not without the detail, ma petite."

She pulled a face and raised her eyebrows as she realised he was right to ask the question.

"It's the sun reflected in the sea just before it sinks below the horizon."

"Ah, bon, it was the absence of the sea that confused me" he replied.

"It needs more detail" she hurriedly agreed.

They kissed and wished each other a 'Joyeux Noël' with Michel promising to visit her regularly as soon as he arrived in Grambois with the family.

It was getting much colder and his back began to hurt as he left Sophia's house and made his way across the square to Jean and Eleanor Manton's shop. The door bell clanged noisily as he entered and he was immediately confronted by a smiling Eleanor.

"Oh, Michel, bonjour ma petite, bonjour" she said excitedly.

"Bonjour, Eleanor."

"It's alright, we're alone, Jean has only just gone to the bar."

"Oh, bon."

"So we have some time to be naughty and play on the table, ma petite" she said with an excited giggle.

"I'm afraid not, I have to return to Marseille immediately, but I came to wish you 'Joyeux Noël' and tell you that I'm coming up with the family after Christmas and I'll call and see you when Jean's not about."

"Oh, that's wonderful because he's going off for a couple of days with the boule team to play a match in Corsica."

"Ah, bon."

"Which means you can stay the night, ma petite."

"Bon" replied Michel thinking that that might not be convenient, much as he would like to spend time in the voluptuous body of the shopkeeper's wife in a warm bed.

"I look forward to us being together after Christmas" he whispered seductively.

"Oh, Michel, so do I" she giggled and she came from behind the counter and gave him a passionate kiss.

"Are you sure you haven't got time for a little quickie? I'm very wet for you."

Michel felt his penis harden. "How can I resist you?" he whispered.

"Hurry then."

He followed her into the back store room where she cleared a suitable space on the table. She turned to face her lover and proceeded to lift up her dress and remove her black lace knickers.

"There" she smiled as she sat up on the table and opened her firm, plump legs for Michel. He was in her moist, comfortable body in an instant and she laid back on the table as he speeded up. He intended the encounter would be quick and Eleanor had only just began to moan gently as Michel climaxed into her.

"Mon Dieu, that was quick" she complained.

"I know, ma petite but it's better than nothing" he replied.

She nodded her head as Michel withdrew from her accommodating body.

"Until after Christmas then" she said solemnly.

"Oui, ma petite."

They kissed for a while, said their 'Joyeux Noël's' and just as Michel was about to leave, Jean Paul Manton returned from the bar and entered the shop.

"Bonjour, Michel."

"Bonjour, Jean."

"You're back quick" said Eleanor to her husband.

"So?"

"Nothing, it just seems everybody's in a rush today" she replied glaring at both her husband and her lover.

"Ah, so joyeux Noël, Jean."

"Bon Noël, Michel."

"I'm sure I'll see you after Christmas" he smiled and gave a little wave as he left the shop.

"What did he want?" asked Jean.

"Nothing, he just came to say 'Joyeux Noël' and told me that he and his family are coming here after Christmas."

"Mmm" replied her husband suspiciously as he went upstairs.

Michel hurried across the square through the archway into Rue Lambert, passed Sophia's house and along to Nicole's home. He hoped she was in as he had just remembered that her daughter, Angelique, was planning to stay at Montelivet for Christmas. He rang the sonnette and hoped she would not demand sexual attention as he was getting very tired.

"Hello" came her sweet voice.

"Nicole, it's Michel."

"Oh, Michel, bon, come in!" she exclaimed with enthusiasm and the door clicked.

He was soon inside the warm little house and in the arms of another of his mistresses, who kissed him passionately.

"I've missed you so much, ma petite" she whispered between kisses.

"I've been very busy in Marseille, ma petite" he replied.

"Too busy even to come and see me?"

"Oui, and I can hardly believe it myself"

"But you're here now and are you staying for a while so we can get to know each other again?"

"Well, er,...."

"Let me get you a drink whilst you're thinking."

Michel was caught for the moment and just mumbled "Pernod, ma petite."

"I remember" she smiled.

Michel slumped onto the settee and moments later Nicole returned with drinks for them both. She snuggled up to him and asked "why have you come to Grambois today?"

"To see you of course and then to make arrangements for Angelique."

"What arrangements?"

"For her to stay with us at Montelivet for Christmas."

"She never told me" replied Nicole.

"Oh, didn't she?"

"Non."

"Is it alright then?"

"I suppose so, but it means I'll be all alone at Christmas unless you plan to stay with me" she smiled.

"I'd love to, ma petite, but I'm needed at home with all my family plus unwanted relations from Le Touquet."

"Oh, you poor thing."

"Oui, I am a poor thing and I'll be bloody glad when Christmas is over."

"So will I if I'm going to be left alone."

"We're all coming up after Christmas, so I'll see you then, ma petite" he said as he kissed her gently on her lovely lips.

"I look forward to seeing you again and again" she murmured and went on "have you time now to have me gently before you rush off?"

"I'm afraid not."

Nicole was disappointed and then changing the subject said firmly "oui, it's OK for Angelique to stay, I'll talk to her when she comes in and find out when I'm expected to drive her down to your place."

"Thank you, ma petite."

"I don't mind being alone all bloody Christmas."

Michel needed to improve the situation and so thinking quickly said "I'll come up on Friday, take you to dinner in Aix and I'll stay the night."

"Oh, Michel" she said and her lovely face brightened.

"Then you could take Angelique back with you and save me a trip" she said.

"That would not be wise ma petite, better you bring her down that morning."

"Ah, oui, otherwise it would be difficult for you to stay."

"Exactly." They kissed again and Michel, leaving his mistress smiling, made his way back across the square and down the steep hill to his villa. He started up the Mercedes, put the heater onto full and drove back to Marseille.

On the journey back Michel used the time to plan various strategies. Firstly, he went to Pierre's brothel at 26, Rue Charbonniere, where he showed his old friend the Christmas cards.

"But they say 'Nappy Christmas' instead of 'Joyeux Noël' complained Pierre as he lounged back in his huge, black leather executive chair behind his magnificent desk.

"I know, but they're English, and that's how they speak, they say *'have a nappy Christmas'*."

"Well what am I going to do with them?" asked Pierre.

"Send them to all your clients" replied Michel seriously.

"I don't think so, Michel, I mean if the picture on the front was of a lovely woman scantily dressed, well maybe, but an old coach up to its axles in snow with a couple of red faced frozen old farts driving it, well it's hardly seductive now, is it?"

"I know, but this year everything English is very chic."

"Maybe in London and Paris, but not down here in Marseille."

"It's a golden opportunity" said Michel.

"It may be for you, but not for me, I'll tell you what, sell them to Gerrard and his mates, they're a bloody nuisance and they certainly need some chic culture. If it wasn't for the chief being a regular customer and a friend of Antone's they'd have closed me down, pompous arses they all are."

"Well couldn't you have some for clients you hate and don't want to see again?" persisted Michel.

"Fuck me, I'd need lorry loads for them!"

"There you are then, buy them from me in bulk, I'll supply them at unbeatable price."

Pierre rocked back in his chair and gazed at the ceiling and then looking hard at Michel replied "leave it with me overnight and I'll think about it."

"OK, that's fine."

"Better go now, I've got a small party of Judges coming in tonight and I want to make sure the girls are all ready and everything is up to scratch."

"Right."

"They're big spenders and demand the best."

"I'll see you tomorrow then."

Michel drove down to the Bourse and parked near the Banque du Sumaris. He made his way down to the strong room with the confident bearing of a wealthy man. After exchanging pleasantries with the staff and signing in, he was allowed into the vault where he opened the wall safe and withdrew his numbered secure box which he carried to the desk in the middle of the vault. If the tax authorities ever saw this they would go mad! It had been a very good autumn. He counted out a large amount and placed it in his inside pocket.

Leaving the Banque he drove straight to Josette's flat in the Rue Benoit Malon where she replied instantly to the sonnette. They kissed passionately for a while before he said "ma petite, I can't stay now, but here is some cash for you as I promised" and he handed his beloved the bundle of notes. Her eyes opened wide and she gasped "oh, Michel, so much, for me?"

"Of course, my darling."

"Oh, you're so good to me."

"I am, aren't I?"

"Oui, you most certainly are."

"Meet me in Ricky's about eight and you can buy me a drink."

"I will, Michel, ma petite" and she kissed him passionately. Lots of money in a relationship certainly makes things run smoothly.

Michel made his way to Jean Gambetta's garage in the Rue de Verdun.

"Jean! Jean! It's Michel" he called as he entered the gloomy interior.

"I can hear you" replied the old man from underneath a battered old Citroen.

Michel stood there whilst the mechanic wriggled out from beneath the vehicle dragging a lead light behind him. The interior of the garage then lit up and for all the world it looked like a poorly lit pantomime stage full of strange dusty shapes.

"Well I suppose you're in trouble with a woman or you've had another accident" said Jean wearily as he removed his Breton beret and replaced in the same position as previous.

"Both actually" replied Michel.

"Go on" replied Jean "and now stun me with the facts."

"She changed lanes and hit my front wing."

"I just knew it would be a 'she' and she's either young and lovely with a firm body or old with drooping tits and loads of money."

"Right first time."

"Young and firm?"

"Oui."

"That means you're going to pay for the repairs and whilst I'm doing the job, you'll be getting your leg over."

"Precisely."

"Why didn't I become a taxi driver?"

"I don't know, but I'm going to see her tomorrow and I'll bring her down for the estimate."

"I look forward to it."

"And be fair to yourself, I've had a good run up since September."

"What, make a profit on one of your jobs?"

"Why not?"

"I guess there's always a first time."

"Always."

"OK, make it cash."

"Don't I always?"

Jean Gambetta grinned at Michel and replied "I'll see you tomorrow then."

Michel drove back to Montelivet to see if Mama and Alexis had arrived and to tell Monique that Angelique would be coming down from Grambois Friday morning. He arrived moments after Mama and Alexis and parked the Mercedes behind Alexis' very battered green Renault, after greeting them he started to unload the luggage and boxes of wine from the car. Mama went into the building followed by Alexis carrying several bags. Mama climbed the stairs slowly and as she reached the very top, Monique opened the door to greet her. At that moment Madame Rochas, from downstairs came out into the hallway to wish everyone 'Joyeux Noël'. Mama turned to return the greeting, lost her balance and plunged backwards into Alexis, who dropped everything she was carrying in an attempt to catch Mama and prevent her falling further. It was to no avail and the two women half fell and half rolled to the bottom of the stairs. Michel heard the rumble accompanied by the screaming and he left the Renault and ran into the hallway. The two elderly women lay in a tangled mass at the bottom of the stairs.

"Mon Dieu! Mon Dieu!" shrieked Monique as she rushed down the stairs to where her Mother and Aunt lay groaning. Michel fairly bounced through the front door and rushed to the inert, tangled pair. Mama was firmly placed on top of Alexis and Michel put his arms round his rotund Mother-in-law and half lifted and half dragged the injured woman to one side. He was relieved to see Alexis move and then sit up. Monique bent down and assisted her Aunt to an upright position saying "are you alright, Aunt?"

"Oui, oui, Monique, I think so, just a little bruised I think."

"Bon, bon."

"Mama, Mama, are you hurt?" enquired Michel of his white faced relative.

"It's my ankle, I've done something to my ankle" she moaned.

Michel looked at it and to him it appeared swollen and possibly was getting worse. At that moment Madame Rochas appeared carrying two tumblers of brandy which she offered to Alexis and Mama.

"Here, my dears, this will help, and as I said 'Joyeux Noël'."

They took the glasses and returned the compliments of the season. Michel thought it was all unbelievable.

"I think we'd better take you both to hospital."

"Non, it's not necessary" said Alexis between mouthfuls of

brandy.

"Oui, it is, now come on. Monique get your coat and help me get Mama into the car."

Half an hour later Michel parked at the casualty entrance of the Hospital de Timone. Alexis was able to follow him, helped by Monique.

"I have an elderly lady in the car with an injured ankle, can someone help please?" he asked the receptionist nurse.

"Of course, Monsieur" she replied and pushed a bell on her desk top as Alexis and Monique arrived. The nurse asked "are you all together?"

"Oui" replied Michel.

"OK, please take a seat and I'll get the duty doctor."

She had just finished speaking when two orderlies arrived with a wheelchair and Michel led them out to the Mercedes where all three struggled to extricate Mama from the back seat. She was now in considerable pain and Michel blessed Madame Rochas for her untimely good wishes.

They placed Mama in a cubicle with Alexis next door. Mama began to cry and Michel went outside to smoke a calming cigarette whilst Monique did her best to comfort her Mother. When he returned the doctor was examining Mama's swollen ankle. He was a little taken aback when he recognised the doctor as the rather severe woman he had brought to the hospital yesterday and had flippantly wished 'have a good day healing'. She glanced up at him and Michel wondered why life was just series of circles, one within another, the same people and situations constantly revolving past at different speeds.

"Bonjour, doctor" he said with a sickly grin.

"Monsieur" she mumbled back and then said to Mama "I think we'd better x-ray your ankle and in any case I want you stay in overnight so we can check you out, OK?"

"Oh, mon Dieu, have I got to stay?"

"Oui, Madame, I'm afraid so."

"You'll be alright, Mama" coaxed Monique.

"Now let's look at the other lady" said the doctor firmly.

After a careful examination it was determined that Alexis was alright except for a few bruises so Michel drove his wife and Aunt back to Montelivet.

"Well what a good start to Christmas this is" complained Monique.

"It was an accident, ma petite" replied Michel.

"If Madame Rochas hadn't come out at that moment...."

"You know the saying 'with 'if' we could put Paris in a bottle'," replied Michel.

"I know, I know" said Monique testily "but if Mama's broken her ankle then it means I've got to look after her on top of everything else over the holiday."

"You've taken on too much as usual, I mean fancy inviting Henri and his wife...."

"It's years since we've seen them and besides if I want to invite them I will!" she snapped back.

They completed the journey in silence and when Michel parked the Mercedes behind Alexis's battered Renault, Monique slipped out and helped her Aunt into the flat without saying a word to her husband. Michel brought the rest of the luggage and wine into the flat and then went back to the Renault and locked it.

"I'm going back to work" he said loftily once Alexis was seated comfortably and Monique had finished fussing round her.

"Are you coming home for dinner?" asked Monique.

"Oui" Michel replied.

Monique just nodded and Michel left quietly.

Relieved to be back at his station Michel drew heavily on a cigarette to calm his nerves. This Christmas was shaping up to a complete nightmare and he began to have deep forebodings. Perhaps things could only get better but somehow he doubted it.

The rear passenger door opened and a fare got in, as he was about to ask for the destination he glanced in his mirror to see the stern face of Gerrard and he realised things were about to get worse.

"Bonjour, Michel."

"Bonjour, Monsieur Gerrard, where to?"

"Out on the Corniche and stop somewhere, we need to talk."

"Oui." Michel started up and swung the Mercedes out and around le Vieux Port and on towards the coast road to Cassis. Gerrard remained silent until Michel pulled off into the usual spot and stopped the car.

"Michel" he began seriously "the telephone number in London that you gave me was passed to my British chums at Scotland Yard, who traced the address."

"Bon" replied Michel, knowing that by the tone of Gerrard's voice it had all gone horribly wrong.

"And they followed it up by raiding the premises, which turned out to be a sleazy massage parlour in the Holloway Road, frequented by two of their MP's."

"Mon Dieu!" exclaimed Michel and then he giggled which made Gerrard furious.

"Do you know what this means, you idiot?" Gerrard shouted.

"I can guess."

"It means, one, the Marseille Gendarmerie and me in particular, have been made to look like incompetent fools, two, Salvator has tricked you and will know who passed on the phone number and three, he has not been arrested and will no doubt return to Marseille looking for a certain taxi driver, who unfortunately no longer has the protection of the police!"

"Bloody good isn't it? I pass on the number given to me by Salvator and you and your 'British chums' cock it up by raiding the place before finding out whether he's there or not and then you have the cheek to blame me!" exclaimed Michel angrily.

"I do blame you, Michel."

"Monsieur Ronay to you from now on, especially as I am no longer receiving any police protection and I'm sure that once I have told Antone all about this and he's chatted to your chief, you also won't be enjoying any police protection either because you'll be back out on the streets in uniform handing out parking tickets!"

That went in deep and they sat in silence until Gerrard said "take me back to le Vieux Port."

They drove back without saying a word and when Michel pulled up at his station Gerrard paid the fare and departed in silence. Michel then drove round to Rue Bonneterie, double parked and went into Ricky's bar.

"Ah, Michel, ça va?" smiled Jacques.

"Ça va, Jacques" he replied as the barman poured the Pernod.

"And how bad is Michel's world today?" asked Jacques.

"A complete catastrophe" replied Michel.

"Nothing changes, mon ami."

"Non, is Antone here?"

"Oui, at the back as usual."

Michel paid and took his drink and went in search of the great man. Antone smiled as Michel approached and waved him to a creaking wicker chair next to him.

"Ça va, Michel?"

"Ça va, Antone."

"You look worried, may I know what's troubling you?"

Michel sipped his Pernod and told Antone the whole story down to the smallest detail. The great man listened in silence and then said "you have done everything asked of you, now leave it to me to have a quiet word in the ear of those who can influence events."

Michel thanked him sincerely and felt much better when he left Ricky's and returned to his station.

It was one of those days, Michel knew it was because the next three fares consisted of couples who argued from the moment they got into the taxi until the moment they arrived at their destination. Michel added an 'argument tax' to each fare to help allay his suffering.

Twice at the taxi station Michel met René who waved, winked and said "Saturday night!". Whilst taking a break and drawing heavily on a soothing cigarette, he glanced at his watch, it was almost eight, time to meet Josette at Ricky's.

Double parking outside he slipped from behind the wheel just as Gerrard appeared from nowhere.

"Let me buy you a drink, Michel."

'Mon Dieu!' thought Michel 'he has got his little shoes on!'

"Why thank you, Monsieur Gerrard" he replied with a smile.

They approached the bar and Jacques poured a Pernod as soon as he spotted Michel and then asked "for you, Monsieur Gerrard?"

"A large brandy, s'il vous plaît."

"Oui, Monsieur."

"Let's sit and talk" said Gerrard as he paid for the drinks. Michel nodded and followed the Gendarme to the back of the bar where they settled into the creaking wicker chairs.

"Cheers" said Gerrard and Michel responded.

"Now then, Michel" began Gerrard, "I feel that when we had

our discussion earlier, well…" he hesitated and Michel knew that Antone must have spoken to the chief, who in turn had clarified Gerrard's thinking, "I was a little hasty, I was disappointed you see that Salvator escaped the net and I allowed it to show."

"I understand completely, Monsieur Gerrard."

"You do?"

"Oui, I would have felt the same, Monsieur Gerrard" replied Michel, letting the Gendarme completely off the hook.

"Call me Cyril" cooed the Gendarme.

"And I just know you'll catch him when he returns to Marseille, Cyril."

"Oh we will, you can be sure of that."

"Bon" replied Michel, secretly hoping that the good looking bastard never set foot in France again let alone Marseille.

"And we want you to go on working with us as before and I assure you that you'll have complete police protection" said Gerrard hastily.

"Well…." began Michel slowly.

"You have the chief's word on that" interrupted the harassed Gendarme.

Michel felt reassured.

"Bon, Cyril, how can I help?"

"From earlier today, we've placed a twenty four hour surveillance team on Edward Salvator, we're monitoring every move he makes and we think Claude will contact his father somehow and then they'll meet somewhere. We will then pounce like a cat on the rats." His eyes gleamed as he said it and he thumped the table with his fist.

"Bon" replied Michel calmly "and what do you want me to do?"

"Just let me know if you see or hear anything from Salvator."
Michel shivered inside and replied "of course, Cyril, I'll let you know straight away."

"Bon, now I must go and see how my surveillance team is getting on" said Gerrard as he finished his drink and then stood up.

'Once a Gendarme always a Gendarme' thought Michel.

"I'm pleased were back working together, Michel."

"Oui, bon, Cyril."

"Stay in touch" he said as he wandered off through the bar and out into Rue Bonneterie.

Michel sat deep in thought when he suddenly became aware of Jacques standing in front of him.

"Guess you could do with another drink after that" said Jacques.

"Oui" replied Michel quietly. As Jacques disappeared the lovely Josette glided through the door and smiled beautifully when she spied her man. Michel beamed at his love as she approached. They kissed and she sat next to her future husband.

"Are you taking me to dinner?" she asked pertly.

"I'm afraid not tonight, ma cherie, I have an injured Mother-in-law in hospital."

"Oh, mon Dieu! What has happened to her?"

Michel explained the whole situation in detail whilst Jacques brought drinks to their table. Josette showed genuine concern and that was another reason that he loved her so. She was gentle, compassionate and caring.

"Dinner tomorrow night then?" she asked determined that nothing would keep her from her Fiancé.

"Oui, I have a job at eight, I have to take Lascelles the politician to see important people in Aix, and then I'll be back, sometime around ten and we'll go to Chez Marius."

"Bon, and you'll stay the night?"

"Possibly."

"I hope so, cherie, I want to talk to you about moving into the new flat."

Michel felt cold inside.

"Oui, of course" he replied.

"I want to move in before Christmas."

Michel felt colder still.

"Before Christmas?" he queried.

"Oui, bien sûr."

The thought of having to be involved with that operation numbed his brain.

"Oui, we must talk and make plans" he replied.

It was an hour later when he arrived home in Montelivet.

"You're late" said Monique firmly.

"I've been very busy" he replied.

"Busy in Ricky's for some of the time, no doubt."

"How's your Mother?" he asked as he slumped down on the settee.

"I phoned at six and the hospital said she had broken her ankle and she's now in plaster."

"Oh, mon Dieu!"

"Precisely, other than that she's alright."

"Bon."

"They're bringing her home in an ambulance tomorrow afternoon."

"Bon."

"She'll have to rest of course."

"Of course."

"So it'll be more work for me looking after her all over the bloody holiday!"

"Get cousin Henri and his wife to help." That made her angry and she replied "how about you helping?"

"I'm too busy working" he replied.

"Hmmm" she mumbled and went out into the kitchen.

Dinner consisted of soup followed by roast chicken and then fruit and cheese. During the meal Alexis became tearful insisting the accident was all her fault and it took some time to convince her that she was blameless.

Michel was glad when it was time to go to bed and when he undressed he decided to sleep in a T-shirt so that his wife would not see the scratches imposed on his body by Sophia.

He fell asleep the moment his head touched the pillow.

CHAPTER 3

Wednesday 17th December.

Michel awoke feeling distinctly hung over. He had drunk too much last night and was now feeling the effects. A shower would do him good and as he struggled out of bed he tossed his T shirt on the floor. He had only gone a few steps towards the en-suite when Monique called out from the bed "how did you get those scratches on your back?" 'Oh, bollocks' he thought as he turned to face his angry wife.

"I expect it was when I was helping your Mother out of the back of the car at the hospital" he lied and he congratulated himself on thinking that one up so quickly and so early in the morning as well.

"Liar" she replied.

"There's a bit of trim that's come loose over the rear door and it caught my back, I'll have to let Gambetta fix it next time the car is in for repair."

"Liar" she repeated and turned over in a sulk. Michel sighed and went into the shower.

An hour later Michel was at his station, clean and feeling refreshed by the hot, black coffee that Monique had made without speaking to her errant husband. The morning was very bright but cold. He sat with the window of the Mercedes closed as he read the morning paper and drew on his first cigarette of the day. As he was reading without paying much attention, he thought of the day ahead, it promised to be busy. One of the first things was to call on Mademoiselle Devaux and arrange for her to bring the battered Citroen to Gambetta's for an estimate. That would be interesting; he wondered what her Mother looked like.

A tap on the passenger window drew his attention. He glanced up to see Sayid's beaming face and Michel wound down the window to greet his friend.

"Bonjour, Michel, ça va?"

"Bonjour, Sayid, get in, it's cold out there." Sayid nodded and joined Michel in the front of the Mercedes.

"Sold the Christmas cards yet?" he enquired.

"Non, but I might know later, I've left a sample or two with various contacts" he replied.

"Bon, now I want you to come and see these cadeaux boxes I've just got in, they're really exquisite" said the Arab.

"I don't think so, Sayid, I've got a lot on my plate at the moment….."

"I promise you, Michel, you'll go mad when you see them."

"Where are they from?"

"Romania."

"I will go mad then, I've still got hundreds of bloody odd sized Romanian sandals in my garage at Grambois!"

"Just discount them and move them on it's easy…."

"How is it that when we do business I never make any money?" interrupted Michel.

"Well neither do I…."

"Why not?"

"Because you never pay me" came the quick reply.

That stopped Michel dead in his tracks for the moment and then he relented.

"OK, mon ami, let's go and see these cadeaux boxes." Sayid smiled and Michel started up the taxi and drove to Sayid's flat.

The boxes were truly exquisite, the colours were scintillating, dark blue, ruby red, jade green and magenta. They were bound in brass with petite padlocks to match and their rounded tops made them look like miniature sea chests, the type that pirates used to keep their treasure in. Michel felt sure he could sell some of these. He examined a box and when he opened it and saw the padded silk lined interior he was very impressed.

"Aren't they beautiful?" asked Sayid as he watched the expression on Michel's face.

"They are" he agreed.

"How many do you want to start with?" asked Sayid.

"How much are they?"

"Whatever I say you know you can double it" came the reply.

"How much?"

"A hundred Francs each."

"I'll take four and see what I can do." Sayid nodded and Michel chose one of each colour. Sayid put them in a cardboard box with some wrapping paper and Michel handed him four hundred Francs.

Michele returned to his station and pulled up behind René. His friend saw him arrive and left his Renault.
"Bonjour, Michel, ça va?"
"Ça va, René."
"It's cold today and no one's about yet."
"Oui, but I've been doing business already."
"Bon."
"Come and see what I've got in the boot."
René joined Michel and peered in at the cardboard box. His face lit up when he saw the boxes.
"Mon Dieu, they look good" he said and then asked "where did you get them?"
"From Sayid, he wants a hundred Francs each for them."
"I'll have a couple" said René.
"OK, choose your colours now, but I want to show them around today, so you can take them later."
"OK, I'll have the red and the green one."
"OK."
"And I'll pay you then" said René. Michel nodded and replied "by the way, they're two hundred Francs to everyone else." His friend grinned.

As René made his way back to his taxi he noticed the scrape on the front wing of the Mercedes.
"Another accident?" he queried.
"Just a little one" replied Michel and he added "but she's going to pay for it!"
"She?" queried René "I might have guessed" and he laughed as he slipped behind the wheel of the Renault.

Within moments a fare arrived in the shape of a large lady in a fur coat, she boarded René's taxi. Michel moved up as his friend swung out to join the morning rush hour traffic in la Canebiére. Suddenly Michel's rear door opened and a slim woman slipped into the back of the taxi and said "Rue Saint Pierre, driver, number forty."

"Oui, Madame" he replied as he started the engine and moved off. 'What luck' he thought 'that's just where Mademoiselle

Devaux lives.'

"A nice day, Madame" he said brightly.

"Oui" came the reply from the back seat.

"Finished your Christmas shopping?" he enquired.

"Haven't started it yet."

"Neither have I."

"I'd cancel Christmas if I had my way."

"Why's that, Madame?"

"It's all too commercialised now, I mean, all we get now from the television is 'buy this and buy that', spend, spend, spend. We're living in a fools' paradise."

'No chance of a tip then' thought Michel.

"It is the time for giving" he countered.

"Maybe, but not when you've got as many relations as I have" she replied firmly.

"Mmm" he mumbled and the thought of cousin Henri and his wife, Jackie, crossed his mind. He had not seen the pair for several years and he was not keen to see them again, especially at Christmas. Henri had inherited a shop selling something or other, from his father and according to Monique he had made quite a success of it. Michel planned to question him closely on that.

Michel turned into the Rue Saint Pierre and his fare reminded him "number forty, driver."

"Oui, Madame."

He stopped outside the block of flats and the woman paid her fare. She paid the exact money and as she slammed the door Michel mumbled 'Joyeux Noël to you too!'.

Driving up the Rue he turned left into Boulevard Fabrici and stopped outside number 23. Spotting the damaged Citroen parked two cars ahead he eased the Mercedes into a very tight gap. Boulevard Fabrici is in a relatively poor area of Marseille near the massive cemetery where generations of Marseille families have their vaults and petite mausoleums.

He rang the sonnette against the name 'Devaux' twice before a gentle voice replied "hello."

"Bonjour, this is Michel Ronay, taxi driver, who was in an accident with Mademoiselle Devaux."

"Oh, Monsieur Ronay, please come in." The door clicked and Michel entered the hallway and made his way up the stairs to the second floor. He recognised the tall woman standing in the doorway of her flat. She was a beautifully mature edition of the young mademoiselle that had collided with the Mercedes.

"Madame Devaux?" he enquired.

"Oui" she replied "do come in."

"Merci" he replied and entered the warm atmosphere of the flat. He followed her into the living room where the delectable Mademoiselle Annette rose from the settee to greet him.

"Monsieur Ronay" she half whispered.

"Michel, please" he smiled in reply.

"Do sit down, Monsieur" said Madame "can I get you a coffee or something?"

"A coffee would be fine, thank you, black and sweet, I was working until very late last night and I'm barely awake yet."

"Of course" she replied and disappeared into the kitchen.

"So you found us alright" said Annette.

"Oui, being a taxi driver made it quite easy" he replied and she blushed at that.

"Of course, how silly of me."

"Not at all" replied Michel and continued "have you been out in the car much since our little mishap?"

"Only once, I'm still a little nervous."

"That's understandable. What did your father have to say?"

"My parents are divorced and my father lives in Paris now."

"Oh, I'm sorry" said Michel warming instantly to the future prospects.

"I don't see him very often" she said sadly.

At that moment the elegant Madame Devaux entered with the coffee.

"I hope it's to your taste, Monsieur Ronay."

"I'm sure it will be, and please call me Michel."

"Thank you Michel, I'm Jacqueline and my daughter is Annette."

"I'm pleased to meet you both" he smiled and sipped the life giving liquid.

"Now Annette has told me all about the accident and it was obviously all her fault...."

"Non, Jacqueline" he interrupted "an accident is never all one persons fault, but let's not go back over that, I've come here to make arrangements for the repairs to both cars and if you or Annette would care to follow me to my contact's garage for the estimate...."

"But whose going to pay, Michel?"

"Well I am, of course."

"You?"

"Oui."

"But why?"

"Because it saves getting the insurance companies involved."

"But Michel...."

"I am happy to pay, the repair bill will not be that much I'm sure."

"You're too kind."

He smiled back and murmured "I know."

"I don't know how we can repay your kindness" said Jacqueline.

'I'll think of something' thought Michel as he carried on smiling.

Jacqueline, accompanied by her daughter, drove the Citroen behind Michel at a safe distance. They arrived outside Gambetta's garage and Michel suggested that they remained in their car whilst he went in to find his friend.

"Jean."

"Oui, Michel" came the reply from the little wooden office at the back of the garage.

"We're here" said Michel as he approached the gloomy shack.

"So I notice" replied Gambetta as he put down his pen on the piles of disorganised and grease smeared paperwork.

Michel smiled and said "I don't think the damage is that bad after all, so if you can keep the price down I'd...."

"Bloody cheek, you told me you were flush and I could make a profit for the first time!"

"Of course, of course, just make it a little profit, that's all."

The old man shook his head and followed Michel out into the bright cold daylight.

"Mon Dieu! Two of them!" exclaimed Gambetta as he approached the Citroen with a smile.

"Mother and daughter" replied Michel.

"Which one's first for rumpy pumpy?"

"Don't be so crude" replied Michel.

"Mon Dieu, Michel, you should be dead by now with exhaustion."

"Well I'm not."

"They'll put your dick in a museum one day."

"Just do the estimate."

Gambetta nodded to Jacqueline and her daughter and then set about examining the dent. With all the necessary breath sucking, gentle one tone whistling, removal of beret and head scratching, he eventually came up with a price.

"How much?" Michel asked in a half choked whisper.

"You heard" replied Gambetta "and that's a good trade price and I haven't looked at the Merc yet."

"Mon Dieu!"

"Exactly, welcome to the real world."

"But….."

"Now you realise how much money it's cost me over the years doing jobs for you that have been a complete loss to me!"

"If your charging that sort of money for car repairs you must be the richest man in Marseille!"

"Possibly" grinned the old man and went on "let's look at the Merc."

Michel wandered, pale faced behind Jean to his taxi. Again, the sighting of the panel followed by breath sucking and whistling produced another staggering price. Michel leaned against the car for support and asked "when can you fit them in?"

"Tomorrow the Citroen and the Merc on Friday."

"You'll get it all done that quickly?"

"Oui, you're my Christmas rush" grinned the old man.

"Mon Dieu, I'm trapped in a life of poverty."

"You'll get over it."

"It's a catastrophe."

"No it's not, and I'll only need the Merc for the day, it's only a little scrape…."

"That's what I said!" exclaimed Michel.

"I know, but I had to verify that professionally."

"And you're going to charge me two thousand Francs for two days work?"

"Oui."

"Mon Dieu!………"

"Bring the Citroen in tomorrow as early as you can, it'll be ready to collect Friday. I'll lend you something for the day whilst I repair your car" interrupted Gambetta.

"At these prices I'll have to consider taking my work elsewhere in future."

"Don't be silly, Michel, I'll see you tomorrow" and with that Gambetta waved to Jacqueline and her daughter, shook hands with Michel and returned to his greasy paperwork.

"It's all arranged" said Michel through the open window of the Citroen to Jacqueline "Jean will repair your car first, he'll start it tomorrow and it'll be ready Friday morning for you."

"Oh, Michel, that's wonderful!" she exclaimed.

"I'll meet you here at about nine in the morning and I'll take you home, is that OK?"

"Thank you so much."

"Not at all, now drive safely" he said as he patted the roof and then waved as his new found friends drove away smiling.

Michel decided to call on Pierre next to see if he could persuade him to buy the Christmas cards in bulk, as he now needed all the money he could get, he parked outside 26 Rue Charbonniere, rang the sonnette and went into the esteemed establishment. Pierre was positively beaming when Michel was ushered into his office by the lovely Christine, one of Pierre's favourite girls.

"Ah, Michel, bonjour, good to see you, sit down and have a drink."

"Oh, bonjour, Pierre, merci, Pernod s'il vous plaît" replied Michel as he sank into the comfortable chair opposite the ever smiling brothel owner whilst Christine poured the drinks.

Michel felt he had a chance to get a sale as it was a long time since he had seen Pierre in such a good mood.

"So, the English Christmas cards then" said Pierre.

"Oui, what do think?" queried Michel.

"I think…..I think, I'll drink to the good health of all the judges in Marseille before I make a decision" he replied, Michel nodded and thought 'it must have been a very good night last night'.

Christine handed the two men their drinks and said with a smile "I'll leave you now and go and help clean up the mess."

"Bless you, ma petite" said Pierre and blew her a little kiss.
"Au revoir, Michel"
"Au revoir, Christine."
"It all went well last night then?" asked Michel as he sipped his Pernod.
"Very well, in fact very, very well and they're all coming back in January with some of their colleagues from Lyon, some judicial convention or something."
"Bon."
"You can say that again, I doubled the prices and threw in lots of extras."
"Go on, like what?" asked Michel eager for information about 'extras.'
"Well, I arranged an early dinner party for them and the sweet was Nicole and Christine stretched out naked on the table and covered with cream. They enjoyed licking it all off and it made the girls so randy with all those tongues working away at them."
"Sounds good" said Michel appreciatively.
"It was good, because when they'd finished that they all wanted to be creamed up and they had all the girls lick them off. Never seen anything like it, a real Roman orgy, and it took 'til the early hours before they were all fucked out."
"Brilliant."
"And then they gave all the girls a thousand Franc tip each!"
"Mon Dieu, they must have been well pleased."
"They were, believe me and I've got the date in January for the next do and they've asked for a couple of young gays to be at the party as some of the old judges are bisexual."
"Have a word with Antone, he has lots of young friends" said Michel helpfully.
"I had planned to do that" replied Pierre as he leaned back in his executive chair and contemplated the ceiling.
"Christmas cards?" Michel reminded him.
"Oui, how many in a box?"
"Ten."
"I'll take ten boxes."
"Oh, bon, merci" gasped Michel.
"Can you drop them in tomorrow?"
"Oui, I must tell you they're a hundred Francs a box."

"Michel, I don't care how much they are, I'm going to send them to the Judges and Gerrard and his silly mates, I want them to enjoy a bit of sophistication from me and the oldest profession."

"You're a great entrepreneur, Pierre, you and the girls will go right to the top."

As Michel left 26 Rue Charbonniere with Pierre's thousand Francs tucked neatly in his wallet, he glanced up to see Edward Salvator leaving his flat at number 12 and getting into the back of his large black Mercedes which then sped away. Seconds later a white Renault with two men in it swung out from the line of parked cars and hurried off in the same direction as the Mercedes. The police tail was well and truly pinned on Salvator.

Michel went straight to Ricky's, double parked the taxi and stepped into the warm, welcoming surroundings.

"Ça va, Michel?" asked Jacques as he poured the Pernod.

"Ça va, Jacques" replied Michel.

"And your world is better today because you're smiling" said Jacques.

"Oui, it is, in fact it's a lot, lot better."

"Bon" Jacques replied and he went off to serve another customer.

Michel sat at the bar, sipped his drink and began to contemplate the day so far and decided to go home for lunch to see if Mama had arrived back from the hospital. He then planned to work right through until he collected Lascelles at eight for the trip up to Aix. He would drive straight back and collect Josette and take her to Chez Marius for dinner. Perfect.

"Bonjour, Michel" said a voice he knew and feared. The hairs stood up on the back of his neck as he turned to face Claude Salvator.

"Bonjour, Monsieur" he replied half choking with a mixture of fear and anxiety.

"Surprised to see me?" asked Claude.

"Oui, Monsieur, I thought you were in London."

"I was, but my Porsche is very fast and it doesn't take long to drive back home."

"Indeed, can I get you a drink?"

"Oui, I'll have a brandy, a large one I think."

"Oui, er, Jacques, a large brandy for Monsieur Salvator, s'il vous plaît." Jacques nodded and Michel turned and smiled at Salvator.

"Saw your father this morning" Michel said hoping to impress.

"Oh?"

"Oui, he was just leaving home."

"Did he say where he was going?"

"Er, no, we didn't actually speak, we just waved at a distance."

"I see" replied Salvator as he picked up the brandy and sipped the golden liquid. Michel could see that Claude was planning something.

"Michel" he said at last.

"Oui, Monsieur?"

"I want you to do something for me."

"Today, Monsieur?"

"Oui."

"I'm afraid I'm very busy today, Monsieur, perhaps….."

"Michel, you didn't hear me, I want you to do something for me today" interrupted Claude.

"Well, I will if I can, of course…."

"You will, Michel, I assure you" replied Claude in a menacing tone.

"Right, what is it?"

"Firstly, someone overheard our phone conversation and got hold of the London number I gave you…."

"Mon Dieu! How did that happen?" gasped Michel.

"I don't know, but the police raided the place soon after, so someone tipped them off."

"You can't trust anyone these days."

"And I want you to find out who told the police."

"Right."

"And I want to know by tonight."

"Right" said Michel as he shivered.

"Secondly, I want you to go and see my father this evening and tell him that I'm back here and I'll meet him in Bandol at midnight."

"Will he know where in Bandol?"

"Oui."

"Wouldn't you rather see him and tell him yourself?"

"Non, the phone is sure to be tapped and Gerrard and his mates are bound to be watching his flat, it's too dangerous for me to go near it."

"Right, so how shall I contact you tonight, Monsieur?"

"Just phone this number" and Salvator handed Michel a business card with a Marseille number written on the back."

"What time will you be there?"

"I won't be there, a woman will take your message and then she'll call me."

"Oh, bon."

"That'll avoid any police raids should that phone number be traced."

"Very wise, Monsieur."

"So, see my father, tell him I'm back and to meet me in Bandol and find out who leaked the London number and don't let me down, Michel."

"Certainly not, Monsieur."

"Call me Claude, after all, you are part of the family" he grinned then finished his brandy and with a little wave of his hand he left the bar.

"Oh, Mon Dieu, Mon Dieu, oh, Dieu."

"Day taken a turn for the worse, Michel?" asked Jacques.

"I'm dead."

"Large Pernod before you die?"

"Oui."

"I should go home after you've drunk this" said Jacques as he filled Michel's glass.

"I will."

Half an hour later Michel arrived back at his flat in Montelivet still shaken by the experience of meeting Salvator so unexpectedly.

"Are you alright?" enquired Monique as he entered the flat.

"Oui, I think so" he replied.

"Bon, Mama's home so go and say 'hello'".

Mama was sitting comfortably in Michel's favourite armchair opposite the television with her plastered ankle resting neatly on the foot stool. Her positioning made it difficult to move easily around the room. 'Bon Noël' thought Michel as he forced a smile and said "Mama, how are you feeling?"

"Not to bad, just a little sore, but I'll be alright."
"Bon, I'm sure you'll be fine by Christmas."
"Oui, it's not long now."
"True."
"And it will be so nice to see Henri and Jackie again."
"Oui" he replied as his heart sank.

Michel sat on the settee and pondered for a moment on the looming Christmas holiday when Frederik came in and interrupted his thoughts.

"Dad, I think Angelique is coming down tomorrow can you meet her at the bus station?"

Michel came back rapidly from his thoughts when he heard that and replied "no, her Mother is bringing her down on Friday, in the morning."

"How do you know?"

"Because I went up to Grambois yesterday and I called in to make the arrangements."

"Oh, thanks, Dad."

"That's OK, son, now, just one thing, where's she going to stay?"

"Here."

"I know, but where's she going to sleep?"

"Don't know, ask Mum." At which point Monique came in followed by Alexis clutching a large glass of red wine.

"Are you staying for lunch?" asked Monique as she fixed her husband with a stony stare.

"Oui, ma petite, and then I'm back to work until late tonight."

"And are you coming home tonight?" she hissed.

"Of course, ma petite, of course, but I expect to be a little late."

"Oui, I expect you will be" and then in a whisper "tell her to get her nails cut."

"What?" enquired Michel only half hearing what she had said.

"Nothing" replied Monique and she returned to the kitchen.

Alexis staggered forward and sat on the settee with Michel, took a sip of wine and said "Mama was lucky not to have been seriously hurt."

"Oui, she was" replied Michel.

"If she hadn't fallen on me heaven only knows what could have happened" said Alexis between sips.

"Oui."

"She could have been killed" and the word 'killed' electrified Michel's thoughts. He had to let Gerrard know that Salvator was back in Marseille before anything untoward happened to him. He picked up the phone and dialled Gerrard's direct line. It rang for what seemed an age before Michel heard the Gendarme's voice.

"Oui?"

"Cyril, it's Michel."

"Is this police business?"

"Oui, of course."

"Call me Gerrard then, you never know whose listening."

"Mon Dieu" sighed Michel in exasperation and then continued "Monsieur Gerrard......"

"Oui?"

"Claude Salvator is here in Marseille...."

"Where?"

"I met him in Ricky's about half an hour ago."

"Why did you not contact me right away?"

"I was so shocked I came straight home."

"Mon Dieu! The trail has probably gone cold by now, I'm very disappointed in you Michel...."

"Monsieur Ronay, s'il vous plaît."

"As I said, I'm very disappointed in you, you're supposed to be working with the police, not against us."

"What do you mean? I'm telling you now aren't I?"

"Oui, but it's probably too late."

"I doubt that."

"What did he say to you?" enquired Gerrard more calmly.

"He wants to know, by tonight, who tipped you off with the London phone number, and he wants me to see his father and give him a message to meet him in Bandol tonight."

"Where in Bandol?"

"I don't know."

"Well how will his father know where to go?"

"Monsieur Gerrard, they both know an address, or a bar, a restaurant where they usually rendezvous."

"Possibly" mused the Gendarme.

"Certainly."

"Well it seems to me that you are in a difficult position,

Monsieur Ronay."

"Oui, I can see that."

"You could be in serious danger, Salvator is ruthless you know."

"I know."

"And if you're not careful you could end up in a fisher man's hut upside down....."

"I know, I know" interrupted Michel testily.

"And I've no spare men to cover you unfortunately, we're under manned as it is, cut backs you understand."

"Oui."

"But I'll make sure my men keep close to Salvator tonight and when he leaves for Bandol to meet Claude, they'll be right behind him."

"Bon."

"Now you make sure you see the father and give him the message."

"I will."

"And if I were you, I wouldn't let Salvator know it was you who gave us the London number."

"Good thinking, Monsieur Gerrard" Michel replied and mumbled 'you prat.'

"Keep in touch."

"I will if I live" and he put the phone down.

"Who was that, Michel?" enquired Mama.

"Just a friend" replied Michel.

"Was it about Christmas?" she persisted.

"Oui."

"Are they coming here?"

"Non, Mama."

"That's good, I think we've far too many already and now I'm in this state I won't be able to help Monique."

"But I will" chipped in Alexis.

"I doubt it dear, remember Hélène arrives tomorrow and you two argue so much and then you always end up crying, well, I mean, you'll be no use to Monique."

"But I want to help."

"I know, but you'd be better off staying in here with me, out of the way of things." At that point Alexis started to dab her eyes between sips of wine and Michel went out to the kitchen.

"Angelique's coming here Friday morning" he said to Monique who was busy dishing up lunch.

"Is she?"

"Oui. Where is she going to sleep?"

"I don't know yet."

"Mmm."

"And this not the time to discuss this."

"OK, and by the way, you're Mother is busy upsetting Alexis" said Michel.

"Mon Dieu, and then Hélène arrives tomorrow."

"And she'll finish her off for Christmas" replied Michel.

"She will" agreed Monique.

"Oui, so joyeux Noël, ma petite" and he kissed his wife on her cheek.

The Ronay family enjoyed a leisurely lunch and Michel was not in a hurry to return to the cold, busy streets of Marseille. It was gone three when he drove down to his station at le Vieux Port and joined the rear of the taxi rank. As fares arrived the taxis left the station and joined the heavy traffic and Michel was soon at the front of the rank. He had just lit another cigarette when the rear door opened and his first fare of the afternoon slipped into the Mercedes.

"Michel" said a gentle feminine voice and he turned to see the lovely Evette Moreau.

"Evette! bonjour, bonjour, ma petite" he exclaimed, delighted at seeing this beautiful mistress once again.

"How are you?" she enquired.

"Bon, and yourself?"

"OK."

"Just OK?"

"Oui."

"Why's that?"

"Well I haven't seen you much since before August."

"I know, ma petite, I've been so busy, I really have."

"Take me home now and you can tell me all about it."

Michel smiled, nodded and swung the Mercedes out into la Canebiére, joining the traffic he headed towards Evette's flat in

Avenue des Mimosas just off the Rue Aviateur. They chatted all the way and Evette reminded Michel that he had called to see her just four times since he returned from his August holiday in Grambois.

"But I have been frantically busy" he said again struggling for sympathy. Michel was a little frightened of her because she was always very sexually aggressive and demanding. She always seemed to be making up for lost time and was a touch desperate on occasions. Michel wanted to keep close to her because not only was she very lovely, but she held a senior position with a Bank, which might come in very useful if he needed an urgent loan. He stopped outside the flat and she said "you'd better come in for a coffee or something, you must be tired by this time of day."

"Oui, it has been hectic" he lied knowing that he was about to enjoy a flurry of sexual activity. He parked the Mercedes and helped carry her shopping into the flat. It was warm and welcoming and as he made himself comfortable on the settee he enquired after her son "how's Roger?"

"He's OK, he's gone to Nice to see his grandmother " she replied from the kitchen.

"Oh, bon" said Michel knowing that, as they would be undisturbed and he had not had Evette for a month or so, he was in for a heavy session.

She returned with two cups of coffee and two tumblers of brandy on a silver tray.

"I thought you might like a little brandy to warm you up."

"Merci, ma petite." He replied as he took the cup and tumbler.

"Here's to us" she said as she sat beside him.

"Cheers."

"It's nice to have you here."

"It's nice to be here."

"Well" she began "since I last saw you I've been doing a lot of shopping."

"Really" he replied as he sipped his black, sweet coffee.

"Oui, and I've got quite an ensemble to show you."

"Bon, I look forward to it."

"Just remind me, ma petite, do you like thigh length leather boots, lace up ones I mean?"

"Oh, oui, I do, I do" he replied almost choking on the hot

coffee.

"Oh, bon, which colour do you like best, black, white or red?"

"Black, I think" he gurgled in reply.

"Bon, I'll start with those then and put the others on later" she smiled.

"Please don't rush on my account."

"I won't I promise you, I'll take my time this afternoon."

"You do that" he smiled.

"Now tell me, what are you doing for Christmas?" she enquired and Michel poured his heart out in great detail and finished with the arrangements for Henri and Jackie from Le Touquet.

"My poor petite fleur" she said in true sympathy at the end.

"Oui."

"You can always stay here for a day or two if it gets too much for you."

"Merci, ma petite, I may well do that."

"Bon, Roger won't mind."

"Oh, bon."

"Now you finish your drinks and relax whilst I get ready" she said and she leaned forward and kissed him hard on the lips. She tasted sweet.

Michel finished the brandy and settled back to await the entrance of Evette. It seemed an age before the door opened and she appeared. She had made her face up with heavy make up and had used a bright red lipstick which made her lips look much more generous. She pouted at him and he felt his penis thickening rapidly. She wore a Cossack style fur hat which matched her knee length fur coat. It all looked very expensive and Michel guessed it was mink. Her black boots clicked on the wood floor as she paraded up and down, pouting all the while. She looked stunning and Michel longed to see what she had on underneath. She turned her back on him and undid the coat and then whirled round. She held the coat open so he could feast his eyes on her. She wore a black choker around her neck with a diamond sparkling at the centre, a black satin basque that was drawn in tight and pushed her ample breasts up over the top and finished on her hips so that the tops of her legs and thick pubic hair were perfectly revealed and it left just a gap of thigh before the tops of her black lace up boots.

Michel gasped and she asked "what do you want to kiss first?"

"Oh, Mon Dieu! Everything!"

"Come here then you naughty fucker" she replied and she stood with her legs open and hands on hips. Michel was at her in a second, first kissing her generous mouth again and again and then down to her hardening nipples and then on his knees burying his face in her pubic hair. She held his head hard against her body and commanded "Just lick, ma petite, until I tell you to stop!" He did as he was told until she was moaning with pleasure and then he put his hands round her bottom and pulled her gently open whilst rubbing his fingers gently round her smooth little hole.

"I'm ready now, Michel, now, now, ma petite, and I want it hard!" and with that she sank to the floor and opened her legs. Michel fumbled with his trousers and underpants to release his rigid penis which he then drove in one long surge right up inside Evette.

"Mon Dieu! You're fucking big but I need it" she gasped as she locked her thigh length boots around Michel's waist.

Michel rode at speed whilst she pushed up hard to maximise his penetration. It could not last long as the pace was too frantic and between deep kisses, Evette screamed out "Now! Now! Now!" and Michel rammed her with all his strength. They ended up panting and wedged against the door, her mink coat providing the most elegant slide across the polished wood floor.

"Mon Dieu, that was good" she said between gasps.

"Oui, it was."

"You'll need to rest, ma petite, there's more to come."

"More?" gasped Michel.

"Oui, you haven't seen the red boots yet."

"Mon Dieu."

"So rest awhile and I'll get you some more coffee."

Michel dragged himself off his mistress and hobbled back to the settee where he flopped down with his trousers and pants still round his ankles. 'More?' he thought, as he rested still panting after the exertion on the floor. Evette went to the kitchen and quickly returned with more coffee and brandy.

"Now drink this slowly and rest, then I'll give you one more show and then I expect you'll want to get back to work." Michel felt weak at the knees, the very thought of work!

"And take your trousers and pants off, ma cherie, you don't

look very elegant like that." Michel did as he was told and then tried to breathe deeply.

They chatted, drank the coffee and brandy and rested for more than an hour before Evette said "I'll go and get ready now, ma petite."

She slipped away and was back sooner than Michel expected. As she entered the room he gasped as this time she was all in red. She wore a red silk top hat, a red tail coat with a red satin basque underneath with red thigh boots. She looked stunning as she paraded up and down flicking the tails of the coat and swishing a wispy black cane that was about a metre long.

"What d'you think, baby?" she cooed as she winked at him.

"Gorgeous" he replied.

"Like my tail?"

"Oh, I do, I really do."

"I thought you might" she smiled and swished the black cane again. She then undid the button at the front of the coat to reveal her breasts pushed up over the top of the basque.

"You look good enough to eat" he gasped.

"Correct, ma petite, I just hope you're really hungry."

"Oh, I am" he replied as his penis hardened once again. She parade some more and then came over to the settee, turned her back on him and bent over. The tails of the coat fell apart and went either side of her bare bottom.

"Now kiss my bum, cherie" she commanded and Michel did so with a passion and then he went on to lick it.

"That's lovely, baby, just keep going." Michel could not stop and eventually pulled her back on to his lap where she expertly guided his penis into her moist body. He thumped her up and down for some while before she rose up and stood, turned and laid on the floor with her legs open. Michel was on top of her in a second and she wrapped her red boots around his waist as her top hat went flying. Michel rode her hard again and this time his pleasure was intensified as she whipped his bare bottom with her swishy black cane. As he had already come once he was able to go on for sometime, encouraged by the whipping of the cane. It was all too good to last and he eventually came with a force that even surprised him. They lay panting and it was only when he disentangled himself from his delicious mistress that he first felt pains from his bottom. He went to the bathroom and check himself in the mirror. His worst fears were realised as he gazed at the many red weal's on his plump behind. 'Oh, mon Dieu!'

Half an hour later Michel had passionately kissed Evette goodbye and had lowered his stinging behind onto the driving seat of the Mercedes. He headed for 12, Rue Charbonniere and Edward Salvator's flat. Michel noticed both the black Mercedes and the white Renault with two men inside, parked nearby. He squeezed into a gap and left the Mercedes as fast as his stinging bottom would allow and rang the sonnette.
"Oui?"
"Monsieur Salvator?"
"Oui."
"It's Michel Ronay, the taxi driver."
"Oh, non, not you again."
"Oui, I have an urgent message from your son."
"Is he here?"
"Oui, Monsieur."
"Come in, come in then."
The door clicked and Michel entered the flat. In a short while he had given the message to Salvator, who appeared delighted at the news. He thanked Michel, gave him a hundred Franc note for his troubles and told him not to tell anyone about Claude or the message. Michel promised that he would not tell another soul, he reasoned that this was OK as he had already told Gerrard and therefore it was a promise he could keep.

Michel drove to Ricky's bar where he remained standing whilst he sipped another brandy and ate one of Jacques delicious ham and cheese baguettes to keep him going until it was time for dinner with Josette at Chez Marius.

It was just before eight that he stopped outside Lascelles flat in Montelivet. He rang the sonnette, announced himself and within moments the politician had joined him in the street.
"Ah, Michel, I'm looking forward to this."
"Of course, Monsieur."
"Let's get going then."
Michel set off at a cracking pace towards Aix as he wished to

deliver Lascelles to the girls and get back to Josette as soon as possible.

"I plan to stay the night, Michel."

"Oui, Monsieur."

"So, can you collect me tomorrow about ten?"

"Non, Monsieur, I have a booking at nine in Marseille and I won't be free until well after ten, midday would be the earliest I could get to Aix."

"That's OK, I'll wait for you then."

"Bon."

They spoke very little from then on as Michel hurried the Mercedes through the night towards Aix. At last they arrived in the Boulevard Turin and Michel followed the eager politician to Maria and Claudette's flat. They were delighted to see Michel and the accident prone Lascelles. Whilst Claudette was talking to the politician, Michel took Maria to one side and whispered "I've got a very sore behind, have you got any ointment?"

"What, have you got piles or something?" she asked with a giggle.

"No, er, a lady friend has overdone the er, whipping."

"Oh, oui, come into the bathroom, we've got something for that."

"I knew you'd understand."

Michel followed the pretty young woman and undid his trousers to reveal his well lashed bottom.

"Mon Dieu!" exclaimed Maria "she's either an amateur or an animal."

"An animal, I assure you."

"Keep still, this may sting a little" she said as she smeared a pink ointment from a large tube onto his pulsating red flesh. It did sting and Michel clenched his teeth.

"There" she said and Michel replied "merci, ma petite."

"Now, whilst were together...."

"Oui" said Michel as he pulled his trousers up.

"We've got a little extra service that your politician friend might be interested in."

"Go on."

"We've got a cameraman, who normally just makes porno video's, who will come in and video a client with us, a sort of 'one off' personal memento of the event so the client can watch it at home, relive the action and play with himself when the wife's out."

"How nice."

"D'you think he'd be interested?"

"Let's ask."

"It is a bit expensive though."

"I'm sure he'll go for it."

Michel's bottom was feeling more comfortable as he explained the new service to Lascelles, who, once convinced that he would have the only tape, agreed with enthusiasm. The cost never came into it and Maria telephoned Joules the cameraman immediately. Michel left them all smiling and assured Lascelles that he would collect him the next day at noon.

An hour later Michel was outside Josette's flat in the Rue Benoit Malon. She was ready and came down immediately to greet him, they kissed passionately once they were in the Mercedes and then sped away to Chez Marius.

George, the owner, was at the entrance, beaming as usual and he showed the lovers to a discreet, candle lit table for two in an alcove at the back of the restaurant.

"I've missed you today, ma petite" Josette whispered over the menu.

"And I've missed you, my darling" he whispered back romantically.

"I so want us to be together."

"So do I, my precious."

"And that reminds me, I've got the date we can move into Rue du Camas, it's Saturday the twentieth, isn't that exciting?" Michel's heart sank right down to his sore bottom.

"Wonderful" he murmured through glazed eyes.

"We can collect the key at ten o'clock from the agent on Saturday, so as we need a bed first we'd better go shopping right away."

"Oui" he murmured through a gritty smile.

"I've got a list, well actually two, the first one is for really urgent things like the bed, and the second is for things like plates and cutlery as I'll bring what I've already got at my flat for the time being."

"Bon" said Michel.

"You don't look very pleased, ma petite" she said with some concern.

"Oh, I am, darling, I'm just very tired, it's been an exhausting day, believe me I feel beaten." Michel always told the truth.

"Oh, you poor angel, we'll eat quickly and go home and you can stay with me."

"Non, I have to go home tonight."

"Why?"

"Mama is in a bad state, and I fear she may have to go back into hospital."

"Oh, dear, I do understand, cherie, we can meet and make all our plans tomorrow."

"Oui."

"Now what shall we eat?"

Michel needed meat, so after a prawn salad starter he went on to demolish a fillet steak followed by his favourite sweet at Chez Marius, the magnificent pear belle Hélène. Josette had a more delicate meal with a melon to start, followed by sea food salad and an ice cream. Two bottles of Cassis rosé completed a satisfying dinner and Michel paid, tipping George well with a fifty Franc note. George beamed as they said their farewells.

They kissed passionately once more outside Josette's flat and arranged to meet in Ricky's for a bar lunch the next day.

As he drove home to Montelivet he wondered how he had become so involved with everything and everybody. He remembered what his Uncle who lived in Tahiti had told him, Tahitians say 'you eat life or life eats you.' He felt he was being distinctly eaten at the moment.

Monique was in bed reading when he arrived home. "I thought you'd be home before this" she complained.

Michel looked at his watch, it was almost midnight.

"Hmm, sorry" he mumbled and he started to undress. He was down to his underpants when the telephone started ringing in the lounge.

"Mon Dieu! Go and answer it quick, Mama's asleep in there" said Monique. Michel rushed in as Mama awoke from her slumbers. Michel snatched up the phone wondering who was calling him at that time of night.

"Oui?"

"Michel, it's Gerrard."

"What do you want?" he demanded, really this was the last thing he needed, a bloody phone call from a stupid Gendarme at midnight.

"You need to know that Edward Salvator is dead."

"Dead?"

"Oui, he was killed in his car on the Cassis road heading for Bandol."

"Mon Dieu!"

"My men were tailing him about an hour ago and his driver realised they were being followed and attempted to shake them off, he was driving too fast round a bend, lost control and went over the edge, his Mercedes fell about two hundred metres."

"Mon Dieu!"

"Salvator and his driver were pronounced dead at the scene."

"Mon Dieu."

"Call me tomorrow around midday and I'll give you further details."

"OK."

"And look out for Claude Salvator, he'll be like a mad dog when he hears the news, bon nuit."

Michel put down the receiver slowly, shocked at the news.

"Was that your friend again?" enquired Mama.

"Oui."

"He's not dead is he?"

"No Mama."

"Oh, good, we don't want anything to spoil Christmas do we?"

"Non, Mama" replied Michel as he wandered back to his bedroom in a daze.

CHAPTER FOUR

Thursday 18th December

Michel had a very restless night, punctuated with thoughts of Salvator's death and the possible retribution of Claude. Gerrard's description 'he'll be like a mad dog' worried Michel, and he tossed and turned, occasionally rolling on his sore bottom. He was glad when it was time to get up and he struggled out of bed trying not to disturb Monique. He went into the shower and pulled himself together under the spray of invigorating hot, little needles. He dried himself, returned to the bedroom and started to dress.

"What are those marks on your bottom?" asked Monique drowsily.

'Mon Dieu' he thought and then replied "I've got a rash through sitting in the car for too long."

"Liar" she said with feeling.

He finished dressing and went into the kitchen and made some coffee for them both. When he returned to the bedroom and handed Monique her coffee he said "I'm going in a minute and then I won't be home 'til dinner time tonight."

"You're going to be home for dinner, and are you staying?"

"Of course, ma petite."

"Bon, and as Hélène arrives today, you'll be here to keep the peace."

"I look forward to it."

Within half an hour Michel was at his station smoking a cigarette to calm his nerves and reading the morning paper. *'MARSEILLE BUSINESSMAN KILLED'* screamed the headline. *'Monsieur Edward Salvator, a leading Marseille businessman, was tragically killed last night in an automobile accident. His Mercedes limousine was being driven by Monsieur Paul Rondel, Monsieur Salvator's chauffer, when it left the Cassis Road and plunged hundreds of metres down a cliff. Police and other services were quickly on the scene, but Monsieur Salvator and his chauffer, had been killed instantly. The cause of the accident is not known, but a spokesman for the Gendarmerie has confirmed that there will be a full inquiry. Monsieur Salvator leaves a widow and one son, Claude, who is at present on holiday in London.'*

Michel was shaking inwardly when there was a tap on his window which made him jump visibly. It was René.

"Bonjour, Michel" he said as Michel wound down the window.

"Bonjour, René."

"A bad business, eh?" René said nodding at the headline.

"Oui."

"Something funny there."

"Oui."

"Rondel knew that road like the back of his hand."

"Oui" agreed Michel.

"I bet the police had something to do with it."

"I wouldn't be surprised" replied Michel.

"Still, he was an evil bastard so it looks like there is some justice."

Michel nodded. It was well known that Salvator was a ruthless man and had hurt many people on his way up. Michel guessed that there would be few tears shed around Marseille at his demise.

"Can I take my cadeaux boxes now?" René asked. Michel had forgotten all about them.

"Oh, René, sorry, I had such a day yesterday I forgot to show them around, tomorrow OK?"

René smiled and replied "oui, but I want them before Saturday, remember you're coming to dinner and it's our big night!"

Michel remembered and hoped his body would hold out until then.

"I'll be there" he replied with a grin and then under his breath 'if I live.'

René smiled, tapped the roof of the Mercedes and returned to his taxi parked behind Michel.

As there seemed little prospect of any business for the moment Michel pulled away from the rank and went round to Ricky's for a coffee.

"Ça va, Michel?"

"Ça va, Jacques, une café, s'il vous plaît."

"Oui."

"Seen the paper this morning?" Michel asked.

"Oui, and I'm glad he's gone, I know you shouldn't speak ill of the dead, but he was evil."

"He was" agreed Michel.

"And now we've only Claude to deal with."

"This is true" said Michel, nodding his head.

"I'm sure Gerrard will get him eventually."

"I hope it's soon" replied Michel gloomily.

"We all do, here's your coffee."

"Merci, now, Jacques, I have to go up to Aix at about eleven and Josette is meeting me here at one for lunch, so if I'm a bit late, tell her where I've gone and give her a drink."

"Of course, Michel, leave it to me. Antone will be in by then and I know he'll want to speak to you about Salvator."

"Bon."

Michel sipped his coffee whilst Jacques served another one of the regular bar flies. He glanced at his watch, it was almost eight thirty and he had to be at Gambetta's by nine to meet Jacqueline and take her home. He sipped a little quicker, finished the coffee and left Ricky's ten minutes later, driving in the bright sunlight to Gambetta's garage in the Rue de Verdun.

Jacqueline was already at the garage when Michel arrived and was in conversation with Gambetta, who was all smiles for the elegant woman and dancing little steps as he re-inspected the damaged Citroen.

"Bonjour, Jacqueline" said Michel as he joined them.

"Bonjour, Michel" she smiled.

"Ça va, Jean?"

"Ça va, Michel."

"Everything alright?" asked Michel.

"Oui, bien sûr, I was just explaining how I would repair Madame's car, it's quite a complex procedure" replied Jean beaming.

"Oh" said Michel "I didn't know that, I thought you just bashed the dent out with a big hammer, filled the rough bits up to make it smooth and then painted it."

If looks could kill!

"It's complex and requires skill and craftsmanship, that's why it costs a lot to body repair cars, and" Jean added with menace "it could cost a lot more if I find extra damage that I haven't quoted for!"

Michel took the point and changed the subject.

"Bon, we leave it all in your capable hands, I'll run you home then, Jacqueline."

"Merci, and thank you, Monsieur Gambetta for taking the time to explain everything to me" she said.

"My pleasure, Madame" replied Gambetta, smiling and removing and replacing his Breton beret.

"See you Friday" called Michel as the couple made their way to the Mercedes.

Gambetta waved and returned to his gloomy garage.

As Michel drove away and towards Boulevard Fabrici he said "I know a quiet little bar in the Rue Saint Pierre, and I think I ought to buy you a coffee or something, it's a cold morning and we both could do with warming up."

"Merci, Michel, that would be nice" she smiled.

He parked right outside the Bar Américiaine in a space just vacated by a large Renault.

"Bon, right outside the door" he said.

"Are you always that lucky?" she asked with a smile.

"Always" he replied and she laughed.

'This isn't going to take long' he thought.

They entered the bar and sat at the back near a large, hot radiator. Michel ordered two coffees and two brandy's from the young waiter as Jacqueline slipped her coat off.

"I'm warming up already" she said with a smile.

"Bon, and you'll feel even warmer after the coffee and brandy" he replied.

"Possibly, I've got to be careful, it's a long time since I've been out drinking with someone" she smiled.

"Surely not, what about your husband doesn't he....."

"We're divorced" she interrupted "he lives in Paris now."

"I'm sorry to hear that" he replied.

"Well that's how it is these days" she remarked with a sigh.

"I know, it's dreadful, I'm going through a divorce right now" he replied.

"Oh, I'm so sorry" she said with concern and her big blue eyes opened up.

Michel was captivated and replied "it's the way we live now, it's modern life, everybody wants too much, expects too much. Once people were content just to be married and have a home, but today…"he raised his eyebrows and shook his head sadly.

"Oh, Michel, what you say is so true, I mean I was content with Eric, we had Annette and we should have been a happy family, but he met this woman at work, well, I can't say what a tramp she was, and they started an affair after she'd had all the other men in the office, and then she got promoted and moved to head office in Paris, and the next thing I knew he was up there with her."

"Mon Dieu, what a fool he must be to have left you and Annette."

"Oh, Michel, you're so kind" she smiled as the waiter brought their order to the table.

Michel picked up the brandy and said "let's drink a toast to us lonely divorcee's."

She smiled, picked up her glass and replied "to us divorcee's." Michel smiled back as they both sipped the golden spirit.

"There, I'm feeling better already, how about you?" he enquired.

"Oui, much better."

"Bon, we should do this more often" he said.

"We should" she replied and laughed. Michel noticed how she laughed with her eyes and he felt that he wanted to kiss the generous lips of this elegant woman right now. He had to have her, there was no doubt in his mind and he determined at that very moment, he would not have Annette, as it would certainly upset Jacqueline if she found out. He thanked God for his humility and consideration.

"After Jean has repaired our cars, let's celebrate with a little dinner party at one of my favourite restaurants and we'll make Annette the guest of honour because she brought us together" he said with an endearing expression on his face.

"Oh, Michel, you're so kind, you don't know what that means to me."

"Oh, I do, for I know what it's like to be unloved by the one you marry and to feel lonely."

"Michel" she whispered.

"Let's make it next Monday evening."

"That will be lovely."

"I'll pick you both up at about eight, will that be alright?"

"Oui, just perfect."

They drank their coffee whilst exchanging admiring glances and then Michel looked at his watch.

"You have to go?" Jacqueline enquired.

"Oui, I'm afraid so, I have to be in Aix soon to collect an important client."

"Don't let me keep you then."

"Non, we have a few more minutes together."

After taking Jacqueline home and saying a tender farewell Michel headed north to Aix. Hoping that Lascelles night of erotic pleasure had gone well Michel tried to calculate what he should charge for the video service. Naturally he would double whatever Joules had asked for but felt that he might be able to extend the margin further if it had been a particularly good night.

He parked in the Boulevard Turin in Aix and rang the sonnette. Maria answered and Michel replied "it's Michel, Maria."

"Oh, bon, Michel, please be quiet when you come in, he's still asleep."

"A good night then?"

"Very, mon ami."

Michel smiled and entered the building. Maria opened the door of the flat and Michel was soon in its warm, perfumed interior.

"How's your bum?" asked Maria in a whisper.

"Much better, thank you" he replied "your ointment was just the job."

"Bon, now remember next time you want a beating, come here, we know how to do it without marking you so badly."

"I will, now how did it go last night?"

"It was quite a session and we've charged accordingly."

"Bon, has he paid you yet?"

"Oui, before we started we took the basic amount but we did tell him there would be more to pay as the night went on, but he was so randy he just agreed to everything."

"Bon."

"We've told him to pay you for the video, your fee and of course the taxi fare."

"Oh, merci, you little angel, now how much does Joules want?"

"A thousand Francs, we've paid him already."

"Right, I'll charge Lascelles double that and give you and Claudette twelve hundred and fifty now, OK?"

"That's brilliant, Michel, thanks."

Just then Claudette came out of the bedroom and whispered "ça va, Michel."

"Ça va."

"He's still sleeping in there, we'll leave him for a bit" said Claudette.

"Not for long, I've got to get back to Marseille" said Michel.

"OK, I'll make some coffee for us all and I'll wake him up" said Claudette.

"Michel's giving us an extra two fifty for the video."

"Oh, merci, Michel, you're too good to us" smiled Claudette.

"I know."

"You'd better pop round soon for a session on the house again" said Claudette.

"Look forward to it" he replied and with that he opened his wallet and gave Maria the thousand Franc note that Pierre had given him for the Christmas cards plus a further two hundred and fifty.

Claudette went off to make the coffee whilst Michel made himself comfortable on the settee.

"So how are things?" asked Maria as she slumped down beside him.

"Pretty awful."

"Oh?"

"Well, I've got all the relations at home for Christmas, my Mother-in-law's broken her ankle and Edward Salvator was killed last night in a road accident......"

"Mon Dieu!" she exclaimed.

"And I've a feeling his son is going to blame me."

"Mon Dieu!"

"And then he'll probably kill me."

"Mon Dieu!"

"Exactly."

"But how could the son blame you?"

"Because...., well, it's a long story."

"Did you crash into Salvator?"

"Non, I was at home when the accident happened, his driver lost control on the Cassis road and went over the side, the car fell about two hundred metres...."

"Oh, Mon Dieu, but you're not to blame then."

Then Claudette appeared with the coffee and asked "what's this all about?"

Michel explained the situation as simply as he could and the girls were very sympathetic and at the end, Maria said "you can always stay here with us if things get too dangerous in Marseille." Michel was touched and replied "merci, ma petites, but I wouldn't endanger you two lovelies, not at any price."

"Oh, Michel, you are a love, you need a little reward, come and have a session before Christmas and we'll dress up for you" said Claudette.

"Why thank you, I'll ring next week and make a date, is that OK?" he asked.

"Oui."

Michel finished the coffee and said "I've got to get going now...."

"OK, we'll get him up" said Maria and the girls disappeared into the bedroom. Michel heard the girls voices and a lot of groaning and it seemed an age before he beheld Lascelles at the door of the living room, supported by the girls, looking like death warmed up and clutching a video.

"Bonjour, Monsieur Lascelles."

"Bonjour, bonjour, I think, what time is it for God's sake?"

Michel looked at his watch and replied "nearly twelve o'clock."

"Mon Dieu, I've got to catch the two o'clock train for Paris, God, my wife will kill me if I miss that train, you see we're going out to a party tonight somewhere or other." Lascelles voice was quite slurred and Michel guessed that the girls had kept him well supplied with alcohol.

"You OK to travel, Monsieur?" asked Michel in a concerned tone.

"Oui, of course, just get me home to collect my bags and then to the station."

"Of course, Monsieur."

Lascelles kissed the girls goodbye, paid them some more money and staggered behind Michel to the taxi. Michel raced the big car back towards Marseille whilst keeping an eye on his pale faced passenger in the back. They arrived outside Lascelles flat in Montelivet in double quick time and Michel noticed that the politician looked a little paler and a touch greener than when they left Aix.

"I think I owe you some money" said Lascelles.

"Oui, Monsieur."

"How much?"

"Well, the video service is two thousand Francs, my introduction fee is…."

"Here, help yourself, just leave me some for the taxi fare in Paris" interrupted Lascelles as he handed Michel his wallet and promptly left the back seat of the Mercedes.

"Merci, Monsieur." Michel counted out the two thousand for the video, five hundred for his fee and a thousand for the fare. A nice round figure of three thousand five hundred Francs. In a while, Lascelles staggered out from his flat with two suitcases that Michel placed in the boot and his passenger resumed his seat. Michel returned the wallet and drove quickly to the station where Lascelles thanked him and said "Joyeux Noël Michel; those girls are worth every Franc they charge, I've never had such a time in my life and I want you to be the first to know that my prick is about to fall off and if I arrive in Paris without it, I'll blame you!"

"Merci, Monsieur."

"Au revoir." and with that he staggered off into the station.

It was almost one thirty when Michel strode into Ricky's with the mornings take nestling in his wallet. The lovely Josette was sitting at the bar and smiled beautifully when she beheld her Fiancé.

"Ma petite" they both murmured as they kissed.

"I'm sorry I'm late, but I've had a busy morning and only just got back from Aix."

"I know, Jacques told me where you were."

"Bon, now what shall we eat?" he asked as Jacques appeared, wished him good day again and poured a large Pernod.

They settled on onion soup followed by Jacques' excellent ham and cheese baguettes. Josette chatted excitedly, between mouthfuls, about the impending move and explained how her packing had been arranged. Michel smiled in all the right places but stopped when Josette said "so let's go shopping for the bed this afternoon."

"Ah" replied Michel, his mind in full overdrive mode trying to think of a real and plausible reason for not going to buy a bed.

"Well, I'd love to go shopping but I'm concerned about Claude."

"Why?" asked Josette.

"Well how he'll react when he finds out about his father."

"What about his father?"

"You don't know?"

"Non" she replied quizzically.

"He was killed in a car accident last night."

"Oh, mon Dieu, mon Dieu" she said with passion.

"I know, ma petite, it's a great shock to everyone."

"But when, I mean how?" she asked pale faced and Michel explained everything slowly and gently to his lovely Fiancé. He remembered that if Claude had not ended the relationship, then Edward Salvator would have probably been Josette's father in law by now. Michel shivered at the thought and remembered that he had to phone Gerrard. He ordered a brandy for Josette, kissed her gently on her forehead and excused himself. Jacques nodded his permission for Michel to use the phone in the little private corridor behind the bar.

Michel dialled the direct number and at last Gerrard answered.

"Oui."

"Monsieur Gerrard" Michel remembered it was police business.

"Oui."

"It's Monsieur Ronay here."

"I know it's you, Michel."

"Bon, you asked me to call you, Monsieur."

"What for?"

"How should I know" replied Michel testily.

"Ah, I remember."

"Bon."

"It's about Claude Salvator, we think he may suspect that you are the cause of some of his problems and coupled with the death of his father, he may become more violent than usual, so my advice is that you keep out of sight until we've arrested him."

"Gerrard, I'm a taxi driver! In Marseille! How can I keep out of

sight? I've got to earn a living for God's sake."
"I realise that, but my advice is to lie low until we catch him."
"When's that going to be?"
"We're closing on him fast."
"Well I need some police protection until you've got him."
"OK, I'll see what I can do."
"Merci, I'd be grateful."
"Phone me later and I'll let you know what I've arranged."
"I will."
"Au revoir."

Michel put the receiver down and joined his Fiancé at the bar. He decided as life was short and his might get even shorter, it probably was a good idea to go shopping while he could.

"So, ma petite, what sort of bed have you in mind?" he asked.

She smiled and replied "a big, soft one!"

Later that afternoon saw Michel and Josette bouncing and sprawling about on the best double beds that Premier Magasin, the large departmental store just off La Canebiére, could offer the discerning home maker. They chose the very best, a top quality, internally double sprung, homeopathic fully approved mattress set on a hand made, blue quilted box base with matching headboard.

"I can assure Monsieur that he'll never suffer with backache again, no matter what the cause" purred the smooth salesman as he looked Josette up and down then calculated his commission for the week so far.

"Bon, can you deliver it before Christmas?" enquired Michel.

"Of course, Monsieur" came the silky reply.

The arrangements were made to deliver it on the Saturday at noon and Michel paid a substantial cash deposit with the balance promised on delivery. Everyone was happy. He drove Josette back to her flat in the Rue Benoit Malon so she could continue to pack and then went round to Sayid's flat to collect the cards for Pierre.

Within an hour Michelle was in Pierre's office, comfortably seated with the boxes of cards neatly stacked at the edge of the brothel owner's executive desk.

"Bad business, Salvator's tragic end" said Pierre.

"Oui, but no one around here will shed many tears" replied

Michel.

"True, true" nodded Pierre as he drew on his cigar, contemplated the ceiling and added "rumour has it that he's got a stack hidden away in a Swiss Bank"

"Wouldn't surprise me" replied Michel.

"I expect Claude thinks he'll get all that" said Pierre.

"He can think what he likes but I'm hoping Gerrard will collar him before he kills me" replied Michel.

"Nothing will happen to you, Michel, believe me, you've got a lot of friends in high places, besides, we need all the taxi drivers we can get!" and he laughed.

"Very funny, but I'm scared of that bastard."

"You worry too much" replied Pierre.

"Possibly." The two men remained silent for a while before Michel changed the subject and said cheerfully "now then, I'm in a position to offer you a new service for your clients."

"Oh, yeah" replied Pierre in a disinterested tone.

"Oui, I can supply a top professional film camera man to video your clients when they're in action with the girls, you can offer a new and expensive video as a memento of their visit."

"Michel, Michel" said Pierre in a tone usually saved for naughty children "I don't want my clients sitting at home watching a video and playing with themselves, I want them here, spending more money, repeat business that's what I'm after."

"OK then, what about out of town visitors like the judges from Lyon?"

Pierre contemplated the ceiling again and replied slowly "good point, good point, I'll give that some thought. How much notice do you want for this cameraman?"

"Well providing that Joules is not filming on location, just a couple of days."

"Bon, and is he discreet?"

"Discreet? That's his middle name, he's filmed top politicians on the job."

"Bon, and how much do you charge for this service?"

"Two thousand Francs per one hour session."

"That's OK, I can add a little margin to that."

They shook hands and Michel left 26 Rue Charbonniere feeling light hearted and drove down to Ricky's in search of Antone.

He found the great man seated at the back of the bar reading the paper.

"Bonjour, Antone, may I join you?"

Antone put down his paper as soon as he heard Michel's voice and replied "of course, Michel."

He sat opposite Antone, sipped his Pernod and said "well he's dead."

"Indeed, and I'm not sorry, not sorry at all" replied Antone.

"And now what happens?"

"The police will arrest Claude and then the organisation will collapse, but, I have only one fear…."

"And that is?"

"Some other evil bastard will try and take over the Salvator's business."

"Is that likely?"

"Indeed, Salvator is rumoured to have a lot of money in a Swiss Bank account."

"So I've heard."

"And that means the operation has been very profitable and where there's money in large amounts then unsavoury characters from all over the place are attracted to the opportunities that exist now that the Salvator's are out of the picture."

"Claude is still about in Marseille" said Michel gloomily.

"He won't be for long, I assure you" smiled Antone.

"I have to survive in the meantime" replied Michel.

"You will, you will, Michel, believe me."

At that moment Gerrard arrived and with "bonjour, Messieurs, may I?" sat at the table opposite Michel. He leaned forward and whispered "Salvator is being buried on Monday at three o'clock. Claude is sure to be there, and so will I, along with my men."

"Bon" whispered Michel.

"And because he may be in disguise, I want you there too."

"Me!" exclaimed Michel.

"Oui."

"Oh, non, Monsieur Gerrard, not me……"

"You will be there just to identify him."

"Oh, non."

"Just in case" said Gerrard.

"Oh, non."

"Oh, oui, and I have arranged for one of my men to be your bodyguard until after we've arrested Claude Salvator." Michel felt a little better after that and managed a slight smile and he looked at Antone, who nodded gently and said "you'll be safe now, Michel."

"OK" he said to Gerrard.

"Bon, now be sure and be at the Saint Pierre cemetery before three, find the Salvator family vault and mingle with the friends and relatives as they arrive."

"Where will you be in case I need you?"

"I will be everywhere and nowhere, but I'll be watching you if I can't recognise Salvator."

"Oh, mon Dieu."

"Nothing can go wrong, I assure you" hissed Gerrard with a demonic look in his eyes.

Michel had heard that before and he groaned inwardly.

"When does my bodyguard start guarding my body?" he asked.

"Tomorrow at nine, his name is Paul Dassault and you can collect him from the Gendarmerie."

"Collect him?"

"Oui, I have no spare police cars unfortunately, cut backs you understand."

"Oui, and does he stay with me all the time until after Salvator's arrest?"

"Non, bring him back at five and then collect him again the next day at nine" replied Gerrard.

"Then who takes over his duties at five?"

"No one."

"No one?"

"Non, you're on your own at night, I'm short of staff, cut backs you understand."

"Oui" replied Michel as his heart sank once again.

"You'll be alright" said Gerrard.

"Well when I've taken Monsieur Dassault back at five, can I keep his gun?"

"Oh, non, non, certainly not, under no circumstances...."

"He won't need it if he's off duty, will he?"

"You can not have his gun, non, that's it."

"Salvator might kill me before the funeral and then where

would you be?" asked Michel.

"You cannot have his gun! Now then, I must go as I have many plans to make. Salvator will not escape this time I assure you."

"Bon."

"I will not see you again until Monday at three, in the cemetery, au revoir."

Michel and Antone watched Gerrard stride out of Ricky's bar and disappear into the busy street.

"I think I'll have another drink to steady my nerves, will you join me, Antone?"

In fact, Michel had several drinks with Antone before he left Ricky's and returned to his station. Although the day was still bright it had become a lot colder and he wondered if it would snow by Christmas. He pulled up behind René who saw his friend and came back to the Mercedes.

"Can I have my cadeaux boxes now?" he asked.

"Oh, oui, René, you'd better take them, I keep forgetting to show anybody" Michel replied glumly. They went to the boot and René took the two boxes.

"Yvonne will love these" he said gleefully "and she's really getting worked up for Saturday night, she keeps on about it."

"Bon" smiled Michel.

"She's got a mountain of food in, so I hope you're going to be hungry."

"I will be" replied Michel.

"Bon, see you then" and with that René returned to his taxi collected a fare and swung out into La Canebiére.

Michel lit a cigarette and thought 'what an uncomplicated life style René and Yvonne have, they have plenty of money, go sailing for the whole of August and have their best friend supplying sexual services for their pleasure.' He drew heavily on his cigarette and went into deep thought. Perhaps this was the secret of life, uncomplicated living leading to true contentment. He decided there and then to change his life irrevocably after Christmas.

After taking three uninteresting fares Michele decided to call it a day and returning to Montelivet.

"Bon, you're earlier than I thought" said Monique with a semi smile as her husband entered the front door.

"Oui, it's been a bloody awful day."

"Never mind, Hélène's here, go and say 'hello' and I'll bring you drink."

"Merci, ma petite" he said and kissed her on the cheek.

He entered the living room to a chorus of greeting. Mama was beaming as she sat comfortably in his seat whilst Alexis and Hélène were perched on the settee and Frederik was sprawled out in the remaining armchair. Michel kissed all the women on both cheeks and then settled down between Alexis and Hélène.

"Had a busy day then?" asked Hélène.

"Oui, and its been difficult."

"Shame."

"It's the time of year" said Mama.

"Christmas is always the same, rush, rush, rush, it was never like this when we we're young" said Alexis solemnly.

"Oh yes it was" countered Hélène.

"It wasn't" argued Alexis.

"I remember Mama crying because she thought she wasn't going to get everything done in time" replied Hélène.

"It was just once, when Aunt Emmanuelle was coming, and Papa kept shouting because he couldn't stand Uncle Jacques" retorted Alexis. 'I know the feeling' thought Michel.

Monique arrived with a tray of drinks and said "you're a noisy lot, I can hear you shouting in the kitchen."

They all took a glass and wished 'Joyeux Noël' and sat quietly for a minute. Michel resolved that this was his last Christmas with all his wife's relatives.

They took their time over dinner and Michel was glad when it was time for bed. He snuggled down with his wife who was feeling passionate and in need. He made love gently to her and it took some time before he came and relaxed inside her. He tried to sleep but the plans and concerns for tomorrow cascaded through his tired mind, eventually he fell into a deep sleep.

CHAPTER FIVE

Friday 19th December

As soon as he was awake Michel wrestled with the decisions of the day. Firstly, the good news was that Gerrard had provided him with a bodyguard, although only nine to five, secondly, Gambetta was going to repair the damaged wing on the Mercedes and thirdly, he was taking Nicole to dinner in Aix. The bad news was that he would have to drive around in one of Gambetta's loan cars and that was always a trial of nerve and determination, it also meant that he could not operate as a taxi and so no income for the day. Although a bodyguard was comforting it meant he was stuck with a Gendarme all day, which might cramp his style somewhat. Deals with Sayid were off the agenda until he was alone again after Salvator's arrest. However, the omens were good and he spent some time in the shower to ensure he was totally fresh for Jacqueline and Nicole.

As he dressed, Monique, all smiles after her needs had been met last night, went to the kitchen and made coffee for them both. As they sat at the kitchen table sipping the awakening liquid Michel said "Gerrard has arranged a bodyguard for me."
"Mon Dieu!"
   "It's nothing to worry about."
   "Really?"
   "Non, it's just until they arrest Salvator, and they plan to do that Monday."
   "Going to give himself up is he?" enquired Monique in a sceptical tone.
   "Non, they plan to catch him at his father's funeral."
   "Bon, I hope you're not going to be there."
   "Well, Gerrard has asked me to...."
   "Michel, you're mad!" she interrupted.
He nodded his head and replied "probably."
   "Just be careful, ma cherie."
   "I will" he nodded.
   "Are you home for dinner?"
   "Non, ma petite, when Gambetta has repaired the car I'll work

all night to catch up on the losses today."

She nodded in a resigned manner.

"We have to go Christmas shopping sometime" she said.

"Oui, perhaps Tuesday?"

"Monday would be better" she replied.

"Monday morning then, Salvator's funeral is in the afternoon."

"OK, we'll make a start Monday and finish off any last bits on Tuesday."

"Bon."

"I'll do some of the basics today with Hélène and Alexis."

Michel raised his eyebrows and said "good luck."

"It'll get them out the house and give Mama a rest" she said in a resigned tone.

"Bon, tell Frederik to stay in because Angelique's coming this morning" said Michel.

"Oh, mon Dieu, I'd forgotten about her" replied Monique.

"Oui, her Mother's bringing her down."

Michel glanced at his watch, it was quarter to nine and he had to pick Jacqueline up before collecting Paul Dassault from the Gendarmerie.

"I must go, ma petite," he kissed his wife and went out into the cold morning air.

Driving quickly in the morning traffic to 23 Boulevard Fabrici, Michele double parked and rang the sonnette. Jacqueline answered in an excited tone and quickly joined him outside the flat.

"Bonjour, Michel" she smiled.

"Bonjour, Jacqueline."

"How are you today?"

"OK, but much better now I've seen you" he replied.

She gave a little laugh and said "merci" as he opened the door of the Mercedes for her.

Michel hurried the car through the narrow streets and arrived at Gambetta's garage in good time. Jacqueline's Citroen was parked outside and was gleaming in the bright morning sunlight.

"Mon Dieu!" she exclaimed "it looks brand new."

"Oui" nodded Michel, knowing the old man had given the car a good clean using polishing compound.

As they strode across to the gleaming Citroen, Gambetta

appeared from the gloomy interior.

"Bonjour, mes amis" he beamed.

"Bonjour, Monsieur" said Jacqueline whilst Michel mumbled a greeting.

"You've made my car look brand new" she said excitedly.

"It's my job, Madame, I'm a professional."

"I can't thank you enough, and the repair on the wing, well you just can't see that it's ever been damaged."

"Oui, Madame, it's called craftsmanship" he replied and glared at Michel.

"It's wonderful" she said.

Michel glanced at his watch and said "I'll have to leave you now as I have an urgent appointment."

"Bon, give me your keys" said Gambetta. Michel handed them over and asked "and what have you got for me?"

"Just a rusty runabout" replied Gambetta and Jacqueline laughed.

"No, he means it" said Michel and she laughed again.

"I'm at home all day so if you have a moment, call in and see me, I'd like to thank you for all you've done" she said to Michel with a big smile.

"Merci, I will, about lunch time?"

"Oui, I look forward to it" she smiled again and then said "au revoir, Monsieur Gambetta" as she slipped behind the wheel of her shiny Citroen.

They watched her go for a moment before Gambetta said softly "leg over at lunchtime, eh, very nice too."

"Your mind" grinned Michel.

"Well think of me at leg over time, bashing the shit out of your front wing and filling up the rough bits before painting it!"

"I will, I promise, and you make sure you've finished it by this evening."

"You've nothing to worry about, it'll be ready by six."

"Bon, now where's this rusty relic?"

"There" Gambetta pointed to a tired looking Renault.

"Does it all work?"

"Like a Swiss watch" replied Gambetta.

"See you at six then."

"Bring the cash, and remember, it might be more than I

quoted."

"Why?"

"Because I haven't made my mind up yet!"

Michel pulled up outside the Gendarmerie and parked the Renault in the only vacant space available. He entered the building and approached the Gendarme behind the imposing desk.

"Bonjour, Monsieur, can I help you?"

"Oui, Monsieur, my name is Ronay and I've an appointment with Gendarme Paul Dassault."

"Ah, oui Monsieur, he's expecting you, just one moment" and he picked up the phone on his desk and dialled a number. The phone was answered immediately.

"Hello, Paul, your man is here, bon." He returned the phone to the desk and said with due solemnity "your bodyguard will be with you in a moment" and then he grinned.

It seemed an age before a door opened in the corridor and a slightly built young man stepped out and came through into the vestibule. He smiled and held out his hand towards Michel and said in a feminine, high pitched voice "bonjour, Monsieur Ronay, I'm Paul Dassault, your bodyguard."

'Mon Dieu!' exclaimed Michel under his breath and then extending his hand, replied "bonjour, Monsieur Dassault."

"Oh, do call me Paul, please" he said as Michel grasped the pale, limp hand of his bodyguard.

"Bonjour, Paul."

"I'm with you all day and every day until five o'clock, then I must be back here."

"I understand" replied Michel.

"Oui, those are my orders from Monsieur Gerrard."

"Oui."

"It's a shame really because Monsieur Gerrard's told me a lot about you and you do seem to be quite a character and I like that in a man, shall we go then?"

Michel nodded and stumbled in a daze to the Renault that now had a parking ticket neatly tucked under the windscreen wiper. As soon as they were in the car Michel asked "have you done this sort of work before?"

"Oh, non, this is my first case" he replied.

"What sort of police work were you doing before?"
"I've just told you, this is my first case."
"What, ever?"
"Oui."
"Mon Dieu!"
"Well, we all have to start somewhere don't we?"
"I suppose so" replied Michel in a strangled voice.
"I've just finished my basic training at Police Academy, and I came top in administration and interview techniques."
"Bon, and how well did you do in unarmed combat or arresting violent criminals?"
"Oh, we don't do that anymore."
"Non?"
"Non, we're much more scientific."
"So what happens if Salvator attempts to kill me?"
"Well, I'll arrest him first of course."
"How will you do that?"
"Leave that to me, Monsieur, just you leave that to me."
"Have you got a gun?"
"Oh, non, Monsieur, I don't need a gun, shall we go now, before you get another parking ticket?"

Michel drove straight to Ricky's bar as he knew he needed a brandy.

"Bonjour, Michel" beamed Jacques.
"Bonjour, Jacques, a brandy s'il vous plaît."
"Bad day already?"
"Oui."
"And what will your young friend have?"
"He's not a friend, he's Paul Dassault, my bodyguard."
"You lucky thing, I've always wanted one of those" smiled Jacques.
"I'll have water, s'il vous plaît" said Paul.
"Still or sparkling?" asked Jacques.
"Sparkling."
"I just knew it" beamed Jacques as he prepared the drinks.
"Is Antone about?" asked Michel as he looked round the bar.
"He'll be in around lunchtime, he's having a rest in bed this morning, had a bit of a party last night and the poor dear's exhausted."

"I understand" nodded Michel, knowing exactly what had been going on in Antone's flat.

"Are you a party goer, Paul?" enquired Jacques with a smile.

"Oh, oui, providing they're not too noisy" he replied and on hearing that Michel took a good swig of brandy to steady himself.

"I know just what you mean" said Jacques.

"If it gets too boisterous you just can't think straight."

"I know, oh, I know and conversation goes right out the window."

"Does it ever" replied Paul as Jacques moved off to serve another customer.

"Drink up" said Michel "I have to go home for something or other."

"Oui, Michel" replied Paul, but before he could finish his sparkling water, Jacques was back.

"Perhaps you'd like to come to one of our quiet parties, Antone and I often hold them, just for a few selected friends."

"Oui, I'd love to."

"Bon, I'll introduce you to Antone later and I know he'll be ever so pleased to meet you."

"Look forward to it."

"Let's go" said Michel impatiently.

Jacques and Paul looked at each other and pulled funny faces.

"Another bad day" mouthed Jacques to Paul as Michel made for the door.

Parking the Renault outside his flat he said to Paul "I won't be a moment, so just wait here."

"OK, Michel" replied his bodyguard.

As Michel opened the front door he heard a muffled noise coming from his bedroom. As he moved closer to the bedroom door he could distinctly hear someone gasping. It sounded like Monique! Was she at it with some bastard? Michel flung open the door and beheld Frederik, naked and on top of Angelique who had her legs wrapped firmly round his step sons waist.

"Dad!"

"Frederik!"

Angelique screamed.

"Shh! you'll wake Gran" said Frederik.

"Oui" said Michel "be quiet and you'd better stop and get dressed before your Mother catches you."

"She's out shopping with Alexis and Hélène" said Frederik.

"I know, I know, now just get dressed will you and I'll make us some coffee" said Michel and he closed the bedroom door and smiled. 'Fancy' he thought 'Frederik's having the daughter in the morning and I'm having the Mother in the evening'. He went into the kitchen and made coffee for the three of them, tiptoed to the living room and opened the door just enough to observe Mama still fast asleep.

In a while Frederik and a blushing Angelique joined him at the kitchen table.

"I'm sorry, Dad, I didn't mean to embarrass you or anything…."

"That's quite alright, now listen to me, what you were doing is quite natural for people who love one another and I'm certainly not going to tell you off."

"Merci, Dad."

"But you must take precautions because I'm sure you don't want to start a family just yet."

"Oh, no, Monsieur" replied Angelique feeling more grown up and less embarrassed.

"Bon, and my advice is not to say anything to your Mother s about this, it had better remain our little secret."

"Oui, merci, Dad."

"Merci, Monsieur" said the relieved Angelique.

"And in future plan to do it where you're as sure as you can be that no one is going to disturb you" said Michel sensibly.

"We didn't expect you to come home now, Mum had only been gone about ten minutes when Angelique arrived with her Mum and with Gran asleep we thought we had plenty of time."

"OK, son, you did your best to be discreet, that's all OK" replied Michel feeling guilty.

Then the phone rang and Michel raced from the kitchen hoping he could get to it before it woke Mama. He did not make it and his Mother in law opened her eyes as he entered the room and said "the phone is ringing."

"Oui, Mama" he replied as he snatched up the receiver.

"Hello"

"Is that you, Michel?"

"Oui" he replied, half recognising the voice.

"It's Tony"

"Tony, bonjour, ça va?"

"Ça va, Michel."

"And all the gang?" he asked as the thought of the statuesque Lisa flashed through his mind.

"Oui, everyone's fine and sends you their love."

"Merci."

"Now Michel, I'm in Marseille right now with Roberto and Lisa and we'd like to meet if that's OK."

"Oui, bien sûr."

"Bon, this afternoon?"

"Oui."

"Where do you suggest?"

"Meet me in Ricky's bar, it's in the Rue Bonneterie, just off le Vieux Port."

"OK, what time?"

"How about three o'clock?"

"That's fine, see you then."

"OK, au revoir." Michel put the receiver down and Mama asked "that's not your friend again, the one that's coming for Christmas?"

"Non, Mama, he's not coming for Christmas."

"That's good because Monique's got far too much to do, especially with Henri and Jackie arriving tomorrow."

"Oui" he replied with a sigh.

Michel returned to the kitchen and chatted to Frederik and Angelique whilst he finished his coffee.

A little while later Michele went down to the car and noticed that the day, although bright, had turned colder.

"Everything alright at home?" enquired Paul.

"Oui, all under control, all OK out here?"

"Oui, no one suspicious hanging about, its just a little cold, that's all."

"Oui, I expect it'll snow by Christmas" said Michel.

"Bon, meanwhile can you put the heater on full?"

Michel obliged as he started the engine and drove off towards the Bourse.

Michel parked as close as he could to the imposing façade of the Banque du Sumaris where he kept his money. Leaving his bodyguard in the car he made his way to the strong room, where after the necessary formalities, he unlocked his personal box and removed some three thousand Francs. Gambetta expected payment and dinner with Nicole in Aix tonight might be a little more expensive than usual.

They then drove to 23, Boulevard Fabrici where Michel parked in a spare gap right outside the flats.

"I'm having lunch with a friend, so I suggest you wander off and have a break yourself."

"Oui, Michel" replied Paul.

"If you go to the Bar Américiaine in the Rue Saint Pierre you'll keep warm and have a good lunch and I'll pick you up in an hour or so" said Michel.

"OK, are you sure you'll be alright?"

"Oui, I'm sure, merci."

The bodyguard left the Renault and wandered off whilst Michel rang the sonnette. He was soon in the warm confines of Jacqueline's flat. The only problem was that Annette was there too, so definitely no chance of any extra carnal activity. After the polite greetings Michel sank into the large settee that dominated the room and the lovely Annette sat next to him.

"It's very kind of you to invite me out to dinner as well as Mama" blushed Annette.

"You are our guest of honour, without you, your Mother and I would never have met" replied Michel.

"Oui, you're just too good to us" said Jacqueline.

"My pleasure" smiled Michel.

"Now you'll stay for lunch?" asked Jacqueline.

"That's very nice of you, but only if it's not too much trouble" replied Michel.

"Don't be silly, now whilst I'm getting something for us, Annette will pour the drinks" with that Jacqueline disappeared into the kitchen and Annette asked "what would you like, Michel?"

"A small brandy, s'il vous plaît."

"Oui" she replied as she left the settee and went to the sideboard where a number of bottles sat on a large tray. Michel watched her in admiration, she was graceful as well as very beautiful.

"Mama's car looks like new, she's so pleased with it" she said as she poured the drinks.

"Bon" replied Michel.

"We are both grateful, it would have been too much for us to pay for the repairs just at the moment."

"Don't think anymore of it, everything is taken care of, I promise you" replied Michel.

"Merci, Michel, without your help, I don't know what we would have done" she said as she handed him a brandy goblet half full of the golden liquid and then sat beside him holding a glass of red wine.

"Mon Dieu, this is a bit generous" he said as he surveyed the amount of brandy in the goblet.

"It'll warm you up" she smiled.

"Overheat me more likely!"

"That's what I've always wanted to do to a man like you" she whispered. Michel did not think he heard her correctly. At that moment Jacqueline entered and picked up a large glass of red wine from the tray.

"There, salute, Michel" she said as she raised her glass and Michel and Annette responded.

"Lunch will be in about ten minutes" she said.

"Merci" replied Michel.

"I've bought us some tender steak, I hope you'll like it" Jacqueline said.

"You're spoiling me, and you know what that means" smiled Michel.

"What?"

"I'll want to come again!" Mother and daughter laughed and then Jacqueline excused herself and returned to the kitchen.

Michel felt slightly uncomfortable with Annette and he just smiled and sipped his brandy.

"Mama tells me your getting a divorce" said Annette.

"Oui."

"Do you think you'll ever marry again?"

"Possibly, if I found the right woman, that is" he replied.

"What's your idea of the perfect woman?"

"I didn't say 'perfect' I said the 'right woman'" he countered.

"Would someone like me be the 'right woman'?"

"I'm not sure, we've only just met and I hardly know you" he replied, feeling a little uncomfortable and hot, 'must be the brandy' he thought.

"But we could get to know each other quite quickly, I mean, I like what I see already, how about you?"

Annette was coming on strong and for once Michel felt at a disadvantage with a young woman. 'She's been reading too many women's magazines' he thought as he struggled for a reply.

"Well, oui, Mademoiselle, you are very attractive and…."

"Would you like to make love to me?"

"Well, of course, what red blooded Frenchman wouldn't? I mean…."

"Don't hesitate then" she said firmly.

"You're very direct and I like that in a woman" he replied.

"I believe you should go after what you want, don't you?"

"Oui" He replied.

"And I want you, and I'm determined to have you before Mama gets you."

"Really?"

"Oui, she's got you all lined up as an after dinner treat next Monday night."

"Really?"

"Oui, her plan is to get you back here, send me to bed and get you too drunk to drive home so you have to stay the night."

"Really?"

"You look surprised" she said.

"Nothing surprises me" replied Michel firmly.

"I don't believe you."

"Really?"

"I think I've surprised you, and stop saying 'really'."

"You're right, you have" he replied lamely.

"Bon, after lunch, you can give me a lift down to the Bourse and we can plan in the car where to meet before Monday."

Suddenly the door burst open "lunch is served, ma petites" said Jacqueline "come along before it gets cold."

Michel followed the two women into the dining room in a daze. 'How do I get so bloody involved?' he asked himself. 'All this nonsense has to stop' he thought 'but on the other hand, it might be that I have too much animal magnetism and it will never stop, c'est la vie'.

He sat at the table and decided to clear his mind of all negative thoughts and enjoy the cuisine before him. Jacqueline had pushed the boat out to impress. A prawn salad starter followed by tender fillet steak, finishing with a gateaux ensured that Michel was both impressed and truly well fed. However, the heavy red wine served with the meal and the brandy aperitif were fighting for supremacy and he asked for a large glass of water in an attempt to subdue the matter.

"I'm going Christmas shopping this afternoon, would you forgive me if I asked for a lift down to the Bourse?" asked Annette with a knowing smile.

"Of course" Michel replied.

"Oh, I'll join you" said Jacqueline.

"Oh, Mama, I thought you had things to do here this afternoon?" queried Annette.

"Oh, the little jobs can wait" she smiled.

"But....."

"I said they can wait" interrupted Jacqueline.

"Why don't you do your jobs and drive down later and pick me up?" asked Annette.

"There's nowhere to park, non, I'll come with you, if Michel doesn't mind?"

"Non, my pleasure" said Michel smiling at the two women and thanking God that he was off the hook, for the moment.

"Bon, we'll go when you're ready" he said cheerfully.

They both looked a little straight faced as they clambered into the rusty Renault. Michel smiled to himself and set off towards the Bar Américiaine in the Rue Saint Pierre to collect his bodyguard. He stopped in a gap a few metres past the bar and said "I have to collect my bodyguard, he's having lunch here."

"Bodyguard?" queried Jacqueline.

"Oui."

"Oh, Michel" she said under her breath as he slipped from behind the wheel and leaving the women with their thoughts, went in search of Paul.

The bar was full and noisy, and he found the young Gendarme

sitting in the corner with a well dressed, middle aged man who had one hand on Paul's knee and the other on his shoulder. Michel approached his bodyguard who looked up and said in a slightly slurred voice "Michel, I thought you'd left me."

"Non, Paul, are you ready?"

"Oui, but let me introduce you to Monsieur Bernard first, he was in the Foreign Legion before he was a Gendarme like me."

"Really?"

Monsieur Bernard blushed and said in a light, delicate voice "I'm retired now."

"Of course, Monsieur" said Michel.

"I'll stay in touch, René, I want to hear all about your exploits" said Paul as he struggled to his feet.

"Bon, I look forward to hearing from you."

"Oui, I've got your card here somewhere" replied Paul patting his pocket.

"Au revoir then" replied René Bernard softly.

Michel led the way followed by the tiddly Gendarme.

After introductions the drive to the Bourse was as quick as it was silent and when Michel pulled up the two women got out of the Renault looking decidedly confused. They said their 'goodbyes' with Michel confirming that he would see them on Monday night and then they drifted off into the crowd of shoppers.

"You look the worse for wear, I think it would be a good idea if you had an early night and I took you back to the Gendarmerie now" said Michel to his pale faced bodyguard.

"Non, Monsieur, I'm staying with you until five o'clock" came the slurred reply.

"OK" sighed Michel and he drove straight to Ricky's as it was nearly three o'clock.

"Ricky's bar?" queried Paul as Michel double parked the Renault.

"Oui, I'm meeting some friends here."

"Mon Dieu, what a life you lead" mumbled Paul as he followed Michel into the bar. Jacques beamed and started pouring the drinks as soon as he saw them.

"Back already?" said Jacques.

"Can't keep away" replied Michel.

"There are two men waiting for you" said Jacques and he

nodded towards the back of the bar. Michel turned to see Tony and Roberto get up from their table and he smiled at them.

"Bonjour, Tony, Roberto, ça va?"

"Ça va, Michel" they chorused.

"Bon, what will you have?"

They ordered more drinks and Michel left Paul in conversation with Jacques and joined Tony and Roberto at their table.

"So, what brings you to Marseille?" asked Michel.

"Business, good business" replied Tony.

"Possibly big business" added Roberto.

"Really?"

"Oui."

"Am I involved?" asked Michel hopefully.

"Certainly are" replied Tony.

"Tell me all about it" said Michel with a smile. And they did. The business plan was simple and direct, they had seen an opportunity to supply very high quality videos and books discreetly to a selected group of customers. Michel's part would be in the selection and initial contact with the clientele followed up by Tony, Roberto or Lisa as appropriate to complete the sale.

"Is Lisa with you?" asked Michel wide eyed.

"Oui, she's at the flat" replied Tony.

"You've rented somewhere in Marseille?"

"Oui, in the Rue Aviateur."

"Bon."

"Come back with us now and we'll show you what we already have here" said Tony. Michel could not finish his drink fast enough. He remembered the previous collection of videos that Tony had given him in August and although he had not been able to sell many, simply because he had been so busy, everyone he showed the videos to had bought immediately, giving him a good profit on the deal. He looked forward in anticipation to the opportunity ahead. He left Paul at the bar in Jacques capable hands, promising the Gendarme that he would be back in time to take him to the Gendarmerie by five.

Driving to Rue Aviateur in Tony's Black BMW they chatted excitedly about the possibilities of the business.

Lisa opened the door to them and gave Michel a big kiss whilst pressing her enormous breasts against him. He was almost overcome with pleasure as the memories of having her naked on the Corniche in August flooded back into his mind.

" Lisa, you look wonderful" he said when the kissing stopped.

"And so do you, ma petite" she replied "now, come and sit down, I know you've a lot to talk about, so I'll get the drinks while you get started."

Tony went into more detail and everything was set to start in the new year. Michel asked if he could have a selection of gay and transvestite videos for Antone before Christmas and Tony was happy to give him four of outstanding quality. Michel felt sure that the great man would be delighted with such a hand picked, quality assured selection.

It was almost five when Michel bade the girls farewell and Joyeux Noël before Tony drove him back to Ricky's.

"Here's to a great new year" said Tony as they shook hands.

"Here's to the new year, au revoir" replied Michel.

Inside Ricky's, the bodyguard, was half slumped over the bar trying to hold a conversation with Jacques, and he was decidedly drunk. Michel sighed as he approached the young man tasked with his personal security against an attack by 'mad dog' Salvator.

"I think it's time I took you back to the Gendarmerie" said Michel firmly.

"Already? Non let's have a drink first" replied Paul.

"I don't think so, it's gone five and it will soon be past your bedtime" replied Michel.

"Nonsense, I want you to know that I'm prepared to go on protecting you until much later, much, much later, provided we stay here of course" came the slurred reply.

"I'm touched by your devotion to duty, Paul, but I'm sure Monsieur Gerrard would not thank me for keeping you out late after your duty roster finishes."

"I suppose not, alright then, hey Jacques, Jacques" he called.

"Oui, mon ami" came the gentle reply from the other end of the bar.

"When's this party of yours?" Paul asked.

"Next Wednesday, Christmas eve, starts at nine, but we won't get going until much later."

"Bon, I shall be there, I've got your address somewhere" he

said, patting his jacket.

"Come on then, off we go" said Michel as he half dragged Paul off the bar stool. They stumbled to the Renault and Michel drove as quickly as he could to the Gendarmerie.

"I'll collect you tomorrow at the same time" said Michel as Paul struggled to open the passenger door.

"Non, it's Saturday tomorrow and I don't work weekends, but I'll see you Monday" replied Paul.

"Don't bother" said Michel and went on "I'll catch up with you after you've arrested Salvator."

"Bon, that's a good idea, well, au revoir, Michel, I've had a wonderful day and met some interesting people." He staggered from the Renault and disappeared into the Gendarmerie.

'Well at least he's home safely' thought Michel as he pulled away and headed for Gambetta's garage.

The Mercedes was parked in the road outside the entrance and Gambetta was lightly polishing the front wing of the gleaming white taxi as Michel arrived. The old man had given the paintwork the same compound and polish that he had lavished on Jacqueline's Citroen.

Gambetta stopped work as Michel approached with a big grin.

"Ça va, Jean?"

"Ça va, Michel."

"She looks beautiful" said Michel.

"Oui she should do, considering the time I've spent polishing her."

"Merci, Jean, merci."

"Don't thank me too much, you haven't seen the bill yet!"

"Oh."

"Oui, you may well say 'oh', the wing was more difficult to repair than I thought" said Gambetta.

"Oh" replied Michel.

"But luckily for you I'm a craftsman."

"Oui" nodded Michel.

"And talking of luck, tell me, did you, er, at lunch time?"

"The daughter was there and…….."

"You had them both?" interrupted Gambetta.

"Non, of course not!"

"That's not like you" replied Gambetta.

"Jean, how much do I owe you?" asked Michel impatiently.

"Better come into the office, I don't want to be seen accepting large amounts of money out here" and he turned and Michel followed him to the wooden office at the back of the garage.

"Now then, I've worked your bill out and" he shuffled through the greasy papers "it's here somewhere."

"You said is was going to be two thousand Francs" said Michel firmly.

"Ah, that was only an estimate" replied Gambetta looking over his glasses at Michel.

"Mon Dieu!"

"Precisely, now then let's see, ah" he said triumphantly "here's the bill for the Citroen, there, not too bad, eight hundred and fifty Francs." He handed Michel a hand written bill.

"Bon" replied Michel.

"Now then, the Mercedes" at that point he whistled a long, single note "is more expensive."

"I guessed it would be" said Michel in a resigned tone.

"Twelve hundred Francs" said Gambetta.

"Oh, bon" said Michel.

"So, make it two thousand for cash" beamed the old man.

"Merci, Jean" replied Michel as he opened his wallet and counted out the money adding a fifty Franc note saying "and here's a tip for the craftsman!" They both laughed, wished each other Joyeux Noël and parted.

Michel headed for the autoroute and Grambois where he knew Nicole would be waiting. Driving the Mercedes as fast as he could to the little village he went straight to her house, parked outside and then rang the sonnette.

"Oui?"

"It's Michel, ma petite."

"Come on in" she replied in a deep, husky voice.

The door clicked and he entered the little, warm house and instantly beheld Nicole at the top of the stairs. She was fully made up and wearing a figure hugging, deep crimson dress.

"How do I look?" she asked.

"Fabulous."

"Really?"

"Really."

"Kiss me then" she replied as she came down to greet him. Michel flung his arms around her and kissed her passionately until she fought for breath.

"Wow!" she gasped "how lucky can a girl get?"

"I've looked forward to this for days" he said.

"So have I, ma petite."

"We're so lucky to have each other" he whispered.

"We are."

"And we must always make the best of our time together" he said seriously.

"Oui, now kiss me again" she commanded.

They kissed for an age, gently swaying, and at last she asked "are you staying tonight?"

"Bien sûr, ma petite."

"Bon, I must have you with me until tomorrow" she whispered.

"Oui, of course" he replied and they kissed again.

Michel savoured the moment as he knew in his heart that with the change of direction that he planned after Christmas, Nicole could no longer be a part of his life.

"Now, I have a big appetite for you, but first I need a little food to keep me going" he said with a smile.

"I feel the same" she laughed.

"So, are you ready then?"

"Oui, Monsieur" she replied coyly.

They set off at a leisurely pace to Aix, chatting about the events of the day and the journey seemed remarkably short. They were still laughing and talking when Michel parked outside the Bistro Romaine at 13 Cours Mirabeau.

"Here we are, my favourite restaurant in Aix" he said. Nicole smiled back at her lover.

"Je t'aime, Michel" she whispered and his heart sank as he whispered back "je t'aime" and he realised that leaving Nicole would be harder than he imagined. 'Perhaps' he thought 'I should reconsider my plans for change'.

"Let's go and eat, I'm starving!" he exclaimed.

They were soon seated in the warm, plush interior of this delightful restaurant, with its ornate painted ceilings and shaped alcoves each containing an elegant sculptured bust of a Roman Emperor. They had been shown, by an attentive waiter, to a discreet table for two which was romantically lit by red candles set in a glittering crystal goblet. The flickering candlelight enhanced the beautiful features of Nicole and at every glance, Michel fell further under her spell. He realised that he could not take his eyes of her. The waiter arrived with the menus and enquired "an aperitif, Monsieur?"

"Oui, Nicole?"

"A scotch and water."

"I'll join you, deaux scotch, s'il vous plaît"

"Oui, Monsieur" and he was gone.

"And to eat?" she enquired with a smile.

"I'll start with you, naked on toast" he replied.

"I'd go better with soup" she giggled.

"OK, providing it's not too hot."

Nicole laughed and consulted her menu. They ordered a sea food platter starter for her and moules for him, followed by roasted lamb cutlet and a large filet steak for Michel. Settling down to eat, with a bottle of rich Burgundy to accompany the food, they took their time and were unhurried both in conversation and their enjoyment of the meal. Michel managed a sweet of ice cream with chocolate sauce, but only just. After coffee, mints and Brandy they were at last ready to leave this paragon of perfect cuisine and return to Grambois for a night of tender love.

As they set off in the Mercedes, Nicole said "I hope the meal has given you plenty of energy, I'm so randy its not true!"

"So am I" he replied.

"I think I'll have to start now" she said as she leaned across and unzipped his flies.

"Nicole."

"Oui?"

"Not while I'm driving."

"Why not?"

"I can't concentrate."

"Of course you can, ma petite, I only want to hold you."

"Nicole, you mustn't, you'll make me come."

"I'll stop before that happens, I promise" and with that she extracted his hardening penis from his underpants and proceeded to stroke it gently until it was rigid. It took less than a minute to accomplish this. Michel started to groan and the Mercedes wandered slightly from side to side as he failed to concentrate.

"Is that good, ma petite?" she asked in a whisper.

"Oh, mon Dieu, oui, it certainly is" he replied.

"How many times do you plan to have me tonight?" she asked.

"Three" he replied.

"Only three? I thought the steak would give you enough energy for six at least" she said firmly.

"Look, stop Nicole because I'm either going to come or crash!" and thought of Gambetta shaking his head as he surveyed more accident damage to the Mercedes acted as a stimulant to Michel and his mind focused immediately and he stopped the car. As soon as it was stationary Nicole leaned across and took him in her mouth.

"Oh, Nicole, stop, stop!"

She did as she was told and said "I told you I was randy."

"We're never going to get home" he said quietly.

"Alright, ma petite, just kiss me and I'll leave you alone until we're home and then….watch out!"

They kissed and eventually set off for Grambois with the concession that she could hold him gently but no stroking. Michel realised that this was going to be quite a night, he hoped he could satisfy his delightful companion.

As soon as they were in the house Nicole closed the door and leaned against the wall and pulled her dress up to her waist. She wore stockings held up by garters and the briefest of black lace panties.

"It's all yours, Michel" she whispered as he dragged her panties down to her ankles. She stepped out of one leg as he fingered her clitoris and kissed her passionately. She fumbled for his rigid penis and having released it from his underwear guided it into her moist and yielding body. Michel rammed her against the wall as she clung tightly around his neck. As soon as he was as far as he could go inside her she wrapped both legs around his waist allowing him to get even further up into her slim body. She gripped him so tightly that he could hardly breath as he thrust up into her with a steady rhythmic pace.

"Mon Dieu!" she mumbled "this is so good, just keep fucking

me all night, all fucking night."

"I'll try" he whispered, but it was not possible and Michel reached his point of ecstasy from which there was no return.

"Oh, my darling" he whispered as he increased the speed of his thrusting and with a mighty rush began to come into her compliant body.

"Oh, Michel, Michel" she called out as he thumped hard into her and squashed her against the wall.

"Oh, mon Dieu" she gasped as he fought for breath and his knees began to tremble.

"I must sit down" he whispered as she unwrapped her legs from his waist and stood shakily against the wall.

"That was good, ma petite" she whispered as he gently slid out of her "you must rest for a while."

He nodded and went into the living room and sank onto the settee. He contemplated the big wet patch around his flies and cursed himself for not taking his trousers off.

"Let me get you a drink" she said calmly.

"A coffee would be nice" he replied and she nodded before disappearing into the kitchen.

They sat and talked for more than an hour before going to bed. Michel lay naked on his back under the sheets and Nicole climbed on top of him. She guided him into her body once again and she rode him gently, kissing him passionately all the while. They continued for some time until at last she began to come and as she tightened Michel released himself gently into her. She kissed him again and again whispering, "je t'aime."

They fell into a deep, dreamy sleep wrapped in each others arms.

CHAPTER SIX

Saturday 20th December

Nicole was up and sitting on the bed calling his name gently as he came to.

"Michel, ma petite, are you awake? I've made some coffee"

"Ah, bon" he grunted as he focused his eyes and gazed at his beloved. He eased himself up and leaned back against the headboard.

"What time is it?"

"Nearly half past eight" she replied as she handed him the mug of coffee. His mind raced and he remembered that Josette was moving into the flat today, Henri and Jackie were arriving and he was having dinner with René and Yvonne. He realised that he could not stand another Christmas like this ever again.

"Merci" he said as he sipped the hot, sweet, black liquid.

"What time are you leaving?" she asked.

"As soon as I've drunk this and got dressed" he replied.

"So soon?"

"Oui, I've a lot to do today, Christmas rush and all that, but I'll be back next week."

"Oh, bon, when?"

"Tuesday or Wednesday, I'll be coming up to see you and I've some things to collect from my house before the holiday" he replied, thinking of the load of Romanian sandals still sitting in his garage since August. The time had come to clear them out and sell them cheap to one of the Arab stallholders in the market at La Plaine.

"Are we going out to dinner again?" she asked.

"Er, possibly, my darling, I have to stay fluid this time of year, I can't be too certain of time" he replied.

"I understand, ma petite, but you will come?"

"Certainly, how could I stay away from you for long?"

"Oh, Michel" she whispered and she kissed him.

Half an hour later Michel was in the Mercedes heading for Marseille with just an hour left before he was to meet Josette and collect the key to the flat in Rue du Camas. Pushing the car as fast as he could on the autoroute he then drove unsympathetically through the busy streets of Marseille. It was a few minutes past ten when he pulled up outside Josette's flat in the Rue Benoit Malon, double parked the car and rang the sonnette.

"Oui?"

"It's Michel ma petite."

"You're late, we're supposed to be at the agents at ten."

"I'm sorry, ma petite, but I've just rushed back from Grambois and the traffic was dreadful."

"I'll be down in a moment."

"Bon."

He returned to the car, slipped behind the wheel and lit a cigarette.

'There's no pleasing a woman' he thought 'even if they love you' and he drew heavily on his first cigarette of the day. A few minutes later Josette appeared and joined him in the car. They kissed and she said "you haven't shaved this morning."

"Not yet, petite."

"Why not?"

"Because I've been busy, now stop complaining and let's get going."

They drove in silence to the agents, where a smart secretary handed Josette an envelope containing the keys and her copy of the lease plus a receipt for the advanced rent. She was all smiles as they made their way to 115 Rue du Camas and Michel parked in a space exactly opposite 116, where René and Yvonne lived. 'How utterly unbelievable' he thought as he switched off the engine. Josette was out of the car in a flash and was through the front door and half way up the stairs before Michel caught up. She opened the door to the flat and entered saying "here we are, Michel, it's all ours!"

"Bon" he replied as he followed her in. The flat was exactly the same as René and Yvonne's but not as well decorated. It was a little musty and was in need of a thorough clean. It was partly furnished with good quality furniture, except for the double bed in the main bedroom, which looked as if it had seen considerable action in the past.

"They'll take this away when they deliver our new one today" she said brightly.

"Bon" replied Michel.

"And you'll stay with me tonight?"

"Oui, of course" he smiled. 'After all', he thought 'I've only got to stagger across the road from René and Yvonne's after the party'.

"Bon" she smiled.

They spent the next three hours moving Josette's small bits of furniture and other bric a brac to the new flat, plus unimaginable piles of clothes, 'why do women keep so much stuff that they'll never wear again?' he mused. In the midst of this tiring operation, the new bed was delivered and the old one removed with much grunting and cursing as it was not only old but extremely heavy. Michel managed to bring a smile to the delivery men's faces with a substantial tip for each of them when it was all over and they wished the lovers a 'Joyeux Noël' with a wink. It was almost half past one when Michel told his Fiancé that he needed lunch and they headed for Ricky's.

"Bonjour, Josette, Michel" beamed Jacques as they entered.

"Bonjour, Jacques" replied Michel quietly.

"Pernod or brandy?" enquired Jacques sensing that it was another difficult day for Michel.

"Brandy for me, and Josette?" Michel enquired of his love.

"Red wine, s'il vous plaît."

"Bon"

"And two of your cheese baguettes" said Michel.

"Bien sûr" replied Jacques.

They sat at a table and sipped their drinks whilst Jacques prepared the baguettes. Michel felt tired and realised he would have to have an easy afternoon so that he could meet the demands of Yvonne later and Josette later still. He knew that she would be keen to test the new bed tonight. He suddenly felt weary at the thought.

"Now this afternoon" said Josette brightly "I'll give the place a good clean and unpack as much as I can."

"Bon."

"Are you staying to help at all?"

"Non, ma petite, I must do some work and I'll have to pop home to see the cousins from Le Touquet" he replied.

"That's OK, I'll probably get on quicker without you there" she said.

"I'm sure" he replied with relief.

"And what time are you coming tonight?"

"Er, it'll be latish" he hesitated.

"How late?"

"After ten I expect."

"After ten? What about dinner?"

"I'll have a snack out, probably here."

"Oh, Michel....."

"I know" he interrupted "but I'll make up for it over Christmas."

"Are you working tomorrow?" she asked in a plaintive tone.

"Oui, I must, we need the money, ma petite." At that moment Jacques arrived with the baguettes and Michel was grateful for the diversion. They had just finished eating when Antone arrived for his lunch and the beginning of his long afternoon of quiet but steady drinking until dinner time.

"Bonjour, mes enfants" beamed the great man.

"Bonjour, Antone" they chorused.

"How are we today?" he enquired.

"Fine, just fine" replied Michel.

"Bon, now, not wishing to disturb you but might I have a quiet word, Michel?"

"Of course" he replied and he excused himself and followed Antone to the back of the bar where the great man lowered his considerable frame into his favourite creaking wicker chair.

"I won't keep you long" began Antone "I just want to warn you that Salvator is somewhere in Marseille as he plans to attend his father's funeral on Monday and then, the rumour has it, that he intends to settle some old scores before skipping off to Switzerland."

"And am I an old score?" proposed Michel.

"Possibly" sighed Antone.

"Mon Dieu!"

"Precisely."

"Gerrard has asked me to go to the funeral to identify Salvator" said Michel glumly.

"Why?"

"Because he thinks he'll be in disguise" replied Michel.

"Be careful, Michel, be very careful."

"I will be, I promise."

"Do you have a gun?"

"Non."

"I'll get you one, just in case" said Antone.

"Oh, non, Antone, I can't manage that, I'd probably shoot myself."

"Very well then, we must just hope that Gerrard and his men arrest Salvator before he causes any more harm." At the words 'Gerrard and his men' a picture of Paul Dassault sprang into Michel's mind and he sighed inwardly, all hope of a powerful arrest gone.

"Oui" replied Michel weakly.

"Have courage, mon brave, I will be at the funeral as well."

"You?" asked Michel in surprise.

"Oui, I want to see that hateful man buried and his evil son arrested, I promise you, I have waited many years for this moment" replied Antone in a slow and determined voice.

"I will see you there then."

"Indeed, now on a lighter subject, have you managed to find me some interesting video's?"

"I have acquired a selection of the highest quality, recommended by the head of the organisation, a perfect choice for the connoisseur" replied Michel.

"Wonderful" beamed Antone.

"I'll drop them in on Christmas eve."

"You're going to make me wait that long?"

"Oui, think of the anticipation."

"I can hardly wait!"

"If I don't see you before, then I'll see you Monday at the funeral."

"Oui, Michel, I will be there."

They said their goodbyes and Michel returned to his Fiancé. She was curious about the private conversation with Antone but Michel dismissed it and drove her back to the flat in the Rue du Camas. Having promised undying love followed by kisses Michel left his Fiancé to clean, unpack and reorganise the flat whilst he headed back to his home at Montclivet to wash, shave and greet

Henri and Jackie. He dreaded the meeting. Pulling up outside the flat he noticed a brand new, top of the range, light blue metallic Citroen parked neatly in front. 'Cousin Henri must be doing well' he thought.

He entered the living room and it seemed as if a sea of faces turned as one to stare at him.

"Bonjour, bonjour everyone" he beamed and a chorus greeted him back.

"I thought you'd be home sooner" said Monique.

"I had planned to be but I've been hard at it since last night."

"He's always working" said Mama "never stops, always at it" and she nodded in the general direction of Henri and Jackie who were perched on the settee like a couple of parrots. Henri got up and held out his hand.

"Good to see you, Michel, you look well" he said.

"So do you" replied Michel as he gazed at his cousin by marriage. He appeared a little fatter than when he last saw him and his hair was a lot thinner with considerable amounts of grey intermingled with the ginger. They shook hands embraced and kissed on both cheeks.

"And Jackie" said Michel as he released Henri from his fond embrace. She stepped up for the same treatment and although she had a plain face there was a distinct sparkle in her blue eyes. It was Michel's opinion that she had worn a little better than her husband, her face was not unduly lined, her complexion looked good and her hair was still blonde. They kissed and she said "it's been so long since we've seen you."

"Oui, time goes by so quickly these days" he replied.

"They say it goes faster as you get older" she said.

"Possibly, now have you all got drinks?"

"Oui" they chorused and Alexis piped up "but I could do with another!"

They all laughed and Monique got up and said "I'll get it" and then as she brushed past Michel she whispered "I'll get you a drink whilst you go and shave, you look a disgrace!"

"Bon, excuse me for a moment everyone, I must go and tidy up" he said and left the room pulling the door to. Monique turned on him in the hallway and said in an angry whisper "where have you been?" and before he could reply she continued "just don't tell me you've been working all night because I don't believe it!"

"I......"

"You've been with some low life tart or other, I know!"

"Listen......"

"Non, you listen, Michel, you pack it in or I'm going to throw you out, do you hear?"

"Oui...."

"I mean it, I really mean it this time!"

"Oui...."

"I've got a houseful of people for Christmas, a Mother with a broken ankle to look after and you, you hopeless, useless, unfaithful bastard of a husband!"

"Oui, but....."

"I'll not put up with it any longer, that's it, now buckle down and help me to get through this holiday or piss off now! Do I make myself clear?"

"Oui, ma petite, you do."

"Bon, now hurry up and get cleaned up!"

She disappeared into the kitchen and he into the bathroom. 'The last Christmas ever like this' he thought as he showered and shaved. In a change of clothes he felt better and relaxed as he rejoined the family in the living room. Monique was all smiles as she handed him a scotch with tinkling ice.

"Well here's to us all, joyeux Noël!" said Michel and the family chorused 'Bon Noël'.

"This will be a Christmas to remember," said Mama "what with my ankle and Henri and Jackie coming to stay, well I'm glad you're all here to help Monique, because I'm pretty useless."

"Oh, non, Mama" they all chorused.

She shook her head "Non, I'm old now and not much good for anything." There were more cries of "non" and Michel sipped his scotch and thought 'the last Christmas'.

"So, are you busy?" asked Henri as he took another sip of wine.

"Oui" replied Michel and added "it seems to get busier every year, so there's either more people in the town, fewer taxis or I'm getting much older."

Henri laughed at that and Jackie managed a smile.

"You're like me, Michel, always working, we never stop, and it's not any good you know."

Michel nodded and replied "you're right but others don't seem to appreciate it" and he looked hard at Monique who tossed her head and turned away.

"I'm always telling you that you work too much but you don't take any notice of me" said Jackie quietly.

"I do" replied Henri in a slightly hurt tone.

"You just tell me I'm nagging all the time and that we need the money and we plainly don't" she replied slightly irritated.

"Let's have another drink" said Monique, determined to try and keep the atmosphere light.

"Good idea" said Alexis.

"I think you've had too much already, dear" chimed Hélène.

"No I haven't and besides it's Christmas and we should enjoy ourselves while we still can, because you never know what's around the corner" replied Alexis waving her empty wine glass at her sister.

"Quite right, Alexis" said Michel "you just never know, I mean look at that crook Salvator, one minute alive and well and making a fortune the next dead at the bottom of a cliff."

"What this?" asked Henri.

"A local so called business man, a rotten crook in reality, was being driven along the Cassis road when his car went over the edge of a cliff and crashed down about 200 metres."

"Mon Dieu!" exclaimed Henri.

"And rumour has it that he has a Swiss Bank account with millions in it" said Michel.

"Money didn't do him any good then" said Jackie.

"Non" replied Michel.

"It's better to be content and happy with someone you love rather than chasing after money all the time" said Jackie with some passion.

"Quite right, I've got the money so I'm just waiting for a drink at the moment and then for the right man to come along" said Alexis still waving her empty glass.

"No one is interested in you dear, you drink too much" replied Hélène.

"You never know, I might catch some toy boy by showing him my Bank statements and then getting him drunk!" replied Alexis.

They all laughed.

"Or round the other way!" she added.

"Oui, I can imagine that after a night out 'would you like to come up and see my Bank statements'" Michel laughed as he said it and even Monique had to smile.

Alexis was enjoying being the centre of attraction and Michel was pleased because she was so often bullied by Hélène who had such a strong and sometimes overbearing character.

Michel also felt the tension between Henri and his wife and he guessed that Henri was more interested in money than his rather plain wife. He wondered if Henri had a mistress or two, but looking at him, he doubted it. He thought it might be interesting to find out though.

Monique disappeared into the kitchen to get more drinks whilst Michel enquired about the long journey from Le Touquet to Marseille. Henri claimed that it was a good run down the autoroute except for the Paris périphérique and the usual hold up around Lyon. They had made a two day run of it and stopped overnight at Macon as Henri felt it would have been too much to drive all that way in one go.

Monique returned with the drinks and Michel asked "where's Frederik and Angelique?"

"Gone out for a walk" replied his wife.

"Oui, young people shouldn't be stuck indoors with old people like us" commented Mama. 'And middle aged people shouldn't be stuck indoors with old people either' thought Michel.

"I'd hoped to see them before I go off to work this evening" said Michel innocently.

"You're going back to work?" demanded his wife angrily.

"Oui, ma petite, I have to make up for lost business when the car was being repaired."

Well, if looks could kill!

"Had an accident, Michel?" asked Henri.

"Oui, only a minor scrape, silly driver changed direction and caught my front wing."

"Easily done these days, everyone's so impatient" said Henri.

"So, will you be home for dinner?" asked Monique.

"Non, ma petite, I'll get a snack while I'm working."

"He never stops" said Mama and Monique sighed and shook her head.

"Are you working all night?" asked his wife, knowing the answer.

"Possibly, but I'll see how it goes" he replied, hedging his bets.

Monique shook her head again and handed out the drinks. The conversation stayed light and easy after that and Michel learned a lot more about his cousins and their business in Le Touquet. Henri had an upmarket shoe shop that he inherited from his father but although the business provided a very good living Henri wanted much more and he told Michel that he saw an opening in the tourist trade. Michel was very interested and Henri said he would go into detail when Michel had finished working.

An hour later Michel was at his station waiting for business. It was now late afternoon and the shoppers were beginning to emerge carrying bags of all shapes and sizes. He took three fares to various parts of the busy city and had just returned to the station when René pulled up behind.

"Michel, ça va?"

"Ça va, René."

"Had a good day?" asked René.

"Not really" replied Michel.

"Oh, why?"

"Couldn't get going this morning" he replied.

"Well, I hope you can get going tonight!"

"I'll try" replied Michel lamely.

"I've never seen so much food, you'd have thought we were starving to death!"

"I can believe it" replied Michel.

"We're really looking forward to it and we've been good all week, we've done nothing so we could save everything for tonight."

"Bon" replied Michel feeling weak.

"I've never known Yvonne so randy, I think it was the sailing and sex on holiday that's done it."

"Oui, it was good wasn't it?" agreed Michel and he smiled when he remembered how many times René and he had had Yvonne on the boat. It had been glorious, naked in the sun and totally abandoned sex with no inhibitions. Michel licked his lips and carried on thinking sexy things as he took two more fares to their destinations. He then drove round to Ricky's for a break and some coffee.

Jacques served him the café noir with extra sugar and enquired after Michel's day so far.

"A slow start but getting better by the minute" replied Michel.

"Bon, we've been worried about you, Antone says it's this damned Salvator business."

"It hasn't helped" replied Michel.

"Never mind, it'll all soon be over, thank God" said Jacques with feeling.

"Oui."

"And where's your little smiling bodyguard today?"

"He only works nine 'til five, weekdays."

"Oh, I wish I could get a job like that, d'you think they'd have me as a Gendarme?"

"No doubt about it, if Paul's anything to go by, your bodyguard material."

"Really, how exciting."

"But you'd miss working here."

"Oh, I would, but I couldn't be a bodyguard."

"Why not?"

"Antone wouldn't approve, he would never let me be put in harms way, no never."

"He's a caring person."

"He is, do you know, I introduced him to Paul and he said straight away that if he came to our little party next week he'd have to stay the night. He said he couldn't stand the worry of that boy going home alone late at night, well what do you think of that?"

"Heart warming" replied Michel.

"Well I think so too" he said as he went off along the bar to serve another customer. Michel had one more coffee before saying goodbye to Jacques and returning to his station.

Michel had only been parked for a few minutes when Sayid appeared and tapped on the passenger window.

"Bonjour, Michel" he beamed.

"Bonjour, jump in" replied Michel and Sayid slipped into the taxi and out of the cold.

"I have some good news for you, Michel."

"Bon, I could do with some" he replied.

"My cousin, Akhmed, well he's not really my cousin but, well it's a bit complicated, he's really a close family friend, but he's more like a cousin really…."

"Sayid, I promise you, I'm now ready for the good news" interrupted Michel.

"He and his brother have a stall on la Plaine and I showed them a couple of samples of the Romanian sandals and they said if you can agree a price, job lot of course…."

"Of course."

"They'll take them off your hands."

Michel smiled and replied "that is good news."

"May not be."

"Why not?" queried Michel.

"You haven't agreed a price yet and Akhmed is a very hard man to bargain with."

"So am I."

"He's very rich" replied Sayid with a smile.

"I'd like to be" grinned Michel.

"If you can do a deal then perhaps you'll pay me?"

"Of course, have I ever let you down?"

"Oui, frequently."

"I always pay you!"

"Oui, eventually, but I'm getting older and I am finding hard to wait."

"Where can I find Akhmed and his brother?"

"Get the sandals and come to my flat and I'll take you to his place and you can do the deal."

"OK, I plan to go to Grambois on Tuesday and collect them, I should be back sometime in the afternoon."

"OK, I'll arrange it all with Akhmed."

"See you Tuesday then, au revoir" said Michel and with a nod, Sayid was gone and had disappeared into the crowd.

Michel prepared to return to le Vieux Port when suddenly the back door opened, he turned to see his fare and stared into the face of Gerrard.

"Bonjour, Michel."

"Bonjour, Cyril."

"Police business, Michel."

Michel sighed and asked "where to, Monsieur Gerrard?" emphasising the 'Monsieur' for effect.

"Drive round the Arab Quarter, slowly, s'il vous plaît."

"The Arab Quarter?" queried Michel.

"Oui, the Arab Quarter, do I have to repeat everything I say to you?"

"Non, Monsieur Gerrard, but you never go there."

"Precisely, I'm looking for someone in the Quarter and I need to talk to you, so I'm combining operations, saving time as well as manpower."

"Bon" replied Michel "we can expect to see a reduction in taxes with these combined operations." Gerrard ignored the remark and Michel started the Mercedes and swung out into the traffic.

"Now drive slowly, this is a police operation."

"Oui."

"Firstly, have you seen Salvator?"

"Non."

"Are you sure?"

"Oui."

"We know he's here in Marseille."

"Oui, so I understand."

"How do you know?"

"Antone told me."

"Does he know where he is?"

"He'd be the first to tell you if he did!"

"Oui, I suppose so."

"I know so."

They travelled in silence for a while before Gerrard said "it looks like we'll have to wait until the funeral on Monday to arrest him. I hope you are prepared" said Gerrard.

"Prepared?"

"Oui."

"What for?"

"To assist in the arrest of course."

"Assist in the arrest?" queried Michel.

"Oui, I expect you to identify him."

"Well you know what he looks like."

"Correct, but he'll be in disguise and we're relying on you to get in close."

"Me?"

"You."

"Look, Monsieur Gerrard, I can't get involved in this without police protection…."

"You've got it already" snapped Gerrard.

"Paul Dassault is a very nice young man but, one, he only works nine 'til five and two, he's hopeless!"

"He's one of my best officers."

"Mon Dieu!"

"Stop the car" Gerrard commanded as he peered out the side window at a number of Arab men loitering outside a bar.

"Who are you looking for?" asked Michel.

"You wouldn't know him" replied Gerrard.

"I might."

"He's an Arab by the name of Akhmed and he has a stall at la Plaine that he owns with his brother Youssef , d'you know him?"

"Never met him" replied Michel honestly whilst a shiver ran up his spine.

"Not surprised."

"What's he done?"

"Can't discuss that, now drive on slowly." Michel did as he was told and the Mercedes eased forward in the narrow street.

"Now then, on Monday, I want you to get as close as you can to Salvator and when you're standing next to him I want you to give me a signal."

"Where will you be, Monsieur Gerrard?"

"I will be everywhere and nowhere."

"Bon, how will you see me then?"

"You will be watched all the time, I assure you, mon ami."

"And the signal?" enquired Michel.

"If Salvator is to your left, then scratch the left hand side of your nose, and if he's on the right, then the right side."

"And if he's in front of me?"

"Scratch the front."

"And behind me?"

"Scratch the back of your head."

"Mon Dieu!"

"Can you remember all that?"

"With difficulty" mumbled Michel under his breath.

"Stop!" Michel did as he was asked and Gerrard peered up a narrow alley between a block of seedy flats and a grocers shop.

"Drive on" he said after a few moments.

"What have these stall owners done?" queried Michel.

"You need not worry about it" replied Gerrard.

"It must be pretty important if you're prepared to spend time and money looking for them on the off chance" replied Michel.

"They're handling a lot of stolen stuff and trying to clear it before Christmas" said Gerrard in an irritated tone.

Michel shivered again. 'Were the Romanian sandals stolen?' he wondered. 'hopefully not, after all, he acquired them in August.' He felt content as he asked "why don't you go up to la Plaine and arrest them?"

"They're not there, some young kid is running the stall at present."

"Oh" replied Michel.

"Non, it's no good, better get back to le Vieux Port, drop me outside Ricky's" ordered Gerrard.

"Oui, Monsieur."

Michel took his time returning through the narrow back streets to maximise the gendarme's fare.

"I'll see you Monday then" said Gerrard as he paid Michel.

"Oui, Monsieur Gerrard, I'll be there."

"Bon, and don't be late" he said sternly.

"Non, Monsieur" replied Michel as he tucked the money into his wallet and Gerrard slipped from the back seat of the Mercedes.

'Mon, Dieu, what a life' thought Michel as he returned to his station.

From then on Michele worked solidly getting the shoppers home to various parts of the sprawling city of Marseille. The time passed quickly and the money plus generous tips mounted up nicely. Returning to his station he glanced at the dash board clock and was surprised to see that it was almost a quarter to eight. He was expected at his friends flat for dinner at eight. Good timing. He drove slowly to Rue du Camas, remembered that there was a small cul de sac just before the end of the street at the junction with the Boulevard Chave and decided to try and park there so the taxi was out of sight of both Josette and René.

He realised that there could be a tricky end to the evening when he left René and Yvonne's and staggered across to Josette's. Perhaps it would be better to stay with René and Yvonne as he may be too drunk to do anything anyway and they would certainly not let him leave if they thought he was going to drive home to Montelivet.

He swung the Mercedes into the cul de sac and hoped for a space to park. At the end he found enough room to squeeze into and leave just enough space for the other parked cars to ease out, relieved he locked the car and made his way back to number 116.

He rang the sonnette, René answered and within moments he was in the warm flat being kissed passionately by Yvonne who said "I've been really looking forward to this evening."

"So have I" replied Michel.

"Bon, René will get the drinks whilst I finish off in the kitchen."

Michel slumped into the settee whilst René poured large scotches for the three of them.

"This could be a night to remember" he said as he handed Michel a tumbler full of scotch and tinkling ice.

"Oui, but if we carry on drinking like this we'll not remember anything!" René laughed as Yvonne joined them. She was all smiles, very well made up, and her hair looked stunning, drawn up into a French roll. Michel was surprised to see that she was wearing a housecoat buttoned up and guessed that some exotic outfit was concealed beneath it. Yvonne liked to tease. She sat next to Michel and raising her glass said "Joyeux Noël, ma petite."

"Joyeux Noël."

"I can guarantee you'll never forget this Christmas!" she exclaimed.

"I'm sure I never will" he replied and he smiled, thinking of his future plans. They drank and relaxed together before Yvonne said

"I've got everything planned."

"I'm sure you have" replied Michel and René laughed.

"We'll eat first, and take our time, and we'll talk about all the sexy things we've done together, here and on the boat."

"Bon."

"And then when we get to the sweets, as I'm the Christmas fairy, I'll start granting wishes for both of you and you'll start granting wishes for me."

"Sounds wonderful" said Michel.

"Oh, it will be, I promise you" she replied.

"Another scotch, Michel?" asked René.

"Just one I think and make it a little smaller."

"Nonsense" said Yvonne "make it a large one, we want you to relax and lose your inhibitions."

"I haven't got any, especially not after the sailing trip in August" replied Michel and René laughed.

"You might have when you find out what I've got planned for you!" she exclaimed.

"Make it a large one then, René."

"Oui, Michel."

René poured the drinks whilst Yvonne busied herself kissing Michel and stroking his face.

"Now I'm going to go and get ready so chat among yourselves until I return" she said and with a final kiss left the room.

"Mon Dieu, she's hot tonight" said René, and added "I hope we can cope."

Michel nodded and took the tinkling tumbler from his friend.

"Salute" said René and they raised their glasses.

Michel began to mellow and relax after a hectic day and he thought that it would be the best idea to stay with René and Yvonne. He realised that he would have to sweet talk Josette in the morning, but he guessed that with the long term arrangements in place he would be able to win her round.

They had just finished their drinks when Yvonne entered with a flourish. The sight of her made Michel break out in a sweat. She stepped forward and twirled round for the men in her life to drink in the sight before them. She wore a silver, sparkly crown on her head, long pendulum diamond ear rings, a thick diamond encrusted choker, a black satin basque with petite black panties and fish net stockings and very high heeled silver shoes to match. As she twirled she enquired "how do I look?"

"Wonderful" said Michel.

"Beautiful" added René.

"I'm your fairy, make a wish" she laughed.

"Give us a kiss and dish up dinner!" exclaimed René.

"Who said romance was dead?" she queried and kissed them both with passion.

"Mon Dieu" murmured Michel.

"Pour the wine and sit at the table" she commanded as she returned to the kitchen.

"I hope your hungry" said René.

"Oui, I am."

"Bon, let's sit up."

The table had been beautifully set up for the three of them. The glasses and cutlery sparkled and the centre piece was a large candelabra set with red candles. René poured red wine into the large glasses and lit the candles. The glow gave a warmth and closeness to the room and Michel sat opposite his friend leaving the seat at the head of the table for the fairy.

Yvonne entered carrying a tray with the first course which consisted of a sea food salad with prawns, baked moules and salmon.

"There, ma petites" she said as she took her place at the table.

With "bon appetites" they began to savour the delights of her cuisine. They toasted each other, as the closest of friends, laughed and chatted as they consumed the salad. When they had finished, Yvonne asked "when did you enjoy me most, Michel?"

"I can't make my mind up between the first time here when you tried on the fur coat or the session we all had together on the deck of the Calypso" he replied.

"Bon, and you, ma petite?"

"In the cabin of the boat when Michel squeezed my balls as I was having you" replied her husband.

"Bon."

"And you?" asked Michel.

"Every time was my favourite" she replied. They all laughed and Michel persisted "there must have been one outstanding moment."

"Oui, when you both had me on the deck of Calypso. It was a lovely warm night and the gentle rocking of the boat as you had me, well, made it all so romantic, and it was so enjoyable, and so sensual having two wonderful, gentle caring men. It's every woman's dream to be loved and gently fucked like that."

Michel and René both smiled and raised their glasses.

"To Yvonne, the loveliest wife imaginable" said René.

"To Yvonne" added Michel as he drank.

"And to you two, the men I both love, but differently" she smiled.

They all raised their glasses and drank.

"Now for the main course" she said and in a moment had gathered up the dishes and returned to the kitchen.

"She'll be a while" said René.

"Why?"

"She's cooking filet steaks, we're having Tournedos Rossini."

"Ah, bon, one of my favourites" said Michel.

"Oui, she thought we needed fresh meat to keep us going" he laughed.

Michel smiled and sipped at the wine, a full and rich Burgundy.

"René, you're my oldest and closest friend"

"Oui, and you're mine" he replied.

"You're very happy with Yvonne and you're very close."

"We are, that's true."

"Are you sure that you're happy with our ménage a trios?"

"Michel, how many times must I tell you, mon ami, I promise you I am very happy, very happy indeed, I have a lovely wife who loves me but enjoys having another man to excite and delight her and I get really turned on watching and joining in. To me it's perfect, my best friend has my wife whilst I watch. What could be better?"

"I don't know, I just……"

"Michel, our arrangements are above board, there is no deceit, no lying, no betrayal, just love and enjoyment between three people who care for each other in different ways, I promise you it's perfect, mon ami."

"You are obviously sure."

"Very sure, you make Yvonne and me very happy. You have added a spice to our lives and I thank you for it."

"Bon."

"Our marriage is much stronger for it."

"Bon."

"I know it wouldn't suit everyone and most men, and women,

go off and have affairs that by their nature have to be surrounded by deceit and hurried liaisons."

"True" replied Michel.

"But we are open and relaxed with all the time in the world."

"Oui" replied Michel as he pondered on his own complicated life.

"We all know that we're going to have session after session tonight until we can't manage any more, and then we'll all go to bed together and sleep like angels until sometime tomorrow."

"Bon."

"So let's enjoy the cuisine, the wine and Yvonne."

They raised their glasses and toasted Yvonne.

"And, Michel."

"Oui?"

"Do relax and stop worrying."

"You're a great friend, René, I promise I'll unwind."

At that moment Yvonne entered carrying a tray with three large dinner plates. Each plate was piping hot with a large filet steak on each set up with the paté and red wine sauce that makes the dish so exquisite. She returned to the kitchen and followed on with numerous dishes containing the vegetables. More wine was poured and the three lovers set about devouring the most delicious main course. The steak fell away from their knives and was full flavoured as well as being as tender as they could imagine. The full red Burgundy flowed faster as they consumed the food until at last they had cleared their plates and were decidedly more full and relaxed than when they had started.

"I think we'll let that go down before we have a sweet" said Yvonne.

"Oui" replied René.

"Meanwhile, I'm ready for some attention" she said.

"Bon, what would you like, Madame?" asked Michel.

"I want to be kissed by my husband whilst my lover squeezes my nipples" she replied.

"As you wish, ma petite" said René as Yvonne undid the lace at the front of her basque and allowed her full breasts to swing free of their confinement. She turned to face René who started to kiss Yvonne whilst Michel stroked her magnificent breasts upwards to her nipples. René kissed as Michel tweaked and Yvonne murmured gently, moaning with pleasure.

Michel felt his penis thicken as Yvonne said "now change over, ma petites."

They did as they were told and Yvonne's murmuring became louder. Suddenly René stood up and undid his trousers, displaying his rigid penis. Yvonne stopped kissing Michel and turned to take her husband in her mouth. Michel returned to her nipples as she consumed as much as she could of René. Michel could wait no longer and also stood and revealed himself to his mistress who reached out and held him for a moment before letting her husband go and turning to Michel taking him firmly in her mouth. Each man toyed with a breast as Yvonne went from one to another in ecstasy.

"Mon Dieu, this is so good" she said between mouthfuls.

"What do you want now, my darling?" asked René gently.

"Have me on the table now" she gasped.

"OK" he replied as she left her seat and laid on the far end of the table.

"You have me first, Michel" she said as she opened her legs, and then she added "come here, René, I haven't finished with you yet."

Michel pulled off her panties as she turned her head to take her husband in her mouth once again. Michel rubbed her clitoris and was about to lick her but she was so wet that he just gently slid into her warm and compliant body. Michel pushed gently with a steady rhythm and gradually moved right up inside her as she opened more and more of her body. Watching her lustily sucking on René was a real turn on and he hoped he could keep going long enough to satisfy her. Michel began to sweat as he moved faster and he could see René arching his back as he forced himself further into Yvonne's mouth. Suddenly it all became too much and Michel could no longer hold on and the unstoppable rush of ecstasy began. He thumped hard into Yvonne and lifted her off the table with his final thrusts. As Michel's action died away, Yvonne pulled away from her husband and gasped "quick, René, finish me, finish me!"

Michel slid out of his mistress as René came from the side of the table and took his place. His rigid penis slid into his wife with ease and started to ram her with some force whilst Michel squeezed her breasts and sucked her nipples. In moments her orgasm began and continued until René climaxed and emptied all he could into her quivering body. They all fell back exhausted. Michel and René slumped in their chairs whilst Yvonne remained on the table gently moaning.

"Oh, mon Dieu, mon Dieu, that was good, just too good, are you going to be able to do it again?" she asked.

"Shouldn't think so" mumbled René.

"Michel?"

"Not for a while, ma petite" he replied.

"Oh" she said.

They all remained silent for a while and then Yvonne sat up and climbed off the table.

"René, pour some more wine while I get the sweet" she said. René did as he was asked whilst Yvonne wandered off into the kitchen.

"What d'you want to do, Michel?"

"Drink that and go to bed" he replied.

René laughed and said "me too."

"That was some session, but too short, we must be getting old" said Michel.

"Oui, I expect you're right."

Yvonne returned with a chocolate gateaux and ice cream. The lovers slowly made their way through the sweet and having drunk their fill of Burgundy moved onto Brandy. They then sat on the settee with Yvonne in the middle, all drifting in and out of sleep as the full effects of a busy day, wine, good food, sex and Brandy took its toll.

"Come on, ma petites, let's go to bed" murmured Yvonne.

They put up no resistance and followed her into the bedroom, soon they were naked and snuggled under the sheets. The last thing they remembered was Yvonne kissing them goodnight as she wriggled down between both of them.

CHAPTER SEVEN

Sunday 21st December

Michel awoke with a thick head and a mouth like a parched desert. His eyes struggled to make sense of his surroundings. He was on his back staring at the ceiling with someone's arm across his chest. He moved his head to see who was cuddled up to him and gazed at Yvonne's lovely smiling face, still with traces of makeup and lipstick. She was fast asleep with René's arm around her and he was gently snoring. Michel remembered where he was and then wondered what time it was. He focused on his wrist watch and saw that it was almost ten o'clock. It was not a problem as it was Sunday and he had planned to work for a short time in the morning and then go home to Montelivet. Then he thought of Josette and he realised he would have to see her and explain why he had not returned to the flat last night to stay with her and christen their new bed. This might be tricky. He attempted to sit up slowly without disturbing the others but he failed. Yvonne stirred and opened her eyes.

"Michel, where are you going?"

"Ah, I think it's time I got up" he replied.

"Nonsense, snuggle down, we haven't finished yet" she said as she slid her hand over his thigh and held his penis gently.

"Oh, non, ma petite, not this morning, I have to go to work" he replied.

"Michel, come on, it's Christmas" she murmured.

"Not quite" he replied. At that point René stirred and asked "what's the time?"

"Ten o'clock" Michel replied.

"You working?" asked René.

"Oui."

"Oh, I guess I'd better too" said René.

"Oh, non" said Yvonne.

Whilst Michel and René showered, Yvonne made the coffee. They sat at the table that had seen action the previous night, quietly sipping the sweet, black reviver and slowly eating croissants and honey. After several cups Michel felt better and it was almost eleven thirty when he kissed his friends 'goodbye', promising to see them once more before Christmas, and left the flat, hoping Josette was not looking out of the window opposite.

Returning to the Mercedes Michel was angry when he noticed a dent in the front passenger door, looking around he saw that the other parked cars were in the same positions as when he parked the previous night. Then he noticed the new black bin bags on the pavement. The notorious Marseille bin men had been down the cul de sac collecting the rubbish bags during the night and had obviously reversed their giant rubbish lorry into the door of the Mercedes. Another job for Gambetta. He sighed, slipped behind the wheel and drove down to his station at le Vieux Port to think for a while. The day was bright, cold and sunny.

After parking the Mercedes Michel wandered off to the kiosk for a paper and some cigarettes. He returned to the car, lit his first cigarette of the day and glanced at the news paper. Nothing of great interest but he could not concentrate as he remembered that the funeral of Salvator was tomorrow. He was definitely not looking forward to it for one moment. He was sure that Gerrard and his 'men' would cock it up and Claude Salvator would foil the planned arrest, escape to Switzerland only to return one day and take his revenge. Michel shivered and drew heavily on his cigarette. He thought he had better call on Josette and pacify her before going home to face the music at Montelivet. He glanced around and noticed that the Port seemed unusually quiet this morning. Perhaps everyone had been celebrating last night. He decided not to do any work but go to his Fiancé's flat in the Rue du Camas and start making amends.

He pulled up outside the flat, looked up and down the street to see if René's taxi was parked nearby and was relieved when he realised his friend had gone to work. Hoping Yvonne was not looking out of the window, he was about to ring the sonnette when he remembered he had a key. He fumbled in his pocket and produced the little ring with two keys, one for the street door and the other for the flat. He entered and went up to the stairs and hesitated for a moment. Then he gathered up his courage and opened the door. He was amazed to see the interior of the flat, it had been thoroughly cleaned and almost glistened in the bright sunlight streaming through the window.

"Josette, ma petite" he called gently as went into the living room. She was not about and he only remained there briefly before going into the bedroom. It was dark with the shutters closed and he could make out a little lump in the bed under the bedclothes.

"Josette" he half whispered as he bent over to awaken his Fiancé. He gently pulled the covers back to reveal her lovely face and mop of black hair. She stirred and whispered "Michel."

"Ma petite" he replied.

"Michel" she said a little louder as she came to.

"Ma petite" he whispered again as she sat up in bed.

"Where have you been?" she demanded.

"Working" he lied.

"You were supposed to come home here last night!"

"I know, ma petite, but........."

"I lay awake nearly all night crying over you!" she interrupted.

"I'm so sorry......."

"I've been so worried, I thought you might have had an accident."

"Oh, ma petite….."

"Or worse still, Claude might have found you." Michel shivered at the thought.

"Well, he didn't….."

"Michel, I can't live like this, always worrying where you are and wondering what's happened to you."

"I know, ma petite" he replied trying to pacify her. She put her arms around him and held him tightly to her. Her warm body was soft, compliant and smelling of perfume.

"I love you, Michel, and you've got to take care of me."

"I love you to, ma petite."

"Promise me that we're going to be together always."

"I promise" he gulped.

"Bon, now then, let me get up and get dressed."

"Oui."

"And then you can take me out for lunch, I'm starving."

"Oui, ma petite" he replied, feeling relieved that he had been able to calm her down with his promise.

An hour later the two lovers were sitting comfortably in Ricky's enjoying soup and baguettes. The sun streamed through the windows and Michel felt quite relaxed as he chatted to the lovely young woman sitting next to him. Antone arrived for his aperitif and leisurely lunch before settling down for his steady afternoon drinking; he came over as soon as he noticed the couple.

"Bonjour, mes enfants, how are you today?" he beamed.

"Bon, Antone, and you?" said Michel.

"Very well indeed and now looking forward to Christmas. I am delighted to say that Jacques and I have friends coming round almost every night."

"Bon" said Michel.

"And most of our closest friends are going to stay overnight."

"Bon."

"It makes sense you know, I mean, I just don't want these young men trying to get home late at night."

"I understand" nodded Michel.

"Especially someone like your young friend, Paul."

"Paul Dassault, my bodyguard?"

"Oui, such a nice young man and very sensitive."

"That's true, he's not really cut out to be a bodyguard" said Michel.

"I agree, I'll have to have a word with the Chief about him."

"I think that makes sense" replied Michel.

"Well, a big day tomorrow, Michel."

"Oui."

"And you won't need your bodyguard if everything goes to plan."

"Here's hoping."

"Everything will be alright, I promise you, now, bon appetite, mes enfants" and he gave them a little wave before going to his favourite table at the back of the bar.

Michel had just finished his baguette when the telephone behind the bar started ringing. Jacques answered it and then called out "Michel, it's for you." Michel groaned inwardly, smiled at Josette and went over slowly to the bar. He picked up the receiver.

"Oui" he said.

"Michel?"

"Oui" he replied as he recognised Monique's voice.

"Where have you been?"

"Working."

"Liar!"

"Monique, ma petite............"

"Listen Michel, you get home now!"

"But, ma petite........"

"Alexis and Hélène have had an accident!"

"Oh, Mon Dieu, are they alright?"

"I don't know."

"Oh, what happened?"

"I really don't know."

"Well where are they?"

"At Orange."

"Orange?"

"Oui."

"What are they doing there for God's sake?"

"Alexis went home this morning to get some more wine."

"Why?"

"She didn't think there was enough for Christmas."

"Mon Dieu!"

"And she took Hélène with her for company."

"Mon Dieu!"

"Precisely, and they seem to have had an accident in the car, I can't quite make sense of it all, so just come home now, will you?"

"Oui, ma petite, I'm on my way."

Michel replaced the receiver as Jacques asked "another bad day, Michel?"

"Oui, the very worst, my two Aunts have had a car accident."

"Oh, non, where?"

"At Orange."

"Are they alright?"

"I don't know, I'm going home to find out."

"Bon chance, mon brave."

"Merci, Jacques."

Michel explained everything to Josette on the way back to the flat in the Rue du Camas. Being wonderful, she understood perfectly and only asked that he should phone her the moment he had any news. Before slipping from the Mercedes she kissed him passionately and hoped that he would come to her later.

Michel hurried the car through the traffic and back to Montelivet.

"At last" said Monique as Michel faced her in the living room with Mama, Henri and Jackie looking on.

"We've been so worried" said Mama with tears in her eyes.

"I'm here now, Mama" replied Michel in his manly voice.

"I know, but I feel so helpless with this damned ankle, I mean I'm useless to everyone."

"No you're not, Mama" said Monique testily.

"Well?" asked Michel.

"What d'you mean 'well'?" asked Monique.

"Tell me about the accident" said Michel firmly.

Monique slumped onto the settee and replied "they've had some sort of accident with a man on a bicycle and another car, I don't know the details, Henri then spoke to a gendarme who didn't seem to know much."

"Are they hurt?" enquired Michel.

"We don't know, but we don't think so" said Henri.

"Well I'd better get going to Orange then" said Michel gloomily.

"I'll come with you" said Henri enthusiastically.

"Bon, that's very good of you" replied Michel with a smile. He felt that some sensible male company might be a great help at the moment. Orange is almost a hundred kilometres north of Marseille and using the autoroute A8 to Aix and then the A7 to junction 22, south of Orange, Michel expected to be there in an hour or so.

"Thanks for coming with me, Henri" said Michel as he swung the Mercedes out into the traffic and headed for the autoroute.

"Not at all, Michel, in fact I'm glad to get out for a bit" he replied.

"I know the feeling" grinned Michel.

"I'm sure you do" replied Henri sympathetically.

"I just hope Alexis and Hélène are alright" said Michel.

"When the gendarme phoned from Courthézon he gave the impression that they were a little shaken but otherwise alright and their main concern was getting the wine back to Montelivet" replied Henri.

Michel grinned and said "I can hear them arguing from here!"

Henri laughed and replied "I must admit they do seem to enjoy a little catastrophe."

Michel was beginning to warm a little to cousin Henri and thought that they may have things in common.

"Did the gendarme tell you where they had the accident?" asked Michel.

"Oui, it was on the road to Jonquières, near Cabridon" he replied.

"I know it" said Michel.

"Apparently after the accident a recovery lorry took both cars to a garage in Cabridon where Alexis and Hélène are waiting to be picked up" said Henri.

"Why didn't they go home to Vacqueyras to wait, it's not far from Cabridon?"

"I expect Alexis wanted to keep an eye on her wine!"

Michel laughed and said "I don't blame her, it's very good."

"Oui, Jackie has often talked about Alexis's vineyards and that wine co-operative she belongs to."

"Oui, I think she does very well out of it."

"I wish my father had left me a vineyard instead of a shoe shop" said Henri with feeling.

"I hear you have a good business, Henri."

"Well, it's alright but hard work and not a lot of profit, believe me."

"I'm sure it pays the bills" said Michel.

"Oui, we get a fairly good living out of it, but I want more than a good living, Michel."

"Really" replied Michel with interest as he joined the dual carriageway that was the run up to the start of the autoroute.

"Oui."

"What have you in mind?" asked Michel.

"Several ideas, but I have to be a bit careful because Jackie is dead against anything new or a bit adventurous."

Michel was warming to cousin Henri, in fact he was almost glowing.

"I understand, Monique is the same."

"Women, they're lovely some of the time but a pain in the arse most of the time" said Henri with feeling.

'A little undercurrent of discord there' thought Michel as he replied "true."

"I mean, what do they want out of life?"

"I'm not sure" replied Michel.

"Neither am I" said Henri.

"You marry them, look after them, provide for them and………"

"All they want to do is keep on living the same old boring life" interrupted Henri.

"Quite" replied Michel.

"They have no sense of adventure, none" said Henri emphatically.

"Well some do" replied Michel, as he thought in quick succession of Sophia painting in the nude, Nicole up against the wall, Evette all dressed up, Eleanor on the store room table, Yvonne on the Calypso, Lisa in the open air and Josette, his only love.

"Well your experience with women must be different to mine" said Henri.

"Possibly" replied Michel.

"Jackie's answer to everything is 'no' so what's the question?"

They reached the kiosk at the Peage and Michel took the ticket and accelerated onto the autoroute towards Aix.

"Tell me about some of your ideas" said Michel in an interested tone.

"I will if you tell me about some of your women" replied Henri. Michel was slightly taken aback.

"Women in my life?" he queried.

"Oui, Monique makes no secret about it all, she says you've admitted it all."

"A little indiscretion, some time ago, you understand."

"Michel, I don't really believe you, I think you're at it all the time" and Henri laughed as he said it.

"Henri, really!"

"Come on Michel, I'm eager to find out what you get up to down here in Marseille."

"Really?"

"Oui, the women in Le Touquet are all like Jackie, somewhat proper, cold and distant."

"I don't believe that for one moment" replied Michel.

"It's true, I promise you."

"I'd have to see that for myself before I could believe that" replied Michel.

"OK, why don't you come up in the spring and stay with us and see for yourself."

"That's an idea, I might just do that."

"I'll introduce you to our friends and their frigid wives and you'll see I'm right" Henri laughed.

"It can't be that bad" said Michel.

"Listen, Michel, I run an up market shoe shop and I spend all day with women, massaging their feet into luxurious, soft leather shoes and chatting them up and I assure you, they're all as cold as ice."

"OK, point taken, now tell me about your ideas, I'm always on the look out for a little enterprise and I can tell you that I've got quite a few projects on the go that will beat taxi driving into a cocked hat if they come off."

"Tell me about some of the women first" demanded Henri.

"OK, let me start with Sophia."

"Sounds good."

"She is, believe me."

"Go on" said Henri as Michel prepared to open up to his cousin, confident that it would all remain confidential.

"She's an artist in Grambois, a nude artist."

"You mean she paints nudes?"

"No, she's always nude at home and when I call to see her she just has me to relieve her artistic passions."

"Mon Dieu!"

"I'm just her sex slave."

"Oh, Mon Dieu, how wonderful."

"She is and she has a perfect tan all over because she paints outside on her balcony all through the summer."

"I'd love to meet her" said Henri wide eyed.

"You may do, one day, but I must warn you she has no inhibitions."

"Wonderful."

"And if she decides to have you, then she'll want it there and then, so you've been warned."

"I look forward to it" replied Henri with a glazed look in his eye and added "is she dirty with it?"

"Non, we have to go to Evette or Yvonne for that" replied

Michel.

"Oh, Mon Dieu, what a life you have, Michel."

"Oui, I suppose I do have quite a time really."

"Tell me about Evette first."

"She's very elegant, always beautifully dressed and made up. She works for a Bank, quite a senior management job she tells me, and she likes to dress up in little costumes and she teases before she goes mad and lets her hair down."

"Go on, Michel" Henri said in a hoarse whisper.

"And she's just dirty with it."

"Oh, Mon Dieu."

"My body is not my own and in between what she does with her mouth, breasts, bum and fanny, she makes filthy suggestions using the foulest language" said Michel spicing it up for effect.

"What does she say?" asked Henri.

"I couldn't possibly tell you, Henri, it's just too disgusting."
By now Henri was shaking gently with excitement and he said "tell me about Yvonne then."

"She likes to share me with her husband, René."

"At the same time?"

"Oui."

"I have been missing out."

"You have, believe me."

"Doesn't René mind?"

"Non, he says it turns him on, besides, he'd rather watch me, his best friend have Yvonne than some damned stranger. You see she needs lots of dirty sex."

"Oh, Mon Dieu, I think that's enough for the moment, Michel."

"OK."

"Let me calm down and tell you some of my business ideas."

"Oui."

They drove on for a while and remained quiet whilst Henri regained his composure.

"We have a lot of tourists visit Le Touquet, mostly British, quite a few Americans and they're pretty good on the whole. They spend well and don't complain much, not like the Germans or the Belgians, mon Dieu, do they whine! Anyway, I'd like to get into the tourist trade, supplying services, tours and the like. The Americans are very keen on that as well as the British, but the

Americans have more money to spend."

Michel liked the sound of Henri's ideas and said "go on."

"I've got an old, empty house, left to me by an Aunt, in the Rue de Londres off the Rue Saint Jean, almost opposite Jean's café and The Bar Américiaine. It would be ideal to turn into an office to run a tourist business or something. I mean, it needs developing, but as it's right in the heart of the town with the sea front and beach just a few hundred metres away, it would be perfect."

Michel was positively glowing at the thought of being in the tourist business with Henri. His mind was racing ahead but he played the situation carefully.

"It sounds a great idea, Henri, but could you run this and your shoe shop on your own?"

"Well, I've got Jackie of course."

"Of course."

"But I really need someone to put a bit of money in and join me as a working partner."

"How much are you looking for?"

"Haven't really got down to the figures yet, Michel, it's really all still in the planning stage."

"I see" replied Michel.

They remained silent for a short while before Henri asked "would it interest you, Michel?"

"Possibly, but I've got a lot of business commitments here at present" he replied.

"I understand."

"And you have got Jackie, and she has to be the favourite person for the business" mused Michel, knowing that, judging by what Henri had said about her, she would be a dead loss.

"Well, Jackie's very conservative and I don't know that she'd be that interested in starting a business. She's very much one for leaving everything as it is."

"Quite."

"She's content to just let me run the shop and wait until we retire and then buy a little cottage in Normandy and wait to die" said Henri sadly.

"Oh, dear, that sounds a bit deadly" replied Michel.

"I want much more than that, Michel, I want some real money to spend, I want to buy a boat, something about twenty metres, with two engines, a real sea going luxury cruiser and fill it with good food, drink and women!"

"That's the idea" replied Michel as happy thoughts of Yvonne and René on the Calypso crossed his mind.

"And I want a big car, a Mercedes limousine, with all the extras."

'Quite a shopping list' thought Michel.

"And I want to have some fun with people, friends and women."

"Bon."

"You know, Michel, you're a long time dead and you've got to make the most of every day."

"I agree" nodded Michel.

"In all the years I've been married to Jackie, I've never had an affair."

"Really?"

"Oui, and I believe I must be the only man in France like it."

"Possibly."

"I mean, when I hear about your little escapades I realise what I've been missing, I'm a fool to myself."

"Not necessarily, Henri, I can assure you that affairs come with a high price."

"Go on, tell me."

"Unhappiness at home, mistresses demanding money as well as sex, problems with their husbands or boy friends, all sorts of jealousy, believe me, the list goes on."

"You seem to be alright though."

"Not really, Henri, not really, I have many problems at the moment and I really must sort things out before it all gets much worse."

"You make it sound pretty bad."

"It is, Henri, it really is."

They fell silent for some time and Michel concentrated on his driving as he increased speed on the autoroute. He was thinking deeply about his situation and decided to show a little more interest in Henri's business idea. It could possibly, if handled correctly, get him out of Marseille and into a new and happier life.

"Henri, I think that your tourist service idea is very interesting and I'd like to think about the possibilities of me becoming your partner."

"Michel, I am delighted, I think we could make a great success of it."

"Oui, I think we could."

"After Christmas, when I get back to Le Touquet, I'll get some figures together and a business plan" said Henri.

"Bon, and you must consider Jackie, and how she'll fit into the business, that's if she wants to of course."

"I don't think she'll want to be involved" replied Henri in an off hand manner.

Michel warmed at that and replied "well of course I'll leave you to sort that out."

Henri nodded and said "I think we could have a great future, Michel."

"Let's hope so" he replied.

The Mercedes made good progress and they soon flashed by the junction for Aix and headed towards Salon de Provence. The day remained bright and clear and the traffic on the autoroute was light. Michel was enjoying the drive and felt very content with the proposed business plans. 'Surprising what opportunities can develop from conversations in taxis' thought Michel.

"So tell me more about Yvonne" said Henri.

Michel smiled and replied "where shall I begin?"

"What happened the first time you had her?"

"It was in July, this year, I took a fur coat round to her flat to look after it until I could give it to Monique."

"Go on."

"We were alone in the flat, René was at work, and she went into the bedroom and tried it on. She then came out to show me what it looked like but didn't tell me she was naked underneath."

"Mon Dieu!"

"She then gave me a flash and I couldn't believe my eyes."

"Wonderful."

"It was, she looked spectacular. She has a beautiful sun tanned body, fabulous breasts, large nipples and thick, black hair around her fanny."

"Mon Dieu!"

"So I had her there and then" said Michel triumphantly.

"And René knew about it later and didn't mind?"

"Non, he told me he was delighted."
"I can hardly believe it."
"It's true, I promise you."
"It's lucky we're all different."
"Yvonne's very sexy and needs a lot of attention" said Michel.
"So it seems."
"And in August I went sailing with them."
"And don't tell me that you had non stop sex with them on the boat?" said Henri breathlessly.
"Oui, I did, days and nights of it"

Henri groaned and said "I have to get a boat" and then asked "and since August?"

"Just fairly regular sessions, mostly at lunch time when René was at work and Yvonne would tell him all about it when he got home in the evening."

"Really?"
"Oui, it really turns him on."
"I can hardly believe it" said Henri.

"Oh, it's true, and last night we had a very special dinner party, just the three of us."

"Tell me all about it" pleaded Henri and Michel did, going into every little detail and by the time he had finished, Henri was sweating, and they had passed Salon de Provence and were headed for Cavaillon on the A7.

"Does Monique have any idea how many women you're involved with?"

"Non, and it's best it stays that way."
"I can understand that."

"And if we can start our tourist business and it's successful, then I may leave Marseille for ever and begin a completely new life in Le Touquet" said Michel.

"Are you telling me that you might leave Monique?"
"Oui."
"And all your lady friends?"
"Oui" replied Michel flatly.

Henri remained silent at that and gathered his own thoughts whilst trying to think through the implications of what Michel had just told him.

"A very big step, Michel."

"Ah, oui, but a necessary one, I assure you."

"Why do you say that?"

"Another year like this one and I'll be dead, either from worry or sexual fatigue!"

"I can believe that" replied Henri.

"And if all the women in Le Touquet are as frigid and cold as ice as you say, then I may just survive a little longer than I would in Marseille." Henri laughed at that and replied "I have a feeling that you might find one or two 'hot' ones on the beach for a little romancing."

"Possibly" grinned Michel.

The traffic on the autoroute became even lighter and Michel pressed on faster to Cavaillon.

It was not long before the sign for Avignon came into view and Michel said "not much further now."

"Bon" replied Henri.

"We turn off at Courthézon and head to Jonquières and then into Cabridon. Have you got the name of the garage?"

"Oh, non."

"It doesn't matter, it's only a small place and we'll soon find them."

Michel hoped that Alexis and Hélène would be contrite and he decided that he would play up the 'rescue dash' element should they start arguing senselessly, as usual. He was in no mood to tolerate any silliness today and he would make the point that he was suffering loss of earnings. He hoped that that would keep them both quiet.

They drove on in silence, each of them thinking about the opportunities before them. Henri was delighted that Michel showed such interest in the project and he believed that with Michel's streetwise knowledge and attitude to life, his own existence would be changed out of all recognition.

"Of course, Michel, if you decide to join me in the tourist business you can live in my house in the Rue de Londres, it's spacious and close to the Bar Américiaine" said Henri, hoping to encourage his cousin by removing any obstacles that might deter him.

"Bon" smiled Michel.

"Naturally I'd have it re decorated and furnished to your taste" continued Henri, gilding the lily.

"Merci, Henri, that's very generous of you."

"Not at all, I think it's important that we get off to a good start, should you wish to join me of course."

"Of course" replied Michel smiling. This was getting better by the moment and Michel thought that if Salvator did escape his arrest at the funeral then an unknown address in Le Touquet would be ideal in ensuring safety from any planned revenge. Michel breathed a sigh of relief and said "you're making this business opportunity very tempting, Henri, in a moment I'm going to have to say 'oui' to your propositions and give you a large cash deposit to make sure you don't offer it to anyone else!"

Henri laughed in a confident manner and replied "Michel, I'm sure we'll make a great success of it and believe me, I'm not about to share this with anybody else, in fact if you say 'non', I probably won't go ahead with it." There is nothing like being needed to the exclusion of all else to ensure the answer is 'oui'.

"Let's do it, Henri" grinned Michel.

"Bon, I know you'll not regret it" beamed Henri as they swept passed the sign for Avignon.

Michel could hardly believe his good fortune. Henri was possibly the answer to his prayers, and to think he was not looking forward to seeing his cousin and his wife for Christmas. 'How wrong can you be?' he thought.

"Next year could be the one to remember" said Michel.

"Oui, I can see us on my twenty metre cruiser by the end of the summer" replied Henri.

"Full of food, drink and women" said Michel.

"You can be sure of that" smiled Henri.

"Shall we invite some frigid ones along with the beach beauties?" asked Michel with a smile.

"Non, we only want the beach beauties who are too hot to handle" replied Henri.

"Oh, non, let's have a few frigid ones, they're more of a challenge" said Michel.

"Non, Michel, I want them all slightly drunk and easy!"

"There, Henri, we're having our first row!" and they laughed out loud. Both of them believed that this was going to be good and they were busy spending the money before they had even started. Michel guessed that Henri had a good deal of cash behind him and he liked that in a business partner. The first sign for Courthézon flashed by and at junction 22 Michel would turn off the A7 and head for Jonquières. The traffic became a little heavier and it was not long before Michel pulled up to the Peage and paid the toll.

Some while later they drove into Cabridon looking for the garage. Michel eased the Mercedes round the town square whilst they searched in vain.

"Better ask someone" said Henri.

"Oui" replied Michel as he slowed and stopped outside a small bar.

"I'll go" said Henri and he slipped out of the taxi. He was back in a few moments and said "there's only one and it's on the road to Vacqueyras."

"Bon." replied Michel and they set off in the direction of Vacqueyras, where Alexis lived. They had only been driving for a few kilometres when they came upon 'Autos de Cabridon' and Michel said "here we are."

"I hope they're alright" replied Henri.

"Oui, and Henri."

"Oui, Michel?"

"I'd like to keep our business arrangements totally confidential until we're ready to start."

"Oui, of course, my lips are sealed."

"Bon."

Michel pulled onto the garage forecourt and parked the Mercedes. He saw Alexis battered Renault with the front suspension collapsed, half leaning against a similarly damaged Citroen. What was left of a bicycle was propped up against the fence nearby. At that moment Alexis and Hélène streamed out of the small garage showroom, large enough for one car only, followed by an anxious looking man dressed in a badly fitting suit.

"Michel, Henri, ma petites" cooed Alexis.

"Aunt" replied Michel as he kissed his alcoholic relative and then Hélène. Henri did the same as he enquired "are you both alright?"

"Oui, bien sûr" replied Hélène "but the cyclist has been taken to hospital."

"Mon Dieu! Is he seriously hurt?" asked Michel.

"Non, we don't think so" replied Alexis.

"Was he unconscious?" asked Henri.

"Oh, non, but he was shouting a lot and his language, well, I've never heard anything like it, he kept calling me a, what was it he called me, Hélène?"

"A fucking idiot" replied Hélène calmly.

"Oui, what do you think of that? And he said I'd wrecked his Christmas, well it wasn't my fault" said Alexis.

"Non" said Michel sympathetically.

"This is Monsieur Olivera, he owns the garage and has been very kind, gave us coffee and a little brandy to steady our nerves" said Alexis.

"Monsieur" said Michel as he shook the proprietor's hand and Henri followed suit.

"I was concerned for the ladies, Monsieur's" he said hastily.

"Merci, you're very good" replied Michel.

"Merci Monsieur, luckily the other car driver was unhurt, it seems that only the cyclist has suffered any injury" said Monsieur Olivera.

"Oui, do you know where they've taken him?" asked Michel.

"Oui, the Hospital de Salon in Orange."

"Merci, Monsieur, now then, can you repair the Renault?"

"We could, Monsieur, but I believe that it's beyond economic repair."

"Written off?" enquired Henri.

"Oui, Monsieur, it was quite a collision."

"So I see" replied Michel.

"And now, Monsieur, I'm sure you want to get back to Marseille, so if you would kindly settle the recovery bill then you can be on your way" said Monsieur Olivera and he turned and headed back towards the one car showroom.

"Better start loading the wine into the Mercedes" said Michel to them all as he followed Monsieur Olivera.

Half an hour later they were on their way back towards Marseille with a boot full of wine and the Aunties sat in the back with two cases of wine between them.

"Well what happened?" enquired Michel.

"It was so sudden" said Alexis.

"I'm sure" replied Michel.

"We had just left home and were coming down the road to Jonquières to get onto the autoroute when, as I was telling Hélène about the trouble I've been having with my neighbour, Madame Gilbert, this stupid man on a bicycle swerved across the road, I mean I don't know why he did that I'm sure....."

"He said it was because he lived there" interrupted Hélène.

"And so to avoid an accident I ran into the other car coming towards me."

Michel raised his eyebrows and asked "what about the other driver?"

"Oh, Monsieur Bonnette, he was very nice about the whole thing, he told me he'd been hit there before, just right there, he said he felt as if this was his own place of destiny."

"Mon Dieu" whispered Michel and Henri grinned and looked out of the side window at the countryside flashing by.

"And we called the gendarmes, and they were very nice and told the rude cyclist to stop shouting and using such bad language other wise they'd arrest him, and then later the ambulance arrived and took the foul mouthed creature away" said Alexis.

"Bon, and then Monsieur Olivera came with his breakdown truck and collected you?" surmised Michel.

"Well not right away."

"Oh?"

"Whilst Monsieur Bonnette and I were giving our details to the gendarmes, some woman who knew the cyclist........"

"His wife" interrupted Hélène.

"She came out of the house and started shouting at everyone and after the cyclist told her what had happened, she started screaming at me!" exclaimed Alexis indignantly.

"Lucky I was there" said Hélène "otherwise I'm sure it would have come to blows."

"Mon Dieu" murmured Michel.

"It was awful" said Alexis.

"How is it then, if you swerved into Monsieur Bonnette's car to avoid the cyclist, he's been injured and his bike is in a hell of a mess?" queried Michel.

"You may well ask, Michel, the fact is that he was so busy watching me crash into Monsieur Bonnette that he didn't look where he was going, and he rode straight into a brick wall by the drive way of his house with such force that he and his stupid bike bounced back into the road where a passing van drove over his bike and knocked him flying down the road!"

"Mon Dieu, it gets worse!" exclaimed Michel. What happened to the van and its driver?" asked Michel.

"Well, nothing, the van wasn't damaged, just a scratch or two, and after the gendarmes had spoken to the driver and got his details, they let him go."

"I think we'd better get you back to Montelivet quickly and let you rest, I'm sure you must be quite shaken up" said Michel calmly.

"Well I was until Monsieur Olivera gave me a brandy" replied Alexis.

"Quite so" said Michel.

"I'm alright now" said Alexis.

"Bon."

They continued the journey in silence and just over an hour later they pulled up outside the flat in Montelivet. Monique, Jackie, Frederik, and Angelique rushed out to meet them and with 'mon Dieu's and much 'la la', kissing and sighs of relief, Alexis and Hélène were escorted inside whilst Michel and Henri unloaded the wine and brought it in.

When the two men joined the family in the living room, Mama was crying and the rest of them were drinking either brandy or scotch.

"Oh, Michel and Henri, what would we have done without you?" queried Mama through her handkerchief.

"It's alright Mama, everyone is home, safe and sound and looking forward to Christmas" replied Michel.

"I know" said Mama.

"And now with plenty of wine" added Henri.

"Oui, and I'm sure I don't know why you thought we needed any more, we've got a cellar full" said Michel to Alexis.

"I just thought you might be getting a little low, that's all, besides, you can never have too much, can you?" Alexis countered.

"Possibly not" replied Michel.

They all relaxed back, continued drinking and listened intently as Alexis and Hélène recounted their catastrophe until Monique served dinner. By then every member of the family had been fully briefed, down to the smallest detail, and all questions had been answered.

Alexis had planned to buy a new car in the spring, so the accident had brought that forward. They all knew she had plenty of money so the loss of the old Renault was not a problem to her, in fact it was a bit of a relief.

After dinner, Michel told them all that he had to return to work and try and make up the business he had lost by going to Orange on the rescue mission.

Monique looked daggers as she asked "will you be back tonight?"

"Possibly not, ma petite" he replied to which Mama murmured "he works so hard that boy, he deserves to do well."

Henri grinned as he knew that Michel would not be working all night and somewhere in Marseille some young woman was expecting his arrival and preparing herself.

"We'll see you tomorrow then, Michel" said Henri with a smile.

"Oui, bon nuit" he replied and left the room, put on his short winter coat and went out to the Mercedes.

Michele drove straight to Josette's flat where, after passionate kisses and promises of undying love, he took her to Ricky's for evening drinks and relaxation in friendly company.

"Are your relatives alright?" asked Jacques as he poured scotch for Michel and red wine for Josette.

"Oui, merci, Jacques, they were quite unhurt."

"Thank God, you certainly didn't need any more elderly injured relatives at your home over Christmas" he said with feeling.

"You're right."

"I'll tell Antone when he comes in, I know he'll be relieved."

"Merci, Jacques."

He went off to serve other customers as Michel turned to Josette.

"I'm so glad and relieved you're back safely, my darling" she whispered.

"I only went to Orange, ma petite, not the other side of the world" he replied.

"I know, but I just worry, that's all."

"I understand."

"Let's not stay here too long, darling, I'm very hungry for you and I don't sleep so well in that great big bed alone" she whispered.

"OK, ma petite."

They finished their drinks and after saying goodnight to Jacques, left the bar. As Michel drove away he was sure he caught a glimpse of a black Porsche Turbo following the Mercedes. His hair stood on end as he sensed that Claude Salvator was very close indeed. He accelerated away and drove quickly to the Rue du Camas and parked in the cul de sac at the end of the road.

Hurrying Josette into the flat, he glanced up and down the street to see if the black Porsche had followed them. It had not and Michel was relieved as he followed Josette upstairs to their little home.

Once inside the warm flat, Michel relaxed whilst the lovely Josette poured drinks for them both and then cuddled up on the settee with her Fiancé.

When they went to bed they kissed and cuddled for a while before Michel rolled gently onto her slim body and eased his rigid penis into her very slowly. They made love for a long rhythmic while before he felt her begin to tighten with a perfect orgasm, at which point he released himself into her, giving her immense pleasure as he pushed into her as far as he could possibly reach. They sighed, then warm and exhausted they fell into a deep sleep wrapped tightly in each others arms.

CHAPTER EIGHT

Monday 22nd December

Michel was woken early by Josette kissing him gently.

"Oh, ma petite" she whispered as he opened his eyes.

"Ma petite" he whispered back. She kissed him again as he remembered that it was the day of the funeral and he had promised to go shopping with Monique. He dreaded both situations but knew he had to face each fearful experience with courage.

"I must get up, Josette."

"Ma petite" she whispered "you stay here a little longer whilst I get the coffee."

"Merci, my darling" he whispered back as his Fiancé slipped from the bed and went into the kitchen.

'Today will be a turning point' he thought. He hoped that Gerrard and his team would not fail in their duty; he felt that he was not likely to survive if they did and his only hope then was to go into permanent hiding in Le Touquet.

His angel of love appeared with two cups of steaming black coffee and he sat up in their new luxury bed to sip it gently and revive his sleepy body.

An hour later he had showered, quickly dressed and was on his way to Montelivet. As soon as he entered the flat he said to Monique "I need to sleep for a while before we go shopping, I'm too tired for the minute."

"Oh, really" she said in an unconvinced tone.

"Really" he repeated.

"I'll wake you in about an hour, at nine" she said firmly.

"Merci, ma petite" he replied as he wandered into the bedroom and got undressed. He dozed off quite quickly and in an hour was then aroused, from a deep sleep, by his impatient wife.

"Come on, Michel, wake up, it's shopping time."

"Mon Dieu, already?"

"Oui, already, I've made some coffee, it's in the kitchen."

He staggered out of bed, showered again and had a slow and close wet shave.

After two cups of coffee and a croissant he announced to Monique that he was ready to start shopping.

"How much money have you got on you?" she demanded. Taking out his wallet he counted out six hundred Francs.

"We'll need much more than that" she said with feeling.

"I'll get some more then, now, are you ready?"

"Oui."

Half hour later Michel was at the Bank and in the strong room counting out two thousand Francs whilst Monique waited outside in the Mercedes. He joined his impatient wife and after parking the car followed her into the first of the many large stores that serve the inhabitants of Marseille.

They trudged through every department of each store as Monique consulted her Christmas present list and tutted as she failed to find exactly what she was looking for. Michel stayed close, like an obedient sheep dog, carrying the ever increasing number of elegantly designed carrier bags. The number of shoppers seemed to grow alarmingly as the day wore on and Michel and his wife were jostled and pushed as they made their way from counter to counter searching for the right present. At last, with the purchase of a pair of ladies gloves for Alexis, Monique announced they were done.

"Bon" replied Michel.

"So what are you going to buy me?" asked Monique.

"Anything your heart desires, ma petite."

"Hmm, that could be costly."

"You're worth it, what ever the price" Michel smiled.

"Hmm" she hummed in an unconvinced tone.

"Really" he said.

"OK, I'd like a nice watch."

"Certainly, ma petite" he replied and they made their way down to the jewellery department where after some considerable time, Monique chose a gold wristwatch which had petite diamonds marking out the hours on its golden face.

"Beautiful, Madame, and it suits you so well" said the weary salesman.

"Oui, it is rather nice" she commented.

"Bon Noël" said Michel as he handed over the money to a

much relieved salesman.

"Something special to remember this Christmas by" she said absently.

"True, ma petite, now let me see the time, ah, oui it's three diamonds past two, mon Dieu!, the funeral is at three!"

They hurried out of the store and Michel drove quickly back to Montelivet.

Half an hour later, after changing into his only dark suit and putting on his only black tie, he was racing to the cemetery at Saint Pierre for the dreaded confrontation with Salvator. He rehearsed the signals for Gerrard, who was everywhere and nowhere! Silly arse! Touch left side of the nose if Claude is to the left, right if he's to the right, back of the head behind, front of the nose in front. Mon Dieu, one scratch on the wrong side of the nose could get a perfectly innocent mourner arrested and give Claude the opportunity to escape!

Michel parked the Mercedes outside the gates of the huge cemetery and made his way towards a crowd of people gathered around a family vault. As he drew closer he failed to recognise anyone he knew.

"Pardon, Monsieur" he whispered to one mourner "is this the Salvator funeral?"

"Non, Monsieur, the Cavallon" came the whispered reply.

"Merci, Monsieur."

Michel looked around for another party and saw a large number of people moving closer to a huge cross. He made his way quickly to the spot they were all gathered round. Again he did not recognise anyone.

"Pardon, Madame, is this the Salvator funeral?"

"Non, Monsieur."

"Merci, Madame" he replied and looked round once more for another funeral. He then focused on a group up the gentle slope towards the top of the rising ground. He made his way quickly passed all the family tombs and as he drew close spotted the unmistakable Antone, dressed in a long black coat with a velvet collar with a black felt hat to match and carrying his silver topped cane. He had arrived. Then he saw Madame Salvator, all in black and clutching a handkerchief to her face. As he glanced around the group of mourners he recognised various faces of the gang with women who he presumed were their wives, or possibly relations, of Madame Salvator.

The Marseille Corporation is deservedly proud of the cemetery at Saint Pierre and it employs a number of cemetery gardeners who keep the lawns and pathways in an immaculate condition. But today, there appeared to be many more gardeners than usual, dressed in green overalls with smart matching caps. Michel noticed that they all had shoulder length hair and large droopy moustaches. Although at some distance, they formed a ring around the mourners and Michel thought he recognised the tall form of Gerrard. Some of them were idly sweeping the gravel about with their brooms whilst continually glancing sideways at the mourners. Each gardener had a large round, rubbish container on wheels, painted in green with matching lid. These were being moved a few centimetres at a time to give the allusion of activity. 'Mon Dieu' thought Michel 'there's enough of them, and I expect they're all gendarmes, no one in his right mind has shoulder length hair and a droopy moustache. And their hair is all the same colour, they look like a circus troupe, the magnificent Baloushka Brothers from the Ukraine.'

"Relatives and friends of the deceased, Edward Salvator...." The priests voice caught Michel's attention and he glanced across at Antone, who nodded slowly at him in recognition, and then he began to study the faces of the mourners close by. It was a little difficult as nearly everyone was wearing sun glasses. It was a bright, sunny but cold day and at three in the afternoon the sun was low in the sky. However, there was a man standing just a few mourners to Michel's right who had a familiar look about him. He wore a long black coat and had a black astrakhan hat pulled firmly down on his head. He also had shoulder length hair, somewhat similar in colour to the gardeners. 'Could he be Claude?' Michel wondered. He looked again but tried hard not to stare. The voice of the priest caught his attention once more "and he was a popular and well loved business man, snatched from us by a tragic accident in the prime of his life....."

Michel looked at the mourners grouped around the coffin of the notorious crook and guessed that they all knew what a dreadful, violent person he was. He focused on the man in the astrakhan hat once again and managed to move closer to him. There were now just two mourners, both women, separating Michel from the person who he suspected was Claude. Michel glanced up at the ring of gardeners, still sweeping idly and moving their rubbish bins in unison like some military precision marching squad. 'Mon Dieu, they're a bit obvious now' he thought and he returned his gaze to the man on his right. He stared hard at him and was almost sure it was Claude. Then, as if on cue, the man returned his gaze and in a flash, Michel recognised the cruel, hard face of Claude Salvator. They looked away from each other and Michel nervously started scratching the right side of his nose, hoping that Gerrard and his merry men would not pounce on the two women who stood between himself and Claude. He carried on scratching for what seemed an age before two large hands grabbed at the shoulders of Claude from behind.

"Claude Salvator, you're under arrest!" boomed a voice.

The women screamed and the mourners shouted 'mon Dieu!' as a struggle began. Claude unbuttoned his coat and slid out of it like an eel, leaving a large bewildered gardener in a silly wig and matching moustache holding his expensive coat. Claude was off like a rocket and Michel, fearful of his escape to Switzerland followed in hot pursuit. They ran between the high tombs and family vaults and Michel could see the gardeners moving towards them. Suddenly Claude darted to the right, between two large vaults, and ran at incredible speed towards a wide gravel path at the end. As he reached the pathway with Michel panting after him, a genuine cemetery gardener, quite by accident and totally unaware of what was going on, pushed his green rubbish bin right into the path of Claude. The crook, travelling at great speed, was unable to stop himself colliding with the heavy bin and tumbling over the top of it onto the gravel path.

"Oh, Monsieur, I'm so sorry" began the gardener as he moved forward to help Claude to his feet. At that moment Gerrard and another gardener arrived along with a gasping Michel. In a moment Claude was up on his feet and ready for Gerrard.

"You're under arrest, Salvator!" shouted Gerrard as he grabbed Claude's right arm.

"Dream on, Gerrard" shouted Claude as he pulled Gerrard's wig off with his left hand and struggled to escape.

"Quick, Michel, give me a hand" demanded Gerrard and Michel grabbed at Claude's left wrist and hung on whilst Claude wriggled to free himself.

"Quickly, Dassault, do something" shouted Gerrard and the other gardener balanced himself for a moment and then took a step back before giving Claude a mighty kick in his crutch. Michel winced as the boot went in and he heard the soft crushing sound that accompanies such a kick. The air expelled from Claude's lungs and whistled through his pursed lips as Gerrard and Michel released him. He sank to the gravel, pale faced, and rolled over onto his side clutching his damaged private parts with both hands.

"Mon Dieu, Dassault, when you are arresting a suspect, you do not kick him in the bollocks, you hit him over the head with your truncheon, did they teach you nothing at Police Academy?"

"I'm sorry, Monsieur Gerrard."

"You'll have to explain it in your report later."

"Oui, Monsieur" replied Michel's bodyguard as he removed his cap and wig. He and Michel then nodded in recognition of one another.

"You won't be needing me any more, Michel" said Paul Dassault with a smile.

"Non, thank heavens" replied Michel.

By then all the Baloushka Brothers had arrived along with Madame Salvator and the mourners. Gerrard pulled off his moustache as the gendarmes picked Claude up and sat him on the rubbish bin that belonged to the wide eyed genuine gardener. They handcuffed him before removing his hat, wig and sunglasses. They replaced his hat which was now, without the wig, too big and it sank down to his ears. The gendarme who attempted to arrest him earlier placed the top coat around Claude's shoulders. Madame Salvator began to cry and lamented out loud "first my husband, now my son, I've nothing left but all the money."

"Take him to Headquarters" commanded Gerrard.

The gendarmes then set off towards the cemetery gates, pushing the rubbish bin with a very pale faced Claude perched on top, looking stunned and holding his crutch.

"Well, Michel, I want to thank you for your assistance in the arrest of Claude Salvator" said Gerrard.

"Glad to have been able to help" replied Michel and now,

realising the very real danger he was in, asked "you will be keeping him in custody won't you?"

"Of course, you need not concern yourself."

"Bon."

"Well done Gerrard, that was a brilliant operation" beamed Antone as he pushed through the mourners.

"Thank you, Monsieur" replied Gerrard.

"I will make sure that the Chief knows all about your daring exploits" continued Antone.

"Merci, Monsieur."

"And as for you, Michel, well, what can I say?" said Antone.

Michel shrugged his shoulders and smiled.

"Outstanding, mon brave!" continued Antone.

"Merci, Antone" he replied.

Suddenly the priest arrived, made his way through the mourners and said in a haughty tone "Now, mes enfants, can we return to the funeral in a dignified manner so that we may complete these sad and serious formalities?"

Antone turned to Michel and said "you go to Ricky's and get Jacques to put one of my special bottles of champagne on ice whilst I watch the final proceedings here."

"Oui, I'd be glad to" replied a relieved Michel.

"I must leave you now, my duty is with the prisoner, thank you for your active support, Messieurs" said Gerrard formally as he saluted Michel and Antone. Michel smiled and thought that the gardeners green overalls made him look a bit silly, but it all worked in the end.

"Au revoir, Monsieur Gerrard" replied Michel and Antone nodded at the gendarme.

As Michel drove to Ricky's through the busy streets the feeling of relief flooded over him. Thank God the old bastard was dead and in his keeping and the son was alive and in the gendarmes keeping. He hoped the son would get a very long prison sentence. By the time Claude was released he would be a millionaire living in Le Touquet.

Michele double parked the Mercedes and went into Ricky's with the biggest smile imaginable.

"Ah, Michel, Michel!"

"Jacques."

"It's all over n'est pas?"

"Oui, it's all over, the old one's buried and the young one's in custody."

"Bravo, mon brave, bravo!"

"Antone said 'put a bottle of his special champagne on ice'"

"But of course, what will you have whilst you're waiting?"

"A large brandy, s'il vous plaît!"

"Naturally" replied Jacques as he poured the amber liquid into a large goblet and placed it on the counter.

"On the house, Michel."

"Merci, Jacques, that's very kind."

"It's the least I can do to say thank you, and I know how worried you've been recently."

"Merci, Jacques."

"Now I must go and put the champagne on ice, otherwise I'll get a smacked bottom later!" he giggled as he left the bar and went through into the private corridor beyond.

Michel sipped the soothing brandy and felt the warmth of it spread through his body. Christmas was beginning to look pretty good. The shopping with Monique was finished, the Salvators' were either dead or arrested, Josette was safely in her flat and a wonderful business opportunity was on offer with Henri in the new year. Everything was perfect. Now all he had to do today was to take the Mercedes to Gambetta to arrange the repairs to the passenger door, telephone the girls in Aix for a session on the house and take Jacqueline and Annette to dinner at Chez Marius and then home to Josette for the night. So it was champagne, dinner and unbridled sex, what more could a man ask for? Henri was right, he did have a good life, although somewhat complicated.

It was not long before Antone strode into the bar like a conquering hero. He appeared larger than normal in his heavy coat and large hat.

"Michel" he beamed.

"Antone."

"Thank God it's all over, now, where's the champagne?"

"I'll get it immediately" said Jacques.

"Bon, come and sit with me, Michel, and let's have a little

celebration" said Antone with a large smile. Michel followed the great man to his favourite table the back of the bar and sat opposite him. Jacques joined them with the champagne and three flutes, he popped the cork and poured the sparkling liquid into the flutes then slipped into the chair next to Antone.

"Here's to us and may we always triumph over evil" said Antone.

"May we always triumph" chorused Michel and Jacques before drinking the sweet, sparkling champagne.

"Mon Dieu, this is good" said Michel.

"The very best for the very best" said Antone.

"Tell me all about it" said Jacques.

"Ah, dear Jacques, I will give you a full account, down to the smallest detail, later, but for the moment, I must tell you that Michel acted quickly, decisively and with great courage."

"Formidable" murmured Jacques.

"Single handed, he brought Claude Salvator to the ground, where upon Gerrard and his men over powered him and carted him away to face prosecution. I myself witnessed the whole event, both the arrest of Claude and the funeral of his father."

"Mon Dieu!" exclaimed Jacques.

"It wasn't quite like that" protested Michel modestly.

"But it was, mon brave, I saw you chase Salvator from the mourners when the gendarme failed to hold him...."

"Oui, but...."

"No, 'buts', mon brave, I saw you chase him through the cemetery and then when he was about to escape, you caught him and threw him over a rubbish bin!" insisted Antone.

"Mon Dieu!" exclaimed Jacques.

"Precisely" replied Antone.

"I think he fell over it, actually" said Michel honestly.

"Non, a desperate, viscous crook trying to evade capture does not fall over a rubbish bin, I assure you" said Antone firmly. Michel decided not to argue and just replied "it was nothing really."

"Nothing really? Mon Dieu, after Michel had brought the man down, Gerrard arrived and was unable to hold him, it was such a fight and I'm sure he would have escaped if Michel had not come to the assistance of Gerrard!" exclaimed Antone with passion.

"Mon Dieu!" said Jacques.

"Indeed, Michel lunged at Salvator and pinned his arm back just after Salvator had torn Gerrard's wig off."

"Gerrard had a wig on?" mused Jacques.

"Oui, he and his men were in disguise" replied Antone.

"Were they dressed up like women then? Transvestites?" queried Jacques.

"Non, they were disguised as Corporation gardeners" replied Antone.

"Oh, interesting" said Jacques.

"And then young Paul Dassault ended the matter with a mighty blow to Salvator's crutch!"

"Bravo, bravo, another hero!" exclaimed Jacques.

"Quite so, another hero, and so young." whispered Antone.

"He'll be able to tell us all about it when he comes to our little intimate party" said Jacques with a smile.

"Indeed" replied Antone and Michel sipped at the champagne whilst they all fell silent for a moment.

"Michel, this is incredible, I'm sure you'll get a medal or something" said Jacques seriously.

"I doubt that" replied Michel.

"Well, I for one will recommend it" said Antone.

"Surely not" protested Michel.

"You are a brave and modest citizen of Marseille, much respected by all those who know you, and by your brave actions you have managed to arrest a known, dangerous criminal, you definitely deserve recognition for what you have done today" said Antone firmly.

"Well, merci, Antone, Jacques" and Michel raised his flute to them.

"Go and put another bottle on ice, this one's nearly empty" whispered Antone and Jacques slipped away immediately.

By the time they had finished the second bottle, Michel's head was spinning.

"May I have some coffee, Jacques?"

"Bien sûr" he replied.

"And I'd better have something to eat to soak up all this champagne" said Michel.

"Leave it to me, I'll do one of my very special baguettes for you."

An hour later Michel drove, a little unsteadily, to Jean Gambetta's garage.

"I wondered if I'd see you again before Christmas" said Gambetta as Michel entered the little office in the gloomy place full of dusty cars.

"Well you were right, here I am again, bringing you more profitable work, making sure that you remain the richest man in Marseille."

"You're too good to me" replied the old man.

"I've got a dent in the front passenger door" said Michel.

"Was she trying to kick her way in or her way out?" queried Gambetta.

"Very funny, it was the bag men actually" replied Michel.

"But I bet there was a woman involved somewhere" said Gambetta.

"I was at Yvonne's and René's place having a meal" replied Michel honestly.

"It must have been a long bloody meal, they don't start collecting the rubbish until about two in the morning" said Gambetta.

"Are you a detective or car repairer?" asked Michel.

"A car repairer who's curious" came the reply.

"Just fix it please, will you?"

"Certainly, but I must warn you, my hourly repair rate doubles Christmas week, it's the rush you understand."

"Rush! What rush?"

"It's all around you."

"These cars have been here for months!"

"I know, and they've all got to be finished by Christmas, that's why it's going to cost you."

"Mon Dieu, you know how to hurt" said Michel.

"Would I hurt my friend's son who now is my very best customer?"

"If Papa was still alive he would have negotiated a special rate for me by now" replied Michel.

"Oui, but my best friend is dead, sadly, and I have to look after his wayward son as well as trying to make a living" said

Gambetta.

"I swear to God, you must be worth a bloody fortune" said Michel.

"Possibly, but you'll never know for sure until after I'm dead" came the reply.

"Well, are you going to inspect the damage?" asked Michel.

"Oui, I'll cast my professional eye over it and give you a rough estimate, which I am bound to increase as the mood takes me."

"Bon, and whilst your casting your professional eye and making up crazy estimates may I use your phone?"

"Oui, providing you're 'phoning a woman" replied Gambetta.

"Why d'you say that?" grinned Michel.

"I don't want you to change your normal behaviour so close to Christmas, it could be very unlucky for both of us" said Gambetta and he left Michel to make his call whilst he inspected the Mercedes.

Michel dialled the number of the girls in Aix and Maria answered.

"Bonjour, Michel, ça va?" she giggled as she greeted him.

"How are my two princesses?" he asked.

"Very well, ma petite" she replied.

"Bon, and are you busy?"

"Oui, but not too busy that we can't fit you in before Christmas as promised" she laughed.

"Bon, you're going to be my best Christmas present yet!" he exclaimed.

"You can be sure of that" she replied.

"When can I come?"

"Just let me look at the diary" she paused and the said "come tomorrow about six, we're a bit busy after eight, is that OK?"

"Oui, two hours with both of you should be ample time to practically kill me" he replied.

Maria laughed and said "see you at six, ma petite, au revoir."

Michel hung up as Gambetta came back into the dusty office.

"All done?" he enquired.

"Oui."

"Bon, now then, luckily it's only a small dent and I can straighten it out with my big hammer and I could do it tomorrow....."

"Non, Jean, I need it tomorrow, I've got to work, it's a very busy time...." interrupted Michel.

"OK, OK, we'll leave it until Christmas eve" said Gambetta.

"Non, I'm too busy, I think we'll have to leave it until after the holiday" said Michel.

"OK."

"Besides it'll be cheaper" said Michel with a grin.

"Oui, I can do a quick, cheap job after Christmas for you" replied Gambetta.

"Bon, I know I can rely on you."

"Have a joyeux Noël, Michel and give my love and best wishes to Monique and all her family, God knows how she puts up with you as well as that lot" smiled Gambetta.

"Merci, Jean, and joyeux Noël to you and your lovely wife, and tell her I might marry her after your dead so I can get all my money back!" replied Michel and Jean laughed out loud at that. They hugged each other and said their 'goodbyes'.

Michel drove round to the Rue du Camas and parked in the cul de sac. Josette was waiting anxiously for him when he arrived.

"Oh, ma petite, are you alright?" she enquired earnestly.

"Oui, oui" he replied as they kissed.

"I've been so worried about you, how did it go?"

"Wonderful, Gerrard and his men were there in force and Claude was arrested."

"Oh, bon, what a relief."

"Gerrard told me that he'd keep him in custody from now on."

"Oh, bon, to think it's all over" she said quietly.

"Oui, and now we can look forward to a quiet Christmas."

"Bon, let's drink to that" she said.

"Oui, but just a little one, ma petite, I have to go out tonight" replied Michel.

"Oh, non, surely not?"

"Oui, ma petite, but I'll be back later, I promise."

"OK, if you promise, I won't complain" she smiled. Josette poured brandy for them both and they sat drinking quietly, comfortable and relaxed.

"Michel"

"Oui, my darling."

"I've been thinking about our plans for the future."

"And?"

"It would be nice if we could see my parents in the new year and officially announce our engagement" she smiled and Michel's blood ran cold at that, despite the best efforts of the brandy.

"It is a little soon, ma petite, I'm not divorced yet" he replied anxiously.

"I know, but surely it won't take long and if we don't start making arrangements soon, everything will be all booked up."

"I doubt it" he replied.

"Michel, it is important to me."

"I know, my darling, we'll get married soon……"

"How soon?" she interrupted.

"As soon as everything has been sorted out, I promise you."

"I'm getting older, and I want to have children you know."

"I understand, ma petite, and we will have lots."

"I don't want lots, Michel, just two, a boy and a girl."

"Excellent, a boy first then a girl two years later."

"Non, a boy and then about four years before the girl, I want the boy off hand when I have the girl" she said firmly.

"As you wish, ma petite" replied Michel feeling slightly harassed.

"Oui, now then, changing the subject, what are you going to buy me for Christmas?" she beamed.

"Anything you want" he replied.

"A nice watch, I've seen the one I want, it's a lovely gold one with diamonds for the hours" she said and Michel felt a touch of déjà vu.

"It's yours, ma petite" he smiled.

"Bon, can we go and get it in the morning?"

"Bien sûr" he replied.

"And, my darling, I need some money" she looked pleadingly at him.

"Oui, ma petite, I'll go to the bank in the morning before we go shopping" he smiled thinking that this was all getting a little expensive.

He sipped his brandy and kissed his beloved between sips hoping it would keep her from making any more plans for a little while.

It was almost eight when he left Josette and drove through the busy streets to 23 Boulevard Fabrici where he rang the sonnette. Annette answered and he was soon in the warm flat, sitting on the settee with a small goblet of brandy in his hand admiring the Mother and daughter before him.

They were both dressed and made up beautifully and if anything, Jacqueline was little more avant-garde than her long legged, full breasted daughter. To the casual onlooker it appeared that the Mother was determined to out perform her daughter. Michel, however, was not a casual onlooker, and decided to have them both if he could, a sort of double Christmas present, an hors d'oeuvres before his double main course in Aix tomorrow night.

"Jacqueline, you look fantastic" he said truthfully, and she did. Her hair was swept back into a French roll, her makeup was glamorous, although a little too heavy; her matching ear rings and necklace were intricate gold and looked expensive, her red dress was off the shoulder and cross pleated at the waist. She wore fish net stockings and very high heeled red shoes, the sort that Henri sold in his upmarket shop in Le Touquet.

"Why thank you, Michel" she replied as she did a little twirl for her admirer.

"I can't believe that you haven't got a queue of handsome, wealthy men waiting to take you out for dinner" he said with a smile.

"Only you, Michel" she replied.

"I'm not handsome or wealthy" he replied.

"Oh, oui, you are" she said with conviction.

"Not both, surely" he grinned.

"Handsome, oui, and I'll find out about the money later!"

"And how do I look?" asked Annette with a smile.

"Absolutely gorgeous" he replied honestly. Her shoulder length hair was swept back, lightly and naturally, her makeup was minimal allowing her beautiful young skin to show, her ear rings matched a gold locket that was pinned to her black velvet choker. Her short black satin dress was tightly fitted to her lovely figure, it was also off the shoulder, but had a fine black lace top which showed her delicate skin underneath. She wore black stockings and black high heeled shoes.

"I'm a very lucky man tonight" beamed Michel.

"Luckier than you know" murmured Jacqueline under her breath.

"Shall we go then?" asked Annette.

"Oui, Chez Marius awaits, and I'm hungry" said Michel.

"And so am I, very hungry" said Jacqueline and Michel noted the inference.

They arrived at Chez Marius where a beaming George showed them to a discreet, candle lit table for three in an alcove near the roaring log fire. It was romantic and wonderfully relaxing. They drank Cassis rosé, nicely chilled, as they perused the extensive menu.

"I feel like letting my hair down tonight" said Jacqueline with a suggestive smile.

"Please do, have anything you want, make it an early Christmas present" replied Michel.

"So" replied Jacqueline, pausing for effect "I can have anything I want?"

"Oui, anything you fancy" said Michel, playing up to her in full.

"Bon, I'll remember that" she smiled as she carried on reading the menu.

"Annette, see anything you fancy?" asked Michel.

"Oui, lots and one thing in particular" she replied.

"Bon."

George then arrived at the table and asked "are you ready to order, Monsieur?"

"Oui, I think so, Jacqueline?"

"I'll have moules marinieres, followed by langouste thermidor."

"Bon, Madame" said George as he scribbled down the order, "and for you, Mademoiselle?"

"Paté and then boeuf bourguignon, s'il vous plaît."

"Oui, and you Monsieur?"

"Crevettes' and then Tournedos Rossini."

"Merci, Monsieur, and to drink?"

"A bottle of Côtes du Rhone and another of Cassis rosé."

"Merci" replied George as he bobbed a little bow and left them gazing into one another's eyes.

"Well who'd have thought that a little accident in a busy street could lead to this?" queried Michel.

"Oui, it's strange how things happen isn't it?" said Jacqueline.

"It's fate" said Annette.

"Indeed it is" said Michel.

"And where will fate lead us next?" queried Jacqueline.

"Who knows" replied Michel and Jacqueline and Annette both grinned at that.

"So, what are your plans for Christmas?" asked Jacqueline.

"I intend to work for most of the time" replied Michel.

"Aren't you going to spend some time with your wife and family?" persisted Jacqueline.

"I shouldn't think so, after all, I am in the middle of a divorce you know."

"Oh, I know, it's so sad when marriages break up" said Jacqueline sympathetically.

"Oui, but it's a reflection of modern life" replied Michel with a sigh.

"Will you ever marry again?" asked Jacqueline softly.

"Oui, if I'm lucky enough to meet the right woman" he replied.

"Oh, you're lucky, Michel, and you'll meet someone soon, I'm sure" said Jacqueline.

"I'm not so sure" he replied.

"Perhaps you'll stay single and have lots of mistresses who adore you" said Annette, hitting the nail right on the head.

"Possibly" mused Michel "but what I really want with a woman is a very full physical relationship that's deep and beyond understanding and that….."

"Oh, Michel" whispered Jacqueline.

At that moment George arrived with the starters.

"Bon appetite" he said as he placed the dishes before the distracted diners.

"Merci" they murmured and Michel was now sure that both Mother and daughter were ready for unbridled sex but how could he keep them separate while he attended to each? He decided not to worry about that problem for the moment, perhaps events would unfold and allow him to take advantage at the right time. They settled down to the delicious meal and other than little sly innuendoes from both women, Michel kept the conversation light and on an even keel whilst allowing little subtle promises that he was ready for love with the right people and they may be the very ones that he had been hoping to meet. Their conversation became less discreet as the food and wine had their effect. Michel was left in no doubt that full and decadent sexual activity was certain back at the flat in Boulevard Fabrici with both of them.

"We're hungry women, Michel, who need satisfying" whispered Jacqueline as she spooned the ice cream from her pear belle Hélène into her generous mouth.

"So I understand" replied Michel.

"And I need to experience a real, mature man" whispered Annette as she sucked at her sorbet.

"Of course" smiled Michel.

"Can you manage both of us tonight if you stay?" asked Jacqueline in a whisper.

"I'm sure" he replied, somewhat surprised that a Mother should be so unconcerned about sharing a man with her daughter. Michel decided to ask that question when he was alone with Jacqueline.

They finished the meal with a small cognac and coffee consumed at a gentle pace, then Michel asked for the bill. George obliged with a bob and a smile and was grateful for the cash that Michel placed over the bill on the tiny plate. The tip was generous and Michel wished George and his staff 'Joyeux Noël' as the diners left the warmth of the restaurant.

They drove back to the Boulevard Fabrici listening to the car radio and quietly enjoying the soothing and romantic music being broadcast to the late night listeners. Once in the flat, Jacqueline poured a large goblet of cognac for each of them and then slumped onto the settee next to Michel.

"It's too late and far too cold for you to go home, Michel, I think you'll have to stay here with us tonight" said Jacqueline firmly.

"Really?" he replied with a grin.

"Really" said Annette.

"Have you got room for me?" he asked in a knowing way.

Jacqueline replied "oui, there's quite a lot of space in my bed to start off with....."

"And if you find that you haven't enough room with Mama, you can come to my bed, where there's lots of room!" interrupted

Annette.

"Exactly" said Jacqueline. So that was the plan, Mama first followed by daughter. 'Age has its privileges' thought Michel and then he remembered his promise to Josette to go home. Somehow he would escape.

They finished the cognac and Jacqueline looked hard at Michel and said "I'm ready for bed, Michel, how about you?"

"Oui, ma petite, you lead the way" he replied as he stood up unsteadily.

Annette jumped up, put her arms around his neck and kissed him passionately and said "don't be too long with Mama, remember I'm waiting for you."

He nodded and then followed Jacqueline into the hallway. As he entered her bedroom Annette whispered "I'm in here" and pointed at the door opposite. Michel nodded again, pinched himself and thought 'this is unreal'.

Jacqueline closed the door after switching on the bedside lights which were discreetly dim.

"Now, Michel, undress me" she demanded before she kissed him passionately. Her tongue was extremely long and he almost choked on it.

"Oui" he whispered. She turned to face a long mirror fitted to the ward robe and Michel stood behind her, kissing her slender neck and her ears. He unzipped the dress, which fell easily to the floor revealing a red lace bra and tiny matching lace panties from which her thick pubic hair protruded. He undid the bra and eased it off her magnificent breasts and she shuddered as he stroked them forward and squeezed her jutting nipples.

"Mon Dieu, this is good" she whispered.

"It certainly is, ma petite" he replied.

He caressed her breasts for some while before stroking down over her firm stomach and then sliding his fingers into her panties eased them down to the floor. She opened her legs and as he stood up she reached behind for his trouser zip and deftly opened his pants and released his rigid penis.

"That feels very good" she whispered.

She guided it under her bottom and Michel pushed against her and watched in the mirror as the top appeared in her pubic hair.

"Doesn't that look wonderful?" she asked.

"Oui" he replied as he pushed gently backwards and forwards. She was very moist and the pleasure for them both was sensational.

"Oh, Michel, this is so good."

"It is" he replied as he stroked her heaving breasts.

"I'm going to come in a minute if you don't stop" she gasped.

"So am I" he replied.

"Have me on the bed now" she pleaded.

"Non, I think I'll make you come like this" he teased.

"Michel, stop, oh, stop!"

He did as he was asked and Jacqueline slipped from his embrace and lay on the bed with her legs wide open.

"Come on, Michel, hurry up and finish me" she gasped. Michel almost fell on her and she guided him in with ease and then wrapped her long legs around his waist and squeezed.

"Ram me, ram me, Michel and for fuck's sake don't stop!"

He gathered his strength and went as fast as the evening meal and cognac would allow. He thought of Henri and the business as he concentrated hard on holding himself back from ecstasy. Suddenly he was aware of Jacqueline shouting.

"Oh, oui! Oui! Oui!" and then she screamed and squeezed the very breath from his body. He relaxed and rammed her until he felt the surge of pleasure begin and he continued until there was nothing left for her in his body.

"Oh, Mon Dieu, that was so good, Michel" she gasped as beads of perspiration appeared on her forehead.

"It was" he whispered in reply.

"Now don't move" she commanded "stay in me."

He lay like a beached whale on top of her and she in return just gently relaxed the scissor grip she had on him. Michel began to doze off and remained half asleep, embedded in his latest mistress. Jacqueline also began to doze and soon they were both fast asleep. Suddenly, she developed cramp in her legs and she awoke to a searing muscle pain.

"Michel, Michel, wake up, wake up, get off me, I've got cramp in my legs!"

Michel rallied round and slid obediently from her body as she lowered her legs and sat up to massage her calf muscles.

"Are you alright?" he asked.

"Oui, I'll be alright in a moment" she replied.

"Bon."

They remained silent for a while before he asked "are you concerned about Annette?"

"Why should I be?"

"Well, you don't seem to mind sharing me with her" replied Michel gently.

"I don't intend to share you with her, I'm just going to let her have an experience with a mature man instead of all those pimply, adolescents who come as soon as they see a naked woman."

"I can have her once then?"

"Oui, just once, then she can spend her time looking for a real man who'll satisfy her."

"You're very understanding."

"Just practical, Michel, and once you've satisfied her, I want you back in here for the rest of the night" she said firmly.

For once Michel was a little afraid, in fact on reflection, very afraid. Jacqueline was a strong individual who obviously intended to nail him down. There would be no escape.

"Well, I'd better go and do my duty" he said.

"Oui, and don't be too long about it" she replied.

Michel heaved himself up from the bed and pulled his trousers up and said "I'll be back soon, ma petite, you rest now and then we'll cuddle up for the night."

"Bon" she replied and she slipped under the sheets. Michel closed the bedroom door after him and then tip toeing passed Annette's room, made his way to the front door of the flat. Within moments he was out in the cold street and in the Mercedes. He raced back to Rue du Camas and parked in the cul de sac. When he climbed unsteadily out of the car he breathed the cold night air and was relieved that he had made the decision to flee from Jacqueline and Annette. He made a mental note to be a little more careful in future as such women could be very dangerous.

Josette greeted him with a huge smile and kissed him passionately.

"Has it been a hard night, ma petite?" she enquired.

"Very" he replied.

"I expect you'd like to go straight to bed now" she cooed.

"Oui, but only to sleep, ma petite."

She looked disappointed but smiled when he said "I've got to save all my strength for shopping tomorrow!"

She laughed and kissed him. They were soon in each other's arms, snuggled down under the sheets and fast asleep.

CHAPTER NINE

Tuesday 23rd December

It was just after nine o'clock when Michel, washed and shaved and refreshed by Josette's coffee wandered down to the kiosk at the end of the Rue du Camas for a newspaper and some cigarettes. The day was cloudy and cold and the weather forecast predicted snow sometime over the Christmas holiday. Michel did not relish the prospect and he shivered at the thought of driving around on icy roads. He asked for a packet of cigarettes, picked up the paper and glanced at the headline which surprised him. In bold black type the paper announced '*CLAUDE SALVATOR ARRESTED AT FATHER'S FUNERAL*', Michel read on as the woman behind the counter held out his cigarettes.

'Claude Salvator was arrested yesterday afternoon by a team of highly trained gendarmes whilst attending his father's funeral at the cemetery of Saint Pierre. Although he attempted to evade the gendarmes he was chased and overpowered by Michel Ronay, a local Marseille taxi driver. Monsieur Ronay bought the suspect to the ground before gendarmes, under the command of Captain Cyril Gerrard, arrived and made the arrest, during which a violent struggle took place and Monsieur Ronay again came to the aid of the arresting officers.

Captain Gerrard commented to reporters after the arrest 'We are very grateful to Monsieur Ronay for his assistance in this matter. I can now reveal that he has been working undercover for the police for some time and had managed to infiltrate the illegal business empire of the Salvator family'.

"Oh, Mon Dieu!" whispered Michel and he cursed Gerrard for what he had said to the press. He realised that he was now a target for all of Salvator's gang and Le Touquet never looked so good.

He read on: *'Monsieur Ronay, a mild mannered man, well respected in the community, went straight back to work to cope with the Christmas rush. Late last night his wife, Monique, said that she hadn't seen him for days'.*

"Your cigarettes, Monsieur" said the woman from behind the counter.

"Merci" he replied absently and handed her a note. He was in a daze and started to wander away and only when she called "your change, Monsieur" did he return to reality.

Arriving back at the flat he was greeted by a smiling Josette, all dressed and waiting to go shopping.

"I'm ready, ma petite" she said.

"Bon" he replied.

"What's the matter?" she asked realising something was wrong.

"You'd better read this" he said as he handed her the paper.

She took it and began to read the report as he slumped down on the settee and lit a cigarette.

"Mon Dieu" she whispered "you are so brave, ma petite."

"Non, I'm not."

"But you are!"

"I tell you I'm not, Claude fell over a rubbish bin and then Gerrard grabbed him, couldn't hold him, so I grabbed his wrist whilst Dassault kicked him in the bollocks!"

"Mon Dieu!"

"And that's the truth."

"But you did help Gerrard."

"Just a little, but he hasn't helped me, has he?"

"What do you mean?"

"Telling the press that I'm an undercover man, mon Dieu, every one of the gang plus half the other riff raff in Marseille will be after me now."

"I see what you mean, ma petite."

"Bon."

"Perhaps we should leave Marseille and start a new life somewhere else" she said quietly. Michel hesitated for a moment and then decided not to tell her about the opportunity in Le Touquet with Henri.

"Perhaps" he mumbled.

"Anyway, let's go shopping" she said brightly.

"Why not" he replied.

An hour later, after Michel had been to the bank and collected several thousand Francs from his deposit box, the lovers were examining the wrist watches in the jewellery department of Marseille's premier shop.

"This is the one I really like, ma petite" cooed Josette.

"You shall have it then" he replied and the salesman smiled and added "an excellent choice, Mademoiselle, if I may say so, it represents the finest quality gold watch that we have at the moment."

"Bon" she said.

As the beaming salesman placed the glittering, diamond studded time piece into its blue velvet gift box, Josette turned to Michel and gave him a little kiss on the cheek and whispered "merci, ma petite, and whilst we're here, can we look at the engagement rings?" Michel suddenly felt trapped, as he had last night with Jacqueline and her daughter. It was the same ghastly feeling of being drawn into something that he did not really want at the moment; commitment.

"Of course, ma petite" he replied with a nervous smile.

Michel paid the salesman as he presented the bill and Josette picked up the watch. They then made their way across the department, sinking gently into the plush dark blue carpet, to the display counter where hundreds of diamond rings sparkled under the hidden lighting of the counter.

"Mon Dieu, aren't they wonderful?" said Josette quietly.

"Oui" replied Michel and thought 'they're all a wonderful price too'.

"I like that one, very much" she whispered as an immaculate female sales assistant glided up as if on roller bearings.

"May I help, Mademoiselle?" she purred in a deep voice through her perfect lips.

"We're just looking" said Michel hurriedly.

"Is there anything that catches Mademoiselle's eye?" purred the immaculate one, totally ignoring the mere male before her. She had seen his type before, poor, nervous and afraid of that commitment that meant life together until death do part.

"Oui, I like that one" she replied, pointing to a modest little ring with three diamonds mounted in a cross over band of gold.

The assistant had the display counter open in a trice and the ring was placed on a blue velvet cushion for Josette to examine it more carefully. She picked it up and said "it's really beautiful."

"Oui, it is" said the immaculate one giving a hard stare at Michel whilst calculating her commission so far this week.

"May I try it on?" asked Josette and the assistant just smiled and bobbed her head as Josette slipped the pretty piece onto her third finger. It fitted perfectly and she held her hand out to admire it.

"What do you think, ma petite?" she asked.

"It's perfect, Mademoiselle" purred the immaculate one before Michel could reply.

"It's very nice" said Michel.

"Can I have it then?"

Michel trembled inside as the immaculate one gave him her 'don't you dare say 'non' look.

"Well" he hesitated and the assistant's stare intensified, "isn't there any others you would like to look at first?" he asked, mentally struggling with the situation.

"Non, ma petite, I really want this one" she replied still waving her hand gently in the air whilst admiring the sparkle of the diamonds.

"Well then" he began as the assistant smiled coyly, knowing that he was sunk without trace, "we'd better have it."

"Oh, Michel, thank you so much, ma petite" said Josette as she kissed him on the cheek.

The immaculate one smiled and purred "that'll be fifteen hundred Francs, Monsieur."

"Right" replied Michel in a strangled tone and he counted out the money from his wallet.

"Merci, Monsieur, now, shall I wrap it for Mademoiselle?"

"Non, merci, I'll wear it" replied Josette.

They left the grande magasin and once outside Michel said "I think I need a coffee or something stronger at Ricky's."

"But we haven't finished the shopping yet" protested his Fiancé.

"We have for the moment, ma petite" he replied firmly.

They walked the short distance from the shop to le Vieux Port and round to Ricky's at a brisk pace. Once inside the warm familiar surroundings Michel felt safe for the moment. He knew that his nerves could not stand much more today and a rest would be appreciated.

"Bonjour, grand hero" said Jacques as they approached the bar.

"Bonjour, Jacques, a brandy and a rosé for Josette, s'il vous plaît."

"Another bad day?"

"Possibly."

"Well now you're here, I'll let the press know" said Jacques as he poured the drinks.

"What!" exclaimed Michel.

"I'll let 'em know you're here."

"Why?"

"They spent all yesterday evening looking for you, and when they interviewed Monique, she told them that you'd be in here. I've had to deal with a lot of pushy press people who drink too much, asking me questions about you, well now you're here, you can tell them, at least they'll stop 'phoning me every ten minutes. As he spoke the telephone rang.

"Oui, Ricky's bar, oui, oui, he's here, oui, he's here now, bon, au revoir" said Jacques and he put the receiver down.

"They're on their way now" he added.

"Oh, Mon Dieu!" exclaimed Michel.

"You're famous now, Michel, and the press want the inside story, straight from the horses mouth!" and with that he wandered off to serve another customer.

"What are you going to do, ma petite" asked a worried Josette.

"Face them, I suppose, it's no good running away. They'll just keep on following me."

She nodded and sipped at her glass of wine. They had just ordered more drinks when the journalists arrived, there were four of them with two photographers.

"Monsieur Ronay?" enquired a thin faced man in a badly fitting raincoat.

"Oui" replied Michel.

"Ah, bon" they chorused as the photographers began to snap from every angle.

"I'm from the Citizen" said a middle aged woman in a green coat "can you tell us exactly what happened when you overpowered Salvator?"

By now the occupants of the bar were gathered around Michel and Josette, sitting on bar stools, and people passing by outside were stopping and then coming in to see what was going on.

"It was nothing really" said Michel modestly.

"Captain Gerrard thought your actions were outstanding,

what do you say to that?" she persisted.

"Well........." he was interrupted by a little fat man in a black coat who asked "when did you first infiltrate the gang?"

"I didn't really."

"Gerrard said you did" the fat man countered.

"I know, but....."

"Can you look this way, Monsieur?" asked one of the photographers, a young, anxious looking man with an unruly mop of hair. Michel did as he was asked and the young man said "put your arm around the lady, please." Michel did as he was asked and the flash went off as the woman in green demanded "who is this young Mademoiselle?"

"I'm Josette Le Franc, his Fiancé" she replied with a smile and held out her hand to show off her glittering new ring. Both camera men flashed again and again at the couple as Michel's heart sank to his boots and he thought 'I'm really in it now, Jean was right, my balls are going to end up on a pole outside this place'.

"I thought you were married, Monsieur?" said the woman in green.

"Only on paper" volunteered Josette "and his divorce will be through in the new year."

Michel cringed and thought that the case for escaping to Le Touquet grew stronger by the moment.

"Mademoiselle Le Franc, when did you find out that your Fiancé was working undercover?" asked a bespectacled young woman in a mauve anorak.

"Well, it was........." she began but was interrupted by the woman in the green coat.

"You must be very proud of him."

"Well, I am......" she replied.

"Have you and Monsieur Ronay been engaged for long?" asked the fat man in the black coat.

"Non, we officially got engaged just today" replied Josette sweetly and Michel's heart sank lower into a black hole of total despair similar to those found in outer space from which there is no escape.

"Congratulations!" exclaimed the press pack as one and Michel tried hard to smile as the cameras flashed incessantly.

"Quite a memorable day for you, Monsieur Ronay" said the

thin man in a raincoat.

"You can say that again" replied Michel.

"Does your wife know that you were getting engaged today?" asked the bespectacled one in mauve.

"Well, actually......"

"Quite a surprise for her then" said the bespectacled one not waiting for Michel's answer but guessing the truth.

"Will you go on working undercover for the police?" asked the woman in the green coat.

"Hardly, not after all this publicity........."

"There's talk of a civic reception and commendation for you, what do you say to that, Monsieur Ronay?" asked the thin man.

"I think that's unlikely" replied Michel.

"Your wife says we could always find you in here, is Ricky's your favourite bar in Marseille?" asked the bespectacled one spitefully.

"Oui, it is" replied Michel.

"What's the barman's name?" asked the young photographer.

"Jacques" replied Michel.

"Jacques, Jacques, here a moment" called the photographer and as Jacques arrived back at the end of the bar the photographer said "Jacques, just pose in between Monsieur Ronay and his Fiancé will you?"

Jacques beamed and stroked his hair before replying "certainly."

The cameras flashed again as both photographers called out in turn 'smile' and 'this way, Jacques' and 'look at Mademoiselle Le Franc' and 'give her a kiss, Michel'. It seemed it would never end and Michel guessed that when all of this fiasco appeared in tomorrows newspaper his life would not be worth living. He decided to end it by saying "now if there are no more questions, Mademoiselle Le Franc and I have some shopping to do before I go back to work."

"Have you set a date for the wedding yet?" asked the bespectacled one in mauve.

"Non, but it will be sometime in the spring" replied Josette with a big smile.

"Just one more shot of you both with your arms around each other" said the young photographer and Michel obliged with a heavy heart. The cameras flashed and at last the torment was at an end.

With 'au revoir's' and 'bon chance' ringing in their ears the couple escaped out of Ricky's onto the busy street and headed for the shops whilst the journalists crowded up to the bar.

"Mon Dieu, that was a bit of a nightmare" said Michel.

"Oh, I enjoyed it" beamed Josette, realising that she had at last captured Michel with the maximum publicity possible. Buying the ring earlier had been a wonderful stroke of good luck.

"I have to go to Grambois this afternoon to pick up the sandals I bought in August and then deliver them to a business man in Marseille."

"Oh, I'll come with you, ma petite" she replied.

"I'm afraid there won't be room for you in the car" said Michel firmly.

"Oh" she said.

"I'll get some more money out of the Bank and you stay here shopping this afternoon and I'll be home later."

"OK, are we going out to dinner tonight?" she asked.

"Oui" replied Michel and remembering his date in Aix at six o'clock he added "it might be a bit later than usual, but we'll go to La Galleot."

"Bon" smiled Josette.

Michel returned to the Bank, withdrew another substantial sum and gave half to Josette and with a passionate kiss left her to wander off into the shops.

As he headed out of Marseille towards Grambois he breathed more easily and determined not to worry about the storm clouds gathering over his head. If the worst came to the worst he would leave Marseille immediately and join Henri and Jackie in Le Touquet. The fact that Henri had offered him his inherited house to live in meant that accommodation was not a problem and with one swift move he would be free of his life in Marseille and all the past. In any event he felt that a life change was inevitable. He had reached that middle age when suddenly he realised his own mortality. The autoroute was busier than he expected and only when he turned off and headed towards Grambois did the traffic ease.

At last he swung the Mercedes into the driveway of his villa and parked outside the garage door. He went into the house and checked that everything was in order, remembering that the whole family would descend on the place on Boxing Day. 'Poor villa' he thought 'you really don't deserve my noisy, squabbling family to invade your peace and tranquillity'. When he was content with the house he locked up carefully and then went to the garage, opened the door and surveyed the boxes of odd sized Romanian sandals stacked along the wall, where they had been since August. He knew he would not get them all into the car but he determined to take as many as he could. He first filled the boot and crammed as many boxes as possible into every available space. Then he filled up the back seat and piled them up to the headlining, making it impossible for him to see out of the rear of the car, finally he filled the front footwell and passenger seat up to the top of the dashboard. When the loading was complete he locked the garage and, after lighting a cigarette, wandered around the garden to calm down and enjoy some fresh air.

He realised that he needed peace and quiet to survive, just a few weeks would do. He decided he would go to Le Touquet after Christmas and he would go alone. He finished the cigarette and surveyed the garden, remembering the fire in August and all the subsequent commotion. Slipping behind the wheel of the Mercedes he drove the short distance to Sophia's house and rang the sonnette till the nude artist said 'hallo'.

"It's Michel" he whispered and she screamed back "Michel! Michel! Entre! Entre!"

Within moments he was in her studio lounge admiring the artist. To his surprise she was fully dressed in a neat black tunic dress and wearing a petite fur hat and black boots.

"Are you just going out?" he asked.

"Non, ma petite, I'm working on a spectacular snow landscape and it makes me feel cold just painting it."

Michel laughed and she then said "but I've got nothing on underneath!"

"Ah, bon, normal couture" he replied.

"Oui, let me get you a drink, ma petite."

"Merci, a scotch with ice."

"Bon, are you staying long?" she enquired as she poured the

drinks from the litre bottle of Bells on the sideboard.

"Non" he replied.

"Long enough to satisfy me before Christmas, I hope."

"But of course, ma petite."

"Thank God for that, I was worried that you might not come to see to me before the holiday, and it's bad enough being on your own over Christmas without being frustrated as well."

"Would I ever let you down?" he asked as she handed him his scotch.

"Non, Michel, but you might let others down" she replied.

"Like who?" he asked.

"Nicole, for instance, she's very much in love with you, you know."

"I know" he replied quietly.

"I mean, to me, you're just a sex plaything that releases my inner artistic self, so that I am free and not bonded by trivial life, to express my true being in my painting" she said solemnly.

"Possibly" he replied.

"What d'you mean 'possibly'?"

"Well possibly you're an over sexed woman who likes painting and doesn't want the bother of a full time man about the place."

"Possibly" she replied and they both laughed.

"Salute and merry Christmas" he said.

"Salute" she replied and they clinked glasses.

They drank heavily and finished the scotch before she asked "another one before we start?"

"Why not" he replied and as she refilled their glasses she asked "what are your plans for Christmas?"

"Working up to Christmas eve and then the day at home with the relatives and then we're all up here for Boxing Day."

"Oh, bon, so I'll get seen to right after Christmas as well?"

"If you're good" he replied.

"You know I can be very good" she said in a husky voice as she handed him his drink.

He laughed and as she sat beside him on the settee she said, in a serious tone, "please go and see Nicole, and make a little fuss of her, she really is quite desperate about you."

"I plan to, after I've taken care of you."

"Bon, I don't think she needs raw sex, just a loving fuss, and then you can tell her that you'll fuck her after Christmas, it'll give her something to look forward to."

"You're all heart."

"It is the festive season" she replied.

"Now then, before we start, what do you think of my snow scene entitled the 'French Alps at dawn'?"

Michel peered at the large white canvas on the easel and other than a few black dots in the middle he really couldn't see much so he remarked diplomatically "it'll be easier to comment when you've put a little more detail in."

"Can't you see, they're the skiers" she said firmly.

"Well as I say, a little more detail is needed."

"I haven't painted in the snow yet, perhaps that's what's confusing you" she said.

"Possibly" he replied "but I'll see it when you've finished it after Christmas."

"Bon, and I'll want some sensible critique then."

"You shall have it, meanwhile, shall I have you?"

"Oh, oui, I'd thought you'd never ask" she replied as she gulped down the last of her scotch and stood up.

"Hang onto your hat and let's make it fast" she said as she unbuttoned her tunic dress and opened it to reveal her tanned naked body.

"Wonderful" said Michel as he unzipped his trousers and produced his hardening penis.

"Do I still look as good as ever?" she asked as she twirled round and then bent over to show her bare bottom to her lover. Michel admired the smooth roundness of her sun kissed bum and her black pubic hair enhanced by her thigh length black boots.

"Good as ever" he replied.

"Excellent, now is it hard enough for me to sit on yet?" she enquired.

"Just give me a moment more" he replied

"Hurry up, ma petite, I'm very hungry and wet!"

"Come on then."

She backed slowly towards him and he held her hips as she lowered herself and catching his rigid penis with her left hand she guided it smoothly into her warm, compliant body.

"Mon Dieu, that's fucking good" she gasped as she took his

full length and relaxed onto his lap. He slid his hands up her sides and massaged her full breasts forward, teasing the nipples with his fingers as she started bouncing up and down on his lap. She went at a steady pace whilst Michel braced himself against the back of the settee and enjoyed the sensation.

"I'm not going to be long" she gasped.

"Bon" he replied.

"It's amazing how hungry you get without realising" she said slowly between each downward thump into his lap.

"So true" he replied.

"Not long now, ma petite!" she exclaimed as she increased the speed of her rhythm. She went faster at that moment and began to tighten on him and then with a gasping yell of pleasure, she reached her climax. Michel was ready for her, he relaxed and came with a mighty thrust up into her. She slowed to a full stop quite quickly and as she fell back against him, still shaking, she said "mon Dieu, that was good, so good."

Michel kissed the side of her face and replied "it certainly was."

"I feel so uninhibited now" she proclaimed.

"Bon."

"I'll be able to paint the snow this afternoon."

"Bon, I'm sure it will look even better now your relaxed" he replied.

"Let's have another drink before you go" she said as she raised herself up from his lap.

"Good idea" he replied as he watched her totter unsteadily towards the Bells on the sideboard.

They sat drinking and talking for sometime before she said "you'd better go now and see Nicole."

"Oui."

"Give her my love and promise me you'll make a fuss of her."

"I promise" he replied.

After passionate kisses and promises of never ending sex, 'Joyeux Noël's' and big hugs, Michel left the artist and walked along to Nicole's house. It was getting colder and he fancied he saw little, light flurry's of snow drifting by in the wind.

"Nicole, it's Michel" he said when she answered the sonnette.

"Michel! Michel! Entre!"

Once in the warm little house he embraced her and then kissed her passionately.

"Oh, ma petite, I'm so glad you've come to see me" she said between kisses.

"I couldn't let you down, Nicole" he replied.

"Are you staying?"

"Non, unfortunately, I have to go back to Marseille on business."

"Oh" she replied with disappointment.

"But I can stay for a while."

"Bon."

"Long enough to tell you that I'll be back to stay on Boxing Day."

"Oh, bon!" she exclaimed, her eyes brightening.

"Oui, and I'll see plenty of you then."

"Wonderful, now, let's have a drink" she said.

"Scotch for me" Michel smiled

Nicole poured two large glasses of the amber liquid and handed one to her lover.

"Tell me first of all, is Angelique behaving herself?"

"Oui, she's being very good" replied Michel as the memory of her and Frederik naked together on his bed flashed by, "and she seems to be enjoying herself with Frederik."

"Bon, I'm glad."

"Salute and joyeux Noël " he said and they clinked glasses.

"Salute" she smiled.

After sipping their drinks she asked coyly "have we time for a little……"

"I'm afraid not" he interrupted "but I could do with something to eat."

"Oh, of course, some soup and baguettes?"

"That would be wonderful" he replied.

After finishing their drinks Michel followed her out into the kitchen where she heated up a vegetable soup, he stood behind her with his arms around her waist, gently kissing the side of her face.

"Stop it, ma petite, you're getting me all hot and very randy" she said.

Changing his mind to match the circumstances he said "hurry up with the lunch then, and we'll have time for a quick session up the wall."

"Bon, can you manage luke warm soup?"

"Oui."

"And eat your baguettes in the car?"

"Oui" he replied.

"Bon, keep on kissing me then and the soup will come to the boil at the same time as me" she said.

Michel did as he was asked and then started to stroke and hold her breasts firmly through her lace blouse.

"Oh, mon Dieu" she whispered as he started to squeeze at her nipples.

"Soup's ready and so am I" she gasped as she turned the gas off and Michel spun her round and held her up against the kitchen wall. He kissed her passionately as she undid his trousers and pulled up her skirt. She had no panties on and she guided his penis into her moist, soft body. Michel was surprised that he had become rigid so quickly after Sophia, but he realised that Nicole really excited him. It was going to be very hard to leave all these lovely women after Christmas. As he rammed himself up into his beautiful, gasping mistress he reconsidered the merits of leaving all this behind and decided to delay any impetuous move to Le Touquet until he had time to soberly consider the situation.

"Oh, Michel, that's wonderful, keep going, just like that!"

His rhythm was steady and he was purposefully using long strokes to excite her quivering body.

"Oh, Michel, Michel, soon, I'm almost there!"

He continued, increasing speed with each thrust until her gentle moaning became more of a scream and he felt her body tighten on him.

"Oh, Mon Dieu! Now! Now!" she cried out as she struggled to push against his body.

Michel with mighty thrusts reached his own climax and lifted her off her feet, pushing her slim body up the wall. They clung tightly together as they climaxed and stayed like that until their passions subsided. They kissed a long unbroken kiss whilst their bodies calmed down.

"That was so good" she said.

"It was, and you are wonderful, ma petite."

"I love you so much, Michel."

"And I love you too, Nicole" he said it before he realised what he had said but it was too late to retract.

"I know, ma petite, we were made for each other" she whispered.

"I have to go soon" he said hastily thinking of the sandals, Sayid, the girls in Aix and then dinner with Josette. 'My life is just getting too busy' he thought as they untangled themselves and Nicole staggered to the stove to dish out the soup.

Half an hour later, after soup, passionate kisses and promises of undying love, Michel was heading back to Marseille, munching a large cheese and ham baguette. He kept thinking of Nicole and began to worry a little about the future. However, some dreadful driving by the other motorists helped concentrate his mind on just surviving the journey.

At last he reached Marseille and drove directly to Sayid's flat. He double parked the Mercedes and rang the sonnette.

"Michel, where have you been?" wailed Sayid.

"Had some business to attend to and I had to go to Grambois to collect the sandals" he replied.

"OK, OK, I'll be right down."

Within moments Sayid opened the door and joined Michel in the street.

"We'll have to hurry, Akhmed usually closes his stall by now" said a flustered Sayid.

"OK, let's go" replied Michel.

When Sayid realised the car was full of boxes he asked plaintively "where am I going to sit?"

"Oh, mon Dieu" replied Michel.

"We'll have to unload those boxes out of the front seat and leave them here."

"OK" replied Michel and they set about the task. Soon they were on their way to the market on la Plaine where most of the stalls are owned by the Arabs.

"How much is he prepared to pay for the sandals?" asked Michel.

"I've no idea, Michel, but if I were you, I'd accept anything he offers, because you'll never sell them."

Sayid's remarks did not please Michel and they remained silent for the rest of the short journey through the crowded streets. He parked the Mercedes as close as he could to the bustling market and the followed Sayid to Akhmed's stall.

"Akhmed" said Sayid as they greeted each other in a friendly manner with hugs and kisses "this is my good friend, Michel Ronay."

"Ah, bonjour, Monsieur" replied Akhmed, and they shook hands as Michel replied "bonjour."

"Sayid tells me that you have some sandals that you want to sell."

"Oui, Sayid said you might be interested."

"I might be, he has shown me one or two pairs and they look alright" said Akhmed.

"Bon, I've got a car load if you want them."

"Bon, I might be able to shift a few before Christmas."

"Bon."

"How many have you got in the car?" asked Akhmed.

"Don't know, but the car's full" said Michel truthfully.

"I'd better have a look" he replied and the called to a young man standing at the back of the stall "Youssef, mind the stall, I'll be back in a minute." Youssef nodded and the three men made their way to the Mercedes.

After Michel opened the boot, Akhmed opened several boxes and looked carefully at the contents of each. He peered inside the car and noted the boxes piled high on the back seat. He then turned to Michel and said "I'll give you a thousand Francs for the lot."

"A thousand Francs! You mean two thousand!" exclaimed Michel.

"Non, I mean a thousand."

"But...."

"Michel" interrupted Sayid.

"I think that's an unreasonable offer" said Michel.

"Take it or leave it, mon ami" replied Akhmed.

"I'm not going to.........."

"Michel" interrupted Sayid again with more of a warning tone.

"So, it seems we've no more to discuss" said Akhmed as he turned to walk away.

"Ok, ok" said Michel, realising he was beaten.

Akhmed stopped and took out his wallet and handed a thousand Francs to Michel and then offered his hand. Michel shook it and said "we'd better help you with them."

After unloading the car, Michel drove Sayid back to his flat complaining all the time that he had been robbed.

"Michel, it was the best possible thing you could do, I promise you."

"Well, I've still got some left at Grambois, perhaps I can sell them and at least get my money back."

"Bon." Then Michel thought of Henri's shop in Le Touquet. Perhaps he could off load them onto the frigid women of that place and bring a little Mediterranean sunshine into their unhappy lives. He felt better after that thought.

Outside Sayid's flat Michel said goodbye to his friend and promised to collect the sandals that he left behind before they went to La Plaine, after Christmas. With 'Joyeux Noël's they parted and Michel drove round to Ricky's for a sobering coffee before his journey to Aix.

"Things any better?" enquired Jacques as he prepared his second best customer's coffee.

"Oui, marginally" replied Michel as he sat up at the bar.

"Bonjour, Michel" boomed Antone's voice as Jacques best customer entered the bar.

"Bonjour, Antone" replied Michel as he smiled at the beaming person.

"Bring your coffee and come and join me" he said. Michel nodded and Jacques said "you go on with him, I'll bring your coffee."

"Merci" said Michel and followed the corpulent form to his favourite table and sat opposite, waiting for his coffee to arrive.

"I hear the press were here this morning to interview the hero" said Antone with a smile.

"Oui, and it was a bit of a do."

"Always is with that lot" replied Antone. "Jacques tells me you've announced your engagement to that pretty little Josette."

"Oui"

"Was that wise, considering you're still married to Monique?"

"Non, but it all came about by accident really" replied Michel.

"Really?"

"Oui."

"I've noticed that about you heterosexuals, you're prone to accidents and impatience" replied Antone haughtily as Jacques arrived with Michel's coffee and a cognac for his lover.

"Merci, Jacques" said Michel.

"You should be a little more circumspect" said Antone quietly before sipping his cognac.

"I know."

"And your story will be all over the papers tomorrow, accompanied by photo's of you and petite Josette, showing off her engagement ring." Michel shivered inwardly at that and sipped at his black coffee.

"I presume you are prepared for the marital storm and counterblast?" enquired Antone.

"Non, not really."

"Have you a hiding place?"

"Non."

"Pity, I would try and find one in the next few hours if I were you" said Antone gravely.

"A good idea."

"And when you've found one, don't go there until you've given me the video's you promised me. The chief and I would be so disappointed not to enjoy them over the Christmas holiday."

"I promise that you'll have them tomorrow night" replied Michel.

"Excellent" beamed Antone "I'm really looking forward to Christmas now."

"Bon" replied Michel in a cheerless tone.

"Come on, Michel, try and see the bright side of it all, remember, you've only got yourself to blame, and when Monique divorces you, Josette's there, already waiting to marry you, so, for you, it's out of the frying pan and into the fire!" and he laughed and Michel had to laugh with him.

They spent an hour talking and laughing and when Michel left the genial man he felt uplifted and quite good about himself.

The journey to Aix seemed to take for ever in the busy rush hour traffic and Michel expected he would be late arriving at the honey pot flat in the Boulevard Turin. He began to make up some time as the traffic thinned a little on the autoroute but even so, it was almost six thirty when he rang the sonnette.

Claudette answered and he was soon inside the perfumed flat and admiring the two lovely women before him. They were both dressed in little red dresses with hems and cuffs of wispy white fur, white stockings and red high heeled shoes. Their thick black hair was swept up and they wore glittering little tiara's on top. They looked divine and Michel kissed them both passionately.

"Ma petite princesses " he murmured as he went from one to another. They both giggled with pleasure.

"You look wonderful" he gasped as he held them close and caught the gentle scent of their expensive perfume. They laughed and Maria said "merci, Michel, now you're a little late and we'll have to hurry you, we've a very busy evening in front of us."

"I promise it won't take you long to finish me off" replied Michel truthfully.

"A drink first" said Claudette "to relax you."

"Oui, a petite scotch."

"Nonsense, it's Christmas" she replied as she poured a good generous measure into a cut glass tumbler.

"Ice?"

"Merci."

He slumped onto the settee as she handed him his drink.

"Now then" began Maria as she sat next to him "we'll have a quick drink with you and then give you a little show before you can have us both in here or the bedroom, whatever you prefer."

"The bedroom sounds comfortable" he replied as he sipped the scotch.

"Right."

Michel relaxed back and hoped that after Sophia and Nicole he could manage twice more with these two and he guessed that Josette would be disappointed tonight, but she would just have to wait until tomorrow morning before he could satisfy her.

The girls finished their drinks and whilst Michel sipped on, Maria put on the gentle mood music as Claudette began parading up and down for his pleasure. Maria joined her and they did a little erotic dance, gyrating and pouting at their friend on the settee.

Michel was soon aroused and unbelievably he felt the stirring in his loins. 'Mon Dieu, these two are good' he thought as in total unison, they undid their little red dresses and gave him a flash of what was underneath. Before he could take it all in they covered themselves up and turned away, but he had seen white lace bras with black nipples showing through cut outs and matching panties with slits showing the gentle sexual folds of their shaved bodies. They continued to gyrate and pout before turning their backs on him, bending over and flashing for a moment, their sweet little black bottoms enhanced with the slender strip of lace neatly caught and half hidden between their cheeks. Michel groaned "oh, this is too good" and undid his trousers to free his penis from the confines of his pants. The girls continued dancing and then with a flourish removed their fur trimmed dresses and tossed them aside. Michel was now free to enjoy the beautiful sight before him. They both looked fabulous in their white lace, peek a boo bras, matching panties and white stockings held up with red satin garters. They pouted and squeezed their breasts at him and tickled each others nipples for their mutual delight as well as his.

'Not long now' he thought as Maria approached him and took hold of his rigid penis and asked "how's this coming along?"

"Very well indeed" he replied at which point Claudette bent over and kissed him passionately before saying "squeeze my nipples and tell me when you're ready to go into the bedroom to finish off."

Michel did as he was told and murmured "now, please."

The girls turned away and he followed them, discarding his trousers, pants and shoes as he went from the lounge to the bedroom. The girls had his shirt and vest off in a trice and he lay naked on the soft bed as the two of them went to work on his body. As he stroked them they used their lips, mouths, nipples and finally their shaven little bodies in every way known to women to arouse a man to perfection and at last when he laid back on the bed, Maria straddled him and Claudette guided his penis into her. By then he was just about ready to explode. In fact he did very soon after the delightful young woman started bouncing up and down on his body as Claudette, now bra less, rubbed her hard nipples around his lips. They were too much for any red blooded Frenchman to handle for long. In a great surge, Michel heaved himself up from the bed to bury his penis as deep as possible into Maria's accommodating body.

"Oh, mon Dieu! mon Dieu!" he shouted as a very severe orgasm racked his body and he felt pain as he continued to thrust into her.

"That was good" said Maria.

"It looks like you've drained him completely" giggled Claudette "and now there's none left for me!"

Michel was sweating and at last when he calmed down he was able to say "that was fantastic, and I'm sorry Claudette, you're right, I'm totally fucked and I just can't manage you."

"Well, as long as you don't go away disappointed, then that's OK" she smiled.

"Mon Dieu, you're both gorgeous" he said.

It was almost half an hour before he could get off the bed and the pretty women helped him dress. Maria made a strong coffee for him which he drank slowly before kissing them both goodbye and wishing them a very 'Bon Noël'.

Michel took his time driving back to Marseille and it was almost nine when he parked in the Rue du Camas and went up to the flat to collect his Fiancé and take her to dinner.

"Where have you been, ma petite, I've been worried about you" she said gently.

"I've had a hell of a day since I left you to go shopping" he replied.

"Tell me all about it over dinner, I'm starving" she said. He nodded and they went to La Galleot where over a long lingering meal he told his Fiancé everything except the fact that he had had three women in the course of the afternoon and evening.

As they finished the meal and Madame Charnay brought the bill, Josette said sadly "I expect your so tired you'll just want to go to sleep when we get in."

"I'm afraid so, ma petite, but I'll make it up to you, I promise. You've had quite a good day, haven't you?"

"Oui."

"A new watch and a lovely engagement ring" he said with a smile.

She smiled back and they returned to the flat where Michel fell exhausted into bed.

CHAPTER TEN

Wednesday 24th December

Christmas Eve was grey, overcast and cold. The Mistral blowing down from the Alps was increasing in speed and the forecast was for snow on Christmas day or at the latest, before dawn on Boxing Day.

Michel awoke after a good night's sleep but still felt tired. Josette had managed to snuggle up so close to him during the night that she somehow had wriggled underneath his left side as he lay face down on the soft mattress. She was still asleep and he kissed her head gently before untangling himself from her soft, warm body and slipping from the bed.

He went into the kitchen and slowly made a large pot of coffee, poured a cup for himself and gathered his thoughts. The next couple of days looked difficult and he needed to think and act quickly to lessen the almighty row that would inevitably engulf him. First thing was to buy a paper and see exactly what the reporters had written about him and his Fiancé, then get home to Montelivet to pacify Monique. He reasoned that if he went home soon he might get a chance to talk to Monique before she saw a paper or one of the neighbours brought the matter to her attention. He took a cup of coffee into Josette and awoke her by kissing her nose and gently calling her name. She smiled when she came to and kissed him on his lips.

"I'm just going to shower, then I'll go to the kiosk and buy all the papers to see what they have to say, ma petite."

"Bon, I can hardly wait" she replied.

Half an hour later Michel was at the kiosk buying cigarettes and all the papers. He and Josette were on the front page of every one of them. Some editors had chosen a photo of them both with Jacques beaming face in the background and others chose either them kissing or Josette showing off her engagement ring. Headlines such as 'Hero Ronay relaxes at Ricky's bar' and 'Ronay plans spring wedding' coupled with lurid details, exaggerated beyond all reason, of his deadly and dangerous undercover work. Editorials posing the question 'how many more Marseille taxi drivers are working undercover for the police?' were on every front page. He sighed, paid for the papers and cigarettes and retraced his steps to the flat. He just put the key into the street door when a voice he knew called out "Michel! Michel!" and he turned to see René crossing the road from his flat opposite. His heart sank to his boots.

"René, ça va?"

"Michel, ça va, what are you doing here?"

"I've a close friend who lives here" he replied.

"Well who's that then?" queried his friend.

"Josette Le Franc" he replied.

"Josette lives here?"

"Oui."

"Didn't she live in Salvator's flat in the Rue Benoit Malon?"

"Oui, but she's moved, just before he was arrested."

"We know about the arrest, the papers are full of it, and Yvonne and I are very proud of you."

"Merci, René, but I guess you won't be so pleased when you read today's papers" and he held them out to his friend who looked shocked as he read 'Ronay plans spring wedding'.

"You're going to marry this girl?"

"Oui."

"What about Monique?"

"She'll divorce me."

"How can you be so sure?"

"Because she doesn't love me and this will be the final straw."

"Don't be too sure, mon ami, she loves you a lot and remember, you're a hero and all women love a hero."

Michel did not know what to say to his friend and his thoughts tumbled into confusion. He always had assumed that Monique would divorce him, but if she did not, then she would have to accept the way he lived and he would be free to carry on his adventures with all his mistresses. What a turn up for the book. He reasoned that if he stayed married he would have the added bonus of all the money from Mama, the Aunt s and their property. The situation looked decidedly brighter.

"Well, we'll have to see" replied Michel.

"We will, and I have to tell you that Yvonne will not give you up, no matter who you're married to, so I hope your new wife will understand" said René forcefully. Michel was surprised at that as he always assumed that Yvonne would only be happy sharing him with Monique. He guessed that he had made a greater impact with his best friend's wife than he had imagined.

"Oh" he said absently.

"Oui, you've made a real difference to our marriage, Michel, and we're very grateful, very grateful indeed" René smiled at him.

"Bon."

"Now remember to call in tonight sometime so we can wish you a 'joyeux Noël'."

"I will, I promise" Michel replied and the friends shook hands before René hurried away to his taxi parked further along the road.

Michel went upstairs to the flat and spread the newspapers out over the dining room table then he and Josette read through them with interest and for her part, some excitement.

After more coffee, Michel kissed his Fiancé goodbye and said "I must go to work now, I'll be back tonight and if it's not too late, we'll go out for dinner."

"Bon, I've got quite a lot of food shopping to do, ma petite, so I'll be busy too."

"Bon."

"Can you let me have some money for the food?" she asked gently.

Michel took out his wallet and gave her the entire contents, some twelve hundred Francs, and said "I'll go to the bank for some more later."

Half an hour later Michel parked the Mercedes outside his flat in Montelivet and went in to face the music.

"I won't ask where you've been since I don't know when, and have you any bloody idea how worried we are about you?" demanded Monique with blazing eyes as he entered the front door.

"I can explain everything, ma petite."

"You'll never live long enough" she replied.

"Have you seen the papers, ma petite?"

"We have."

"And did you read what Gerrard said about me being undercover and how grateful the Police are to me?"

"We read that" she replied with eyes firmly fixed on her

wayward husband.

"And?"

"And what?"

"Surely you realise that I've had to go undercover again, for your safety?"

"My safety?"

"Oui, and Frederik and Mama and the Aunts."

"Why?"

"All of Salvator's gang are looking for me and Gerrard advised me that as he was withdrawing my bodyguard" Monique sucked in her breath at that "because of cutbacks and shortages, I was on my own, and he advised me to lie low. So I went to Grambois, because I didn't want them to follow me home here and possibly endanger my whole family."

"Oh, Michel" she cried out and with tears in her eyes flung her arms around her husbands neck and said "I'm so sorry, ma petite, I had no idea, I just thought you were out, messing about with other women, can you forgive me?"

"There's nothing to forgive" he replied honestly and hoped her penitence and goodwill would carry on when she read the latest editions. He realised by what she said that she was totally ignorant of today's headlines.

They went hand in hand into the living room where the whole family was assembled and Michel was greeted by cries of welcome and adulation.

"You're so brave, Michel" said Mama dabbing at her eyes and continued "if only Papa was alive, he'd be so proud of you."

Alexis burst out crying at that and nearly spilt her glass of wine and Hélène smiled and said "I've always known you had the guts for something special!"

"Bravo, Michel" said Henri and Jackie chorused "bravo."

"Glad you're back OK" said Frederik with a grin and Angelique just smiled coyly.

"Well, merci, all of you, I'm glad to be home, now then, I don't know about you lot, but I could do with a scotch" said Michel and immediately Monique kissed him on his cheek and said "I'll get it, ma petite, you sit down and take it easy."

René was right, everyone loves a hero, and Michel was beginning to enjoy the role. Perhaps he would not rush off to Le

Touquet to soon after Christmas, he thought, take a little time to take stock and then reposition himself.

"Tell us all about it then, Dad" said Frederik and Michel, now clutching a large scotch and ice, went though the whole escapade, exaggerating every little detail for effect. He had finished by lunchtime and was glad to sit back and answer questions from his adoring family whilst Monique aided by Jackie and Angelique served the meal.

Like most French families, the Ronay's enjoyed their midday meal on Christmas eve knowing that it would be their last until after midnight mass, when, after a light supper and sleep a huge traditional feast would be consumed later Christmas day. Michel informed his adoring wife and admiring family that he would work up until this evening and then return to begin the festivities. Monique planned, with the help of Jackie and Angelique, to prepare all the food that afternoon and evening whilst Alexis and Hélène kept Mama company and tried not to argue. Henri and Frederik were at a loose end and Michel promised to pop back around six, if he was not too busy, and take them down to le Vieux Port for a quick look round and a drink in Ricky's. Henri looked much relieved at that suggestion and Michel knew only too well that his cousin must be tired of being hemmed in with a flat full of women.

The first thing Michel did after leaving the flat, was to drive to the Bourse and return once more to the Bank to draw out more money from his secure box in the strong room. Having accomplished that he parked at his station by le Vieux Port and awaited his first fare of the day.

The rear passenger door opened and an elegant lady slipped into the back of the taxi with several carrier bags emblazoned with the names of the premier shops and chic boutiques.

Michel looked in his rear view mirror to see the face of Madame Veron, a regular and long standing customer, just as she said '12, Rue Audibert, please, driver.'

"Oui, Madame Veron" he replied with a smile.

"Oh, Michel, Michel" she cooed.

"Oui, Madame"

"Ah, Michel, ça va?"

"Ça va, Madame?"

"Oui, bien sûr, I'm pleased to see you, Michel."

"Likewise, Madame, it seems ages since I last saw you."

"It is."

"How's Mademoiselle Christine?" he asked as fond memories of having perfect sex with her by the pool at Madame's villa at Cassis sprang to mind.

"Very well, very well indeed and she often asks after you."

"Really?"

"Oui, and now that we've read about your brave exploits as an undercover agent, well, it seems we never stop talking about you" she replied.

"Bon, now then, what have you bought yourself for Christmas?" he asked brightly.

"Oh, not a lot really, just a few clothes and things you know."

"Ah, don't miss the opportunity to spoil yourself" he replied and she laughed.

He then kept Madame amused all the way back to her flat in the Rue Audibert with his version of events surrounding the arrest of Salvator, and after paying the fare and giving him a very generous tip, she invited him in for a drink. Michel courteously refused, excusing himself by explaining that he was very busy but would be delighted to call in the new year. She understood and he was relieved, as he knew that she was a very generous person, wealthy and lonely and he could well spend a long time with her during the afternoon consuming large quantities of her mature, single malt scotch. As he drove away he reflected on her invitation and reasoned that as a hero, he would be foolish to give up so many opportunities that were, and would be on offer to him in Marseille. He would have to think very hard indeed before he rushed off to Le Touquet

Returning to le Vieux Port, Michel parked in line and lit a cigarette. The rank moved forward very quickly and he had only just finished his cigarette when he found himself at the head of the line of taxis.

The rear door opened and a large blonde lady and a thin, grey haired man with glasses struggled into the back seat. The smell of drink enveloped Michel as he asked "where to, Monsieur?"

"Better take you home first, ma petite" said the man in a semi whisper as he kissed the blonde on her flushed cheek. She giggled and replied "Oui, ma petite Papa, wouldn't want your wife to see us together again."

"Well, Monsieur?" asked Michel patiently as he clicked the meter on.

"Er, 36, Rue Aviateur, s'il vous plaît" replied the man in a slurred voice.

"Non, that's your address, silly" said the blonde.

"Oh, oui, er, er, what's your address then?" he asked the blonde.

She ignored him and said to Michel, "take me to 45, Rue de Verdun, and then go to Rue Aviateur for Monsieur."

"Oui, Madame" replied Michel.

"Mademoiselle" she corrected.

"Mademoiselle" repeated Michel as he swung out into the busy traffic.

"Will you miss your Papa over Christmas?" asked the man, as he nuzzled into the blonde's neck.

"You know I will, Papa."

"And I will miss you" he mumbled.

"Oui, no naughty smack bottoms until we're back at the office."

"I know, I'm going to miss that every lunch time."

"Never mind, Papa, it won't be long" she replied.

"D'you really like my present?"

"Oui, Papa, what mademoiselle wouldn't?"

"I only want you to have the best."

"I know."

"You mustn't wear it at work, I don't want any of that lot to know our little secret."

"Oh, non, Papa."

"You promise?"

"Of course, I promise."

"There's a good little Mademoiselle, because I wouldn't want to have to bend you over my desk and smack that pretty bum of yours too hard now."

"Oh, why not, if I've been naughty, I deserve it" she giggled.

"You're never naughty, not really, just very good, now kiss

me" he mumbled and she turned to him and Michel watched in the mirror as the old man fumbled for her mouth and in the process his glasses fell off. With his eyes closed he seemed blissfully unaware and continued to press home his attack on the flushed face of his companion.

When they broke for air and he opened his eyes, he said "where are my glasses?"

"You've dropped them, Papa, they must have fallen on the floor" she replied. They both, in their unsteady state, started to search the floor of the taxi. At that moment a deranged motorist, in a rusty Renault, appeared out of a side road without pausing for a second, causing Michel to swing the Mercedes violently to the left to avoid hitting the lunatic. Michel heard the crunch as he shouted at the foolish driver now accelerating hard away from the taxi.

"I've trodden on my glasses!" wailed Papa as he collected the remains from the floor.

"Mon Dieu! They're broken" said the blonde.

"What am I going to do?" wailed Papa.

"Haven't you got a spare pair?" she asked.

"Non, I've ordered them but they won't be ready until after Christmas" he moaned.

"Oh, dear."

"And I can't see without them."

"Oh, Papa."

"It's all your fault, driver!" he shouted.

"My fault, Monsieur?"

"Oui, your fault, your bad driving made me tread on my glasses!"

"Non, Monsieur, a stupid driver nearly hit us and by my expert driving I saved us from a very nasty accident, then you, Monsieur, trod on your glasses" replied Michel in a truculent tone.

"Don't you talk to me like that!" exclaimed Papa.

"That's the truth, like it or not!" replied Michel.

"I don't like it!"

"That's tough" replied Michel.

"Do you know who I am?" demanded Papa.

"Oui."

"Who am I then?"

"A drunk office manager who's having an affair with his

secretary and who enjoys smacking her bottom whilst bent over his desk, but your name and that of the business is not known to me!"

"You're a disgrace, Monsieur, I'll see you loose your licence!"

"And do you know who I am?" asked Michel.

"Non, Monsieur" replied Papa.

"I'm Michel Ronay."

"The undercover taxi driver, the hero!" squealed the blonde.

"Correct, Mademoiselle."

"I've read all about you in the paper" she carried on.

"Indeed" replied Michel.

"Oh, Monsieur Ronay, I think we'd better go to the Rue Aviateur first and see Monsieur safely indoors, I mean, without his glasses he's helpless, and then you can take me home and tell me all about your very brave but dangerous work" she said breathlessly.

"Nicola!"

"It's best, Papa, I would be so worried about you otherwise."

"What about my wife?"

"I'm sure Monsieur Ronay will see you to your door and I'll hide in the back here."

"Nicola!"

"36, Rue Aviateur, Monsieur Ronay, s'il vous plaît" she said firmly.

"Oui, Mademoiselle" replied Michel with a grin and he took the next turning to his right and began to drive in the direction of Papa's home in the Rue Aviateur. Michel was enjoying being a hero, it seemed to be the answer to every eventuality.

The old man protested all the way home, in one breathe he blamed Michel for everything, then he recanted, claiming he could see well enough with the interior light on. He looked helpless and sad with the light off and without Nicola to look after him. 'Pathetic' thought Michel as they pulled up outside number 36. Nicola then added insult to injury by asking Papa for the fare money which he gave begrudgingly. Michel helped him out of the taxi as he continued to plant kisses on her red lips, wishing her 'Joyeux Noël' with every other breath. Michel struggled with Papa to the door and he then rang the sonnette.

"Oui" came a strong voice of a woman.

"It's me, ma petite, Raymond."

"Bon, at last" came the reply and the door clicked open.

"Bon Noël" said Michel as he helped the old man in through the door and left him in the hall way for his wife to find him, clutching his broken glasses with his face covered in lipstick.

By the time Michel returned to the Mercedes, Nicola was now comfortably seated in the front.

"Now then, Monsieur Ronay, take me home slowly and tell me all about your work, I'm just dying to know all about it" she whispered and heaved her large breasts up and down for effect.

"Oui, Mademoiselle."

"Call me Nicola, Michel."

"As you wish."

"Oh, I do wish, believe me."

Michel believed her and they set off towards her home at a slow pace. He told the story once again, embellishing the details here and there, and was grateful when Nicola drew in a breath and heaved her breasts up in amazement at a moment of intense danger, such as when he was chasing Salvator and drove the Mercedes down a drain and Gerrard shot himself.

"Mon Dieu! You're a real hero, the papers never mentioned that" she said.

"Non, that all happened back in August, when I was deep undercover, I guess the truth will never be known" he replied modestly.

"Oh, Michel" she whispered, breasts heaving.

The journey continued and Michel found himself enjoying the situation more and more. At last they arrived outside 45 Rue de Verdun.

"There, Nicola, you're home safely" he said.

"How can I not be safe with such a man as you, a real hero?"

"You're too kind, that'll be a hundred Francs, s'il vous plaît."

"Here" she said "have that" and she handed him two hundred Francs.

"Merci, Nicola."

"Now, I can't let you go, come in and have a drink."

"That's very kind but…….."

"I insist, Michel, please for me, please" she interrupted.

He smiled, nodded and replied "OK."

He parked the Mercedes and followed Nicola into the building and up to her flat on the second floor.

The flat was warm, neat and very feminine but had a lonely feel to it. He sat on the settee whilst she poured a scotch for each of them. This was the first opportunity that Michel had had to see her clearly. She was about thirty five years old, quite tall with a full figure, large breasts and a mop of blonde hair. She looked dishevelled and her lipstick was well and truly smeared about. Papa must have been sliding about her face in his drunken passion and Michel fancied that Papa was wearing more of Nicola's lipstick than she was.

"Salute and joyeux Noël " she said as she handed him his scotch and sat down beside him.

"Now, tell me all about yourself, what sort of man are you really?"

"I'm a person of no importance, and I'd rather talk about you, much rather."

"Oh, Michel, you know how to handle a woman."

"Non, I'm afraid I don't, I'm an absolute failure with women."

"I don't believe you" she laughed.

"It's true, I can't even get you to talk about yourself!" She laughed out loud at that and then bent forward and kissed him gently on his lips.

"You shouldn't do that" he said as she drew back.

"Why not?"

"Because you are a very beautiful young woman and I'm a red blooded Frenchman" he replied and she gurgled at that, then sipped her scotch.

"And we're alone" he added before sipping his scotch.

"I know" she whispered, "glorious, isn't it?"

"It's too dangerous" he whispered.

"For who?"

"You, Nicola."

"Me, why?"

"Think of yourself, you have possibly upset your boss, he may be in trouble with his wife...."

"Why do you say that?" she interrupted.

"Because when I left him he was clutching his broken glasses and covered in your lipstick!"

"Oh, mon Dieu!"

"And you are now alone with an undercover agent, who can be ruthless when it comes to getting what he wants."

"Oh, Michel, what do you want?" she asked, breasts heaving.

"Only what you want, Nicola."

"I want you, Michel."

"What about Papa?"

"Never mind about that old fool, I don't care about him!"

"I thought as much."

"Oh, Michel, stay with me tonight and make love to me."

"I can't ma petite……"

"Well just a quickie then" she interrupted.

"How can I resist you?"

"Drink up, Michel, I'm impatient and my needs are great."

They finished their drinks and then Nicola stood up and grabbing his hand led Michel into the bedroom.

"We'll be more comfortable in here" she said as she switched on the bedside lamps and closed the door. She then put her arms around his neck and kissed him passionately.

"There" she said "now I'll show you what a grateful secretary looks like." With that she unbuttoned her white blouse, revealing a very pretty lace bra, straining under the weight and pressure of her breasts, undid her black skirt, letting it fall to the floor and then kissed him again.

"Now then, undercover agent, you undo the rest!"

Michel unclipped her bra and her breasts bounced forward towards him, he took them in his hands and massaged them gently.

"That's good" she whispered.

He slipped his fingers down the sides of her matching lace panties and slid them to the floor. She stepped out of them and as he came up he planted a big kiss in the middle of her pubic hair. She moaned and then stepped away before flinging off her high heeled shoes and dropping down onto the bed.

"OK, now let's see what a hero looks like naked" she smiled.

Michel was undressed in a moment and then dived onto the bed next to her. They put their arms around each other and she dragged him on top of her fulsome figure. They kissed passionately and when they broke for air she said, "I'm wet for you, Michel, so just do it."

He pushed at her with his rigid penis and it slipped into her effortlessly.

"Mon Dieu" she whispered as Michel carried on ever upward until he was pressed hard against her body.

"Now slowly, Michel, I want this to last as long as possible."

"Oui, ma petite."

"And then it will be the best Christmas present ever" she whispered.

Michel set a slow rhythm, pulling out a long way before plunging back into her accommodating body. She was a big girl all round and her smooth acceptance of him reminded Michel of Eleanor's comfortable body.

"Oh, mon Dieu" she whispered over and over again as Michel carried on with his slow, relentless rhythm of love. He closed his mind to the young woman beneath him and thought of Henri and Le Touquet. He wondered whether Henri would put the project back six months or so, giving him time to consider all the possibilities now before him. His mind then drifted and he relived all the adventures he had had since the summer and he realised that he was truly enjoying life despite all the problems. Suddenly he became aware of Nicola's cries to God becoming louder and louder and he quickened his thrusting pace as she neared her climax. Then, with unbelievable speed, she wrapped her long legs around his back and then tightened her body on his penis as her orgasm began. She squeezed and then shook him like a dog shakes a rat as he endeavoured to release himself into her. He managed it and then shaking and gasping for breath begged her to let him go. She relaxed her legs and he was able to breathe again.

"Merci, Nicola" he gasped.

"That was so good my hero" she replied.

"Oui, it was."

"Perhaps you'd like another drink before you go" she said, her composure almost completely recovered.

"Oui, that would be good."

"We can sit and make our arrangements for our next date, when hopefully you can stay longer" she said brightly.

"Oui" he replied breathlessly.

Michel determined not to stay too long with his latest conquest and within half an hour he was heading back to Montelivet for a rest before taking Henri and Frederik down to le Vieux Port.

"I've come back a little early" he proclaimed to Monique and the family "as I picked up a drunk man and a woman. It was unpleasant and I felt I needed a break after that."

"Quite so, ma petite" said Monique "let me get you a drink."

"Merci" he replied as he sank down onto the settee.

Henri smiled and said "glad to see you back early." Michel bet he was and smiled in return.

Whilst Monique, Jackie and Angelique prepared the food for the coming Christmas feast, Michel relaxed with Henri, Alexis, Hélène and Mama. Everybody seemed most agreeable and Alexis and Hélène appeared to be on their best behaviour. It was almost six when Michel suggested that he took Henri and Frederik down to le Vieux Port and Ricky's. Henri was ready like a shot but Frederik told his step father that he would prefer to stay with Angelique as they had more presents to wrap and he wanted to remain close to her. Michel understood and set off down town with an eager Henri. They drove around le Vieux Port as Michel gave Henri a running commentary on the sights of old Marseille.

"You'll certainly miss all this when you come to Le Touquet" said Henri seriously.

"Possibly" replied Michel, now truly uncertain about his future.

"It's all a bit quiet compared to Marseille" continued Henri.

"I'm sure, but after the last week or so, I could manage a bit of quiet" replied Michel.

"I can understand that" said Henri solemnly.

Michel double parked outside Ricky's and then strode in like the hero he was, followed by a smiling Henri.

"Ah, Michel" called Jacques from behind the bar.

"Jacques, ça va?"

"Oui, bien sûr. What can I get you?"

"A scotch and, what are you having Henri?"

"A scotch."

"And a scotch for my cousin Henri."

"Ah, cousin Henri" said Jacques as he poured the drinks.

"From Le Touquet" added Michel.

"Ah, Le Touquet" repeated Jacques.

"Oui"

"I'm Jacques, you may have seen my photo in all the

newspapers."

"Non" replied Henri.

"Surely you have, I was the one posing between Michel and his Fiancé."

"Fiancé?" queried Henri.

"Oui, petite Josette, surely you know all about her?"

"Non" replied a dumbfounded Henri as Michel sank further into the abyss of the black hole. Henri looked at Michel, picked up his scotch and said "we'd better sit down somewhere whilst you tell me all about your Fiancé, Josette." Michel nodded and followed his cousin to an empty table at the back of the bar. They sat in the creaking wicker chairs and Henri said "there's a lot I don't know about you, Michel, and I must admit, I'm very curious." He sipped his scotch and waited for Michel to begin.

"It's like this, Henri, the whole thing is both a mistake and a misunderstanding."

"Go on."

"I've known Josette for some time now, and it was in my mind earlier this year, well, summer really, that I considered divorcing Monique......."

"Why?" Henri interrupted.

"Because we'd come to the end of the relationship."

"What does that mean exactly?"

"Henri, stop asking questions and I'll tell you everything."

"OK, carry on."

"And I discussed it with Monique when we were at Grambois in August, and she pointed out certain things...."

"Like what?"

"Advantages. I thought about what she said and I changed my mind about a divorce, but I didn't tell Josette......."

"Why not?" interrupted Henri.

"Henri, stop interrupting me, please!"

"OK, sorry, do go on."

"I didn't tell Josette because she was going through a bad time with Salvator...."

"Oh" Henri nodded.

"And she had, well, we both had, a lot to worry about."

"I understand."

"Then, whilst we were out shopping, I bought Josette a watch."

"Oh, nice."

"And whilst we were in the jewellery department, she asked if she could look at the rings and before I could say 'no' she was picking out an engagement ring, helped, I may say, by a cruel looking, man hating lesbian assistant."

"Mon Dieu, how awful!"

"The worst of it was, believe it or not, the damned ring fitted her perfectly, and so she wore it immediately!"

"Mon Dieu!"

"Precisely, then we came in here for a coffee and the press descended on the place, photographing every move we made, and questions, questions, questions, it was a nightmare."

"Horrific."

"And in the midst of all this chaos, one of the reporters asks who she is, and she says 'I'm Josette Le Franc, his Fiancé, and here's my ring!'"

"Mon Dieu!"

"Then we had to have photos of us with Jacques, kissing each other and so on."

"How are you going to get out of this mess, Michel?"

"I'm coming to Le Touquet after Christmas."

"Who with?"

"Alone, at the moment."

"A very wise move, if I may say so."

"You may." They remained silent for a while, each deep in thought.

Michel had just signalled to Jacques for more scotch when Antone walked in beaming, and whilst waving at some of the other regulars, made his way directly towards Michel and Henri.

"Ça va, Michel."

"Ça va, Antone, and let me introduce you to my cousin Henri, from Le Touquet."

"Pleased to meet you, Henri, I'm sure" and they shook hands. Antone then squeezed his frame into his favourite chair at the next table as Jacques arrived with two scotches and a cognac for Antone.

"Merci, Jacques" said Michel.

"Now then, Henri, what do you think of our hero?" asked Antone.

"I have no words to describe him" replied Henri.

"Neither have we, not only is he a brave hero, but a generous one too."

"Indeed."

"Oui, I know because he told me only the other day that he had a very special present for me, and he was going to give it to me on Christmas eve" said Antone, with a smile.

"Quite right, it's in the car, I'll go and get it right now, and that'll give you an opportunity to talk about me while I'm gone."

They all smiled at that as Michel went out to the Mercedes and brought in the four videos, neatly wrapped in gold gift paper, for Antone and the Chief to enjoy over the holiday.

"Four of the very highest quality, especially for you" he said as he handed the packet to Antone.

"Merci, Michel, I know the Chief and I will enjoy them."

"Oh, you will, I've been assured by the video director himself that these are the very best available anywhere in the world."

"Merci, Michel" smiled Antone "you've made two old men very happy."

At that moment Gerrard walked in and made straight for Michel and his companions.

"Bonjour, Messieurs" he said abruptly.

"Bonjour" they replied in unison.

"May I join you for a moment or two?" asked Gerrard.

"By all means, Monsieur Gerrard" replied Antone as Gerrard eased himself into a chair opposite the great man with the gold parcel of videos on the table between them.

"A drink?"

"Merci, just a small cognac, I'm on duty."

"Of course" replied Antone as he waved to Jacques.

"And who are you, Monsieur?" asked Gerrard looking at Henri.

"Forgive me, Monsieur Gerrard, this is my cousin Henri from Le Touquet."

"Pleased to meet you" replied Gerrard as Michel continued "this is Monsieur Gerrard, who led the daring arrest of Salvator."

"Another hero" said Henri as Gerrard smirked.

"You're surrounded by them" said Antone as Jacques arrived.

"Cognac for Monsieur Gerrard, another one for me and two more scotches, Jacques, and put it all on my bill" said Antone.

As Jacques moved away, Gerrard leaned forward over the table and looked around at their attentive faces.

"Messieurs, I must say this only once, and I must be brief." They all looked at him earnestly.

"I have received information that a certain Monsieur Conrad Montreau, from Lyons, known as the 'Black Snake', has been seen in and around Marseille, talking to some of Salvator's men!" Michel shivered at that.

"Montreau is a well known criminal mastermind who always manages to stay one step ahead of the police" said Gerrard.

"Mon Dieu" whispered Henri.

"We believe he's planning some sort of takeover of Salvator's dirty business, and we will need all the help we can get in tracking this man down and eventually bringing him to justice." 'Oh, non' thought Michel 'not another undercover job.'

"So, Michel, I want you to be on the look out for this man" said Gerrard as he produced from his pocket a black and white photo of an unsavoury looking character with a mop of black hair and a neat moustache.

"Mon Dieu" whispered Henri as Michel took the photo and examined it. He made up his mind there and then to go to Le Touquet immediately after Christmas.

"Right, I'll keep an eye out for him" he replied with confidence.

"Bon" said Gerrard as Jacques arrived with a tray of drinks.

Gerrard finished his drink quickly and wished them all 'Joyeux Noël' before rushing off into the busy streets of Marseille.

An hour later Michel drove Henri back to Montelivet, slowly and now and then, a little unsteadily.

"I will join you in Le Touquet as soon as I can after Christmas, and I'd be pleased if you could just fix me up with a few basics in your old house" said Michel firmly.

"That's fine, Michel, I'll start as soon as I get back."

"And not a word to Monique."

"Non, I promise."

"I'll phone you before I set off" said Michel.

"OK." The dye was cast.

After drinking several cups of black coffee, whilst they inspected the labours of the women in the kitchen, Michel told Monique that he was just slipping out to see René and Yvonne and to see to another little bit of business before returning in plenty of time to take them all to midnight mass and carol singing. She kissed her husband and told him not to be late back. He promised and was gone. Parking in the cul de sac off the Rue du Camas he walked quickly along to René and Yvonne's and rang the sonnette. Within moments he was in the warmth of his friends comfortable flat drinking yet another scotch.

"So you're off to Grambois after Christmas" said Yvonne.

"Oui, for a well deserved rest" replied Michel.

"How long for?" asked René.

"Just a few days" replied Michel.

"We'll miss you" said Yvonne.

"And I'll miss you too" smiled Michel.

"We can make up for lost time once you're back" said Yvonne with a gleam in her eye.

"Possibly, ma petite, but I must tell you that I'm thinking of leaving Marseille" said Michel seriously.

"What?" exclaimed René.

"Why?" enquired Yvonne.

"I have been offered a business opportunity that I'm finding hard to refuse and I'm thinking about it very seriously" replied Michel to his surprised friends.

"Oh, Michel, you can't leave Marseille" said Yvonne.

"As you're my best friends, I've told you first."

"What does Monique say?" asked Yvonne.

"She doesn't know yet" he replied truthfully.

"So you're leaving her" said René in a matter of fact tone.

"Oui" Michel replied.

"And you're going away with Josette?" enquired René.

"Who's Josette?" demanded Yvonne.

"A close friend" replied Michel.

"His Fiancé" corrected René.

"Oh, Michel" said Yvonne in a shocked tone.

"I'm not taking Josette with me" replied Michel.

"Well where are you going?" asked Yvonne in a frustrated tone.

"To Le Touquet."

"With cousin Henri?" asked René.

"Oui, with Henri."

"Oh, Michel, I can't cope with all this, I'm sure, and fancy telling us on Christmas eve, surely you could have left this bad news until you came back from Grambois?" asked a confused Yvonne.

"Possibly, but I might go suddenly from Grambois and I didn't want to leave Marseille without telling you."

"But you will come back from Le Touquet to visit won't you?" asked Yvonne.

"Of course, it's not the other side of the world you know!"

"Bon, let's have another drink" said René.

They chatted on but an air of sadness enveloped them all and Yvonne cried when Michel kissed them both goodbye. He wondered if he was doing the right thing as he crossed the street and let himself into Josette's flat.

"Michel!" she exclaimed as he entered the door and flung his arms around his beloved. They kissed passionately for some time before she said "no more work until after the holiday."

"No more work" he replied.

"Bon, now instead of going out for a meal, I've cooked something special for just the two of us" she smiled.

"Bon, but I have to leave by about eleven, I've promised that I'd take them all to midnight mass."

"Oh, ma petite" she said in a gentle voice.

"I know, but it is the last time you know" and she brightened up at that.

"Oui, the very last time, and then after Christmas our new life together begins" she beamed.

"Oui" he replied not wanting to upset her with his decision to leave Marseille and start a new life alone. He was still unsure about that and he knew he would have to give a lot more thought to the situation before coming to an absolutely final decision. No more 'definitely, may be'.

Michel relaxed with his Fiancé and enjoyed the meal, which was light and delicious. They ate melon with raspberry vinaigrette dressing followed by lobster in brandy with tomatoes and onions, Homard a l'americane, followed by ice cream. At the end of the meal they drank coffee but Michel refused a cognac. He had had enough to drink and he knew that he had to drive back to Montelivet.

With passionate kisses and declarations of undying love he left his Fiancé, promising to see her in the evening of Christmas day.

He drove back to his flat in Montelivet with a very heavy heart.

CHAPTER ELEVEN

Thursday 25th December

It was almost midnight when Michel and Monique led the rest of the family up the hill from their flat to the small church at the crossroad on top of the highest point at Montelivet. As always on Christmas eve the church was full and the Ronay family squeezed in almost at the back of the stone built house of God. The service began and Michel sang the hymns and thought of Josette and his new life without her. He was troubled and saddened by events and not even the colourful tableau of local children, dressed in the traditional Provençal costumes, could lift his spirits, nor the carol singing. He had noticed that Monique and the family had been unusually quiet when he had first arrived home and he put that down to tiredness.

At last the service concluded and he looked around at the faces of his family and resolved sadly that this would be the last Christmas that he would spend with them. Henri kept giving him a knowing look and Michel determined to talk to his cousin privately as soon as he could. He felt that something was up. They walked back from the church briskly as it was becoming colder and flurries of snow whirled around in the sharp wind. Once inside the flat Michel poured drinks for the whole family and wished them all 'Joyeux Noël .' They all seemed somewhat subdued and when Michel followed Monique out into the kitchen, where they were alone, he asked his wife "you're all a bit quiet tonight, aren't you?"

"Engaged to Josette Le Franc are you?" she demanded with blazing eyes.

"I can explain everything" he replied.

"Well, this had better be bloody good, in fact, the best story ever!" she exclaimed.

"You've read it all in the papers……." he began.

"Dead right, Madame Rochas brought her paper up for me to see it and then Frederik went down to the kiosk and bought the rest, how could you do such a thing, Michel, how could you?"

"It's all nonsense…."

"Is it?"

"Look, it all got out of hand and you know what the press are like…….."

"Non, I don't know what the press are like, please tell me!" she interrupted.

"If you'll only let me explain….."

"Well you'd better rehearse this pretty carefully because you're going to have to tell this tale a few times with detailed explanations, Mama hasn't stopped crying since she read it, Alexis hasn't stopped drinking and Hélène just keeps on shaking her head, Frederik has gone very quiet and all in all, the whole family is pretty pissed with you, and never mind how I feel, you lying bastard of a husband!" and she burst into tears and sat down at the kitchen table which was groaning under the weight of prepared food. 'Fuck Madame Rochas' thought Michel 'that busybody, interfering old crow had caused Mama's accident and now had thrown the spanner into the family works on Christmas eve of all bloody times!'

He sat down opposite his distressed wife and decided to try hard to recover the situation. It meant lying much more than usual but he thought of all the options from walking out now and returning to Josette's flat to staying put and showing a brave face. He chose to stay and lie for all their sakes.

"Now, Monique, please listen to me, please" at that she stopped crying and looked at her husband.

"First of all, I want you to know that I love you and I always will, always, you understand?"

She nodded just a little.

"You and Frederik are everything to me and I'm sure you realise that deep down" and she nodded again at that.

"And this business with the Le Franc woman is part of a very elaborate undercover ploy to protect you and Frederik." She looked hard at him as he continued "Gerrard confirmed today that an evil bastard called 'Black Snake' is in Marseille, and he's been contacting Salvator's men in an attempt to take over his operations."

"Really?" she whispered.

"Oui, and here is a photo of Black Snake, he's from Lyon according to Gerrard" Michel produced the black and white photograph that the Gendarme had given him and showed to his tearful wife.

"Oh" she said with a faint smile "he looks dangerous."

"He is very dangerous, and what's more, Henri was with me in Ricky's when Gerrard told us all about this crook, so you can ask Henri yourself about that" said Michel triumphantly. Thank God for Henri.

Monique smiled a little uncertain smile and Michel continued "and my wish as well as my duty, is to protect you and Frederik from this evil man, so, the Le Franc woman was the ideal person to distract Black Snake or any of Salvator's lot from coming anywhere near you!"

"Oh, Michel" she whispered.

"As Le Franc was a former girl friend of Claude Salvator, it was considered very useful to have her involved with me."

"Oh, Michel, I'm so sorry" she whispered.

"That's alright, and believe me, the best way to get maximum publicity for this stunt was to have the Le Franc woman in all the press photo's with me, proclaiming our engagement."

"Michel."

"With that press coverage, 'Black Snake' and all his cronies would know about it and that would make her the target for any revenge attack instead of you, ma petite."

"Oh, Michel, I do love you so" she said as she got up from her chair and came around the table and kissed her husband with a passion.

Michel sighed an inward sigh of relief and asked his wife "shall we now go and tell the family all about it?"

"Oh, oui, ma petite, oui."

Michel followed his wife into the lounge were the subdued family sat gazing into the fire.

"Michel wants to tell you all about his reported engagement to Josette Le Franc" said Monique in a firm voice.

"This'll be interesting" said Hélène as Alexis and Mama burst out crying. Frederik, Angelique and Jackie looked perplexed and Henri looked amused.

Michel told them the same story as he had told Monique in the kitchen, pausing only once to invite Henri to support the conversation in Ricky's with Gerrard, which Henri did with gusto.

The family sat opened mouthed as Michel continued and were greatly impressed when he showed the photo of 'Black Snake' and Henri embellished the conversation with Gerrard so that he might bask in some reflected glory and Michel was grateful for that.

"Mon Dieu!" exclaimed Mama "the family is full of hero's."

Hélène, Frederik and Angelique were smiling from ear to ear and Jackie looked proudly at her brave husband. Alexis carried on crying telling everybody that she was so happy and she knew deep down that there was a rational explanation, and she desperately needed another drink to steady her nerves. The atmosphere in the room changed completely and Michel settled back with a very large scotch brought to him by his adoring wife.

'Christmas might not be too bad after all' he thought as he sipped the golden liquid.

The family were now happy and content and it was time to eat a little before retiring to bed. Monique had prepared a piping hot onion soup poured over bread with grated cheese sprinkled lightly on top. With a few glasses of wine and a selection of cheeses to follow the meal was complete and they were all content to wish each other 'Joyeux Noël' and retire to their beds knowing what was before them.

It was almost eight when Michel was awakened by noises in the kitchen. Monique was already up and attending to a million things that a woman has to do at Christmas, a fact that most men, worldwide, seem oblivious to. Michel staggered out of bed and into the shower where the hot stinging needles of water helped sober him up and reinvigorate his tired body. After dressing very casually he wandered into the kitchen to see Monique, Jackie, Hélène and Angelique hard at work preparing more food. There seemed to be mountains of vegetables being peeled, cheeses being prepared and puddings being mixed.

"Mon Dieu," he mumbled and then asked in a whisper "is there any coffee?"

Monique looked up from the huge turkey that she was busily preparing and snapped "Non, you'll have to get it yourself, can't you see we're all busy!"

Michel attempted the hazardous journey across the crowded kitchen towards the kettle, trying not to get in anyone's way, when

Hélène seeing that he was a helpless male completely out of his depth, broke off from her vegetable peeling duties and said "you go into the other room and I'll make you a coffee."

"Merci, Hélène" replied a relieved Michel as he left the hive of industry.

He discovered Henri alone in the lounge reading yesterday's papers, courtesy of Madame Rochas and the dutiful Frederik.

"Ah, Michel" smiled Henri "sleep well?"

"Like a top, and you?"

"Non, not too well, Madame Rochas spare bed is not the most comfortable and on top of that, Jackie snores."

"Oh" replied a surprised Michel.

"Oui, she's always snored, sometimes it really gets on my nerves."

"I'm sure" replied Michel.

"Have you ever slept with a woman who snores?" asked Henri.

Michel allowed the faces of all his mistresses to cascade through his imagination and truthfully could not think of one.

"Non, I haven't" he replied truthfully.

"You're lucky, Michel, very lucky."

At that moment Hélène arrived with a steaming black coffee and handed it to Michel

"Would you like a cup?" asked Hélène of Henri.

"Non, merci, Hélène" he replied and she returned to her vegetable peeling duties. The two men were alone again and Michel seized upon the opportunity.

"Henri, I want to thank you for your comments last night, it helped a great deal."

"That's OK, Michel, I mean, I did nothing really except report what Gerrard told us in Ricky's."

"I know, but your support was most welcome."

"I'm dying to know if you're really planning to divorce Monique and marry this girl, so, are you?"

"I honestly don't know at the moment, but I am sure that I need to leave Marseille and start our business in Le Touquet" Michel replied.

"Well at least that's a positive decision" said Henri.

"We should do well and I'm looking forward to it."

"So am I" replied Henri.

"A year from now we could be sitting on board your twenty metre boat surrounded by half drunk, loose women!" exclaimed Michel.

"I'm really looking forward to that" replied Henri and they both laughed.

"I wonder what Christmas lunch is like on a boat?" mused Michel.

"Very nice I expect, in the right company" said Henri.

"No wives then" replied Michel.

"Definitely no wives" said Henri firmly.

"Who'll do the cooking?" asked Michel.

"The half drunk loose women of course!" replied Henri and they started laughing again.

"Mon Dieu! I couldn't manage an underdone turkey with an overdone woman serving it" said Michel.

"Really?"

"Well only if she was half naked" said Michel as Henri continued to laugh.

"What's tickling you two?" asked Monique as she burst into the room followed by Jackie and Angelique.

"Something rude, I expect" said Jackie before either man could reply to Monique.

"No it's not" replied Henri and he continued "we were just trying to imagine what it would be like having Christmas lunch on a boat."

"Really" said Monique.

"Take no notice, Henri's off on his hobby horse again, he thinks he's going to find the money to buy a bloody big boat" said Jackie quite angrily.

"Got to have a dream, ma petite, otherwise how can you have a dream come true?" asked Henri with a smile.

"Dream on then, ma petite" she replied sourly and Henri sighed at that and gave Michel a resigned look.

"Right, as soon as Mama and Alexis are awake we'll open the presents" said Monique, attempting to improve the atmosphere.

"Bon" said Michel.

"Hélène is just finishing the vegetables and Frederik is down in the cellar bringing up more wine, and then we'll all be together" said Monique with a smile.

At that moment the telephone started to ring and Monique answered it.

"Hello, oui, joyeux Noël , oui, oui, merci, oui" she then held out the phone and said "it's your Mother, Angelique."

Michel froze slightly and wondered if he would get a chance to speak to his lovely mistress alone in Grambois.

"Hello, Mama" said Angelique as she put the receiver to her ear "oui, joyeux Noël , oui, oui, we're just going to open our presents, oui, non, I don't know, oui, I'll see you tomorrow, au revoir, au revoir." She then held the phone out to Michel and said "Mama wants to talk to you Michel, I think she wants to thank you for having me here."

"Ah" said Michel as he attempted to look pleasantly surprised.

"Hello, Michel speaking."

"Hello, ma petite" whispered Nicole at the other end.

"Oui, joyeux Noël " he replied.

"And joyeux Noël to you, ma petite, and if you were here right now I'd let you have me up the kitchen wall again."

"Oh, that would be nice."

"And I'd make you do it very slowly, very slowly indeed, so what do you say to that?"

"Look forward to it, I'm sure."

"Do you think you could do it once before Christmas lunch and once afterwards?" she teased.

"Certainly could" he replied, sweating a little.

"Bon, I'll stay very sexy and without my panties, ready for you when you come back here tomorrow and make sure Frederik takes Angelique for a long walk in the afternoon, whatever the weather!"

"I'll do that" replied Michel hastily.

"Au revoir, ma petite, keep thinking of me."

"Au revoir, Nicole, au revoir." And he put the phone down and spoke generally to the family "she just thanked me for having Angelique and said she'd be pleased to see us all tomorrow for a drink at her house."

"Bon" said Henri smiling but Monique and Jackie looked a touch suspicious.

Drinks were then poured and Hélène, Alexis and Frederik joined them and finally Mama was helped from her bed to

Michel's chair.

The presents were assembled and carefully distributed and everyone sat and waited for Monique to say "open yours first Mama." She did as she was told and undid a number of little gift wrapped parcels to reveal lace handkerchiefs, a bottle of her favourite Givenchy perfume, various soaps and a book all about Marseille in the thirties when she was a young girl. It was full of sepia tint photo's which brought memories flooding back to her.

The rest of the family followed Mama and with various cries of 'oh' and 'la la' the presents were viewed and admired. Monique and Frederik clubbed together and had bought Michel an expensive camera and he was somewhat touched by this gift. Monique had her watch and Michel had bought Frederik several books on keeping fit and bodybuilding as well as a neat pair of binoculars. Henri and Jackie exchanged gifts that seemed mundane and showed that somehow they had little interest in one another.

They had all finished unwrapping their presents when the door bell rang. Monique got up and went to see who it was. The family remained silent, all straining to catch the conversation at the front door. They heard Monique say "do come in" and Michel's heart sank as he wondered who was next coming through the door. It was Madame Rochas from downstairs.

"Bon Noël everybody" she chirped.

"Bon Noël" they replied in unison.

"I didn't want to disturb you, but I just wanted to wish you all the very best for Christmas and the new year."

"How kind" said Monique and then asked "will you have a drink?"

"Oh, I'm not stopping, Monique, I don't want to interrupt your Christmas" she replied. 'Not much' thought Michel 'because of you, Mama's been injured and I've had to lie more than usual to keep the peace.'

"Please have a drink" insisted Monique.

"Oh, alright then, just a small cognac" she replied as she sat on Monique's chair nearest Mama.

"And how's your ankle, dear?"

"Very painful at night, but I mustn't grumble."

"Non, we do become such a burden as we get older."

"We do, I know."

"My sister broke her ankle, just like you she fell down the stairs."

"Really?"

"Oui, and it wouldn't heal up."

"Really?"

"Oui, and she's younger than you."

Monique handed Madame Rochas her cognac and she called "salute" to the family, took a good swig and continued "oui, and in the end the doctors gave up with it and amputated her foot."

"Really."

"Oui, it was the best thing really."

"Oui."

"Still, I'm sure that's not going to happen to you, I mean you look quite fit and well for your age. How old are you now then?"

"Eighty next year."

"You're good for eighty, and you should be alright providing you don't put any more weight on, that is."

"Oh, I've given up with diets" replied Mama.

"Oh, never give up, dear, I mean look at me, I've never given up."

'You can say that again' thought Michel.

Madame Rochas finished her cognac and Monique invited her to have another.

"Just a small one, Monique, thank you." Whilst Monique attended to the drink Madame Rochas turned her beady eyes towards Michel who guessed at what was coming.

"I couldn't believe what I read in the paper yesterday about you and that girl being engaged, I thought that there must have been some mistake" she said.

"Well oui and non" replied Michel.

"What d'you mean?" she enquired with interest.

"As far as the press and the public are concerned, I am engaged to Josette Le Franc" and at that Madame Rochas drew in her breathe and whispered "mon Dieu!"

"But in reality, we are not engaged, how could I be? I'm married to Monique."

"Oui" came the mumbled reply.

"The Le Franc woman is in fact part of a special police

undercover operation."

"Mon Dieu!" she whispered again as Monique handed her the small cognac.

"Oui, and I must ask you to keep this information to yourself, and I'm not able to go into any more detail, but be assured, Monique knows everything" said Michel with confidence.

Madame Rochas drank her small cognac in one go and said "I think I ought to go now as I'm expecting my sister and her husband later."

'She can't wait to tell her sister and anybody else who'll listen about my engagement to Josette' thought Michel as the old neighbour abruptly wished them all a 'Bon Annee!' and left the room.

"Thank goodness she's gone" said Michel.

"I think I'm ready for another drink" said Henri.

The atmosphere changed and Alexis started to cry, and between tears she said "fancy her poor sister having to have her foot amputated."

"Never mind" said Hélène "it was for the best in the end."

"Can we change the subject?" pleaded Mama.

"Of course, Mama, now not another unhappy word today" said Monique brightly.

The morning drifted on and soon it was lunchtime. Monique, assisted by Jackie and Angelique kept checking on the state of the turkey and when at last she declared it was ready, she was greeted by a chorus of 'oh, la la.'

Once all the women, except Mama and Alexis, were on their feet, the table was laid and the meal was produced. As Michel and Henri sat and watched, clutching their drinks, they were amazed by the amount of food and the speed of its journey from the kitchen to the table. The women seemed to have formed a chain of food bearers whilst Frederik was busy opening bottles of wine and placing them on the already over loaded table.

"OK, I think we're ready" said Monique as she surveyed the mountain of food with her hands on her hips.

"Bon" said Michel as he staggered to his feet, followed by Henri.

Mama of course had to remain in Michel's chair, opposite the television, and she made a little murmur as her daughter asked "what would you like to start, Mama?"

"Oh, just a little of something, don't worry about me" she replied.

"Alright," replied Monique "leave it to me."

By now everyone was seated around the table and they began to demolish the food that had been placed before them. They had a choice to start of mushroom soup or paté which was followed by the roast turkey, all its trimmings and tureens full of piping hot vegetables. Michel carved the magnificent bird a little unsteadily whilst Monique dished out the vegetables. They all talked volubly as they ate and consumed the wine at a great rate. After the turkey roast they had to sit and talk for some considerable time before pressing onto the selection of cheeses. This move also entailed a change of wine to a heavier Burgundy as they tasted and enjoyed a variety of the very best cheese, Michel finished with his favourite, Roquefort.

Again more time was required before moving on to the thirteen traditional deserts consisting of fruits in syrup, meringues, gateaux's of all shapes and sizes, all with cream, finishing with the famous Gateaux du Roi. At last cognac was consumed by all and then sleepily they left the table one by one to either sit in front of the fire or stagger off to bed. Michel casually glanced at his watch and noted it was almost four in the afternoon. He was the last to leave the table and decided to go and lay down on his bed. He staggered past Henri and Jackie dozing on the settee and Frederik propped up in an armchair with Angelique on his lap, her head on his shoulder. Alexis had been helped by Hélène into their bedroom and Monique followed her husband into their room. She kissed him on the forehead as he slipped into a deep and relaxing sleep.

It was almost seven when Michel awoke with a very thick head. The combination of scotch, wine, cognac, turkey, cheese and cream cakes now played havoc with his stomach as well as his head. He felt full and uncomfortable and remembered that he had promised to go to Josette's for the evening. His mind revolted at the thought of more food but he felt he had to go. He staggered out of the bedroom to find Monique in the kitchen looking dazed as she surveyed the place. It looked like the proverbial bomb blast.

"I'm going out for a while, ma petite" he said.

"Where?" she asked.

"Down to le Vieux Port" he replied.
"Why?"
"Don't ask, ma petite, but I'll be back later I promise."
"OK" she smiled and he was grateful.

Half an hour later Michel was in the sweet embrace of his Fiancé.

"Ma petite" she whispered between kisses "I expected you earlier."

"I'm sorry, darling, but I just had to stay at home, I was trapped, you know how it is, but I'm free now and we're together."

"I know" she replied.

"And remember, it is the very last time."

"Oui" she smiled at that.

They sat on the settee and she asked "what d'you want to drink, ma petite?"

"A scotch, just a small one."

"OK" she replied and added "I hope your hungry." Michel's stomach groaned inwardly before he did, at that remark.

"So, so" he answered.

"Bon, I've cooked quite a lot, but I suppose if you've already eaten….."

"Non, ma petite, you dish it up, I'll eat it" he replied bravely.

Josette had cooked beautifully and plentifully and Michel gazed once more at a candlelit table groaning under the weight of the food placed upon it. They started with fruits de mer followed by roast turkey with all the trimmings, but luckily not so many vegetables as Monique had prepared, followed by the cheese dishes and then the thirteen deserts. Michel managed to complete the meal by having very small portions, but he made it. This is the curse of every man with a mistress; two full lunches at Christmas.

They had hardly finished their cognacs when Michel said "let's go to bed and make love right now."

"Oh, Michel, you're so naughty" she replied coyly.

He laid naked on top of the bed as his beautiful Fiancé slipped out of all her clothes and joined him. They kissed passionately for some time before she straddled him and guided his rigid penis into her body. Michel just lay quietly on his back watching Josette move up and down on him and with each stroke she pushed harder to enjoy the very maximum penetration. He watched her breasts bob up and down in the rhythm and got more turned on as her nipples hardened and extended. She began to sweat a little with the exertion and he reached up to her nipples and squeezed them gently as she began to gasp. Her orgasm was not far off and Michel felt her begin to tighten. He was able to relax and flood her body as she went faster and faster to the end. She fell forward and smothered his face with gasping kisses for some while before she regained her composure.

"Mon Dieu, it gets better every time we do it" she gasped.

"It does, ma petite." he replied before falling into a deep sleep.

He awoke at eleven feeling as bad as any man could. He was solid with food and could hardly move. Josette was still fast asleep and he slipped from the bed determined to go home to Montelivet. He dressed quietly and then gently kissed his Fiancé awake.

"You're not going are you?" she demanded sleepily.

"Oui, ma petite."

"Oh" she groaned and turned her head away.

"But I'll come and see you tomorrow afternoon, as soon as I've got them all up to Grambois."

She did not answer him but started crying and he left her with an "au revoir, ma petite" and returned home.

As he parked the Mercedes he noticed that the wind had subsided a little and the flurry's of snow were becoming heavier. He expected a good covering of snow by the morning and he knew the trip up to Grambois would be a nightmare.

Entering the flat he found Frederik, Angelique and Mama watching the television, Alexis asleep on the settee and everyone else had gone to bed. He left them all to it and went into the bedroom to snuggle up to Monique who lay on her back gently snoring. Slipping in beside her, Michel was soon fast asleep, despite being very full of food.

CHAPTER TWELVE

Friday 26th December

Michel did not wake until almost nine. He heard a considerable noise coming from the kitchen and he decided not to investigate until he had showered and was clean shaven. His body felt like solid mud and his head was heavy and made a ringing sound when he moved.

The shower gave him some relief and a wet shave improved his looks as well as his general well being. Clean underwear and shirt lifted him a little and then he decided to look outside. He opened the window inwards and then undid the shutter and gently pushed it open. Everywhere was white and it looked quite deep. His heart sank and his head started ringing all the more. Today was going to be a nightmare, he felt it deep within.

When he ventured into the kitchen he found Monique being assisted by Jackie, Hélène and Angelique, washing up, drying and tidying at a speed which made his head ring even more. They all looked at him as he stood there, mouthing plaintively "any coffee?"

"Oui, you go and sit down, I'll get it for you" said Hélène briskly.

"Merci" he mumbled.

"Want anything to eat?" asked Monique.

"Oh, non, merci, ma petite, merci" he replied before moving off toward the lounge. Henri was sitting on the settee reading the paper and Mama was watching the television.

"Bonjour, Michel" beamed Henri.

"Bonjour, Henri, Mama." Mama just nodded, her eyes fixed firmly on the screen.

"Sleep well?" enquired Henri.

"Oui, unconscious, and you?"

"Likewise, Jackie didn't snore!"

"She may have done but you didn't hear her" replied Michel and Henri laughed and Michel felt the ringing in his head grow louder.

"Have you seen it outside?" asked Michel as he sat down

slowly on the settee.

"Oui, it looks quite deep" replied Henri.

"We always get it a bit heavier up here, I expect it's fairly clear down town and on the autoroute" said Michel.

"What about Grambois?" asked Henri.

"It could be quite bad up there, especially if it was windy last night, the snow will have drifted" replied Michel.

"Think we'll make it alright?"

"Oui, I'm sure" replied Michel as Hélène brought in his coffee.

"Well I'm looking forward to spending a few days up there with a roaring fire and a comfortable bed" said Henri cheerfully.

"Oui, so am I" replied Michel

"And plenty to eat" added Henri.

"I'm not eating now until next Christmas" said Michel with conviction and Henri laughed.

"Severe snow storms expected within the next twenty four hours" said Mama in a loud voice.

"What, Mama?" asked Michel.

"They've just announced it on the news, a severe weather warning" she said firmly.

"Oh, bon" replied Michel.

"We'd better hurry up and get going to Grambois before it hits us" she said.

"Oui, Mama, just as soon as everyone is ready" replied Michel.

"I'm ready now, I'm just waiting for Monique to pack my bags."

"Right."

"I can't do anything with this ankle of mine" she said plaintively.

"I know, Mama."

Alexis then staggered in clutching a large cup of coffee and said "bonjour, everyone, have you seen the snow outside?"

"Oui, and there's a severe weather warning, more heavy snow, it's just been on the news" replied Mama.

"We'd better get going to Grambois then" said Alexis firmly.

"Oui, I've just told Michel, I'm ready to go as soon as Monique has packed my bags" replied Mama.

"I've already packed mine" said Alexis smugly as she sank into the armchair by Mama.

"Bon." Michel sipped his coffee slowly as Henri asked "shall I take Frederik and Angelique with Jackie and me?"

"Merci" replied Michel "I'll bring everybody else."

"Will you have enough room in the car for all our luggage and the wine?" asked Alexis in a concerned tone.

"Oui, Alexis, and I'm sure if I can't get it all in, Henri will have some spare room in his car."

"Oui, of course, you have nothing to worry about, Alexis" said Henri.

"Bon, you see, I wouldn't like to leave any of the wine, just in case we get cut off by the snow in Grambois."

"We do have a village shop" said Michel.

"I know, but they don't stock very good wines do they?"

"They're alright" replied Michel testily.

Monique joined them and said "we're just waiting for Frederik now and we can start getting organised."

"Still in bed?" asked Michel.

"Oui" replied his wife as Angelique and Jackie slipped into the room carrying cups of coffee.

"Angelique, go and wake Frederik up and tell him we're all waiting for him" said Michel.

"OK."

"Will we get to Grambois alright?" asked Jackie.

"Oui, I've just said to Henri, that it's always worse up here, it'll be clear down the town and on the autoroute" said Michel in an optimistic tone.

"Severe weather warning" said Mama loudly.

"When?" asked Monique.

"The next twenty four hours, it was on the news."

"Better get going then" said Monique.

An hour later found the Ronay family packed and almost ready to go. Michel felt much better as he and Henri went down to the cars to clear the snow and make ready for the journey in convoy to Michel's villa in Grambois. The snow was deeper than Michel had at first thought and it took both men some while to clear it from their cars. Michel's door lock was frozen and it required some hot water from the kettle to free it from ice. Once inside the Mercedes he started it up and put the heater on full. Henri did not have any problems with his Citroen and his new car purred into life.

"We'll have a problem getting Mama into the car with all this snow on the pavement" said Michel. Henri nodded and replied "Let's clear a path for her then."

"Frederik can do that whilst we're loading the luggage" said Michel.

"And the wine" added Henri with a chuckle.

"Drive you mad, don't they?"

"Oui, so remember, no old ladies on the boat!" exclaimed Henri.

"Too right."

Frederik brushed the snow to one side for the safe passage of his Grandma whilst Angelique shovelled some of it away the best she could. Michel and Henri struggled down with all the cases, bags of various sizes, bottles of wine and plastic bags containing food with strict instructions from Monique or Jackie to "make sure you keep this one upright in the boot otherwise it'll spill."

At last everything was aboard the two cars and now only the passengers remained. Back in the flat Michel switched off everything he could, did a final walk round check and locked the door of the flat. As he joined the family in the hallway below, Madame Rochas appeared from her flat and asked "are you off now?"

"Oui, Madame" replied Monique.

"Well, have a good time all of you, and mind the snow; there's a severe weather warning."

"Merci Madame, we know" replied Michel impatiently.

"You don't want to get caught in it you know, some people have been trapped for days and some have even died" she droned on.

"And you have a good time too, Madame" said Michel and continued "now let's get going, you lean on me Mama. Monique, you take her arm and Frederik, you open the front passenger door for Mama when we get to the car. Henri, if you'll kindly stay close behind in case I slip over."

"Oui, Michel" replied Henri as the entourage made it's way out of the hallway, down the steps and towards the Mercedes. It seemed to take an age before the group of shufflers reached the car and Frederik opened the door for his Grandma. With great difficulty, Michel aided by Monique and Henri got Mama into the seat and the door closed. Then Alexis, Hélène and Monique clambered into the back of the well loaded taxi. Frederik and Angelique slipped into the rear of the Citroen and with a flash of his headlights Henri indicated he was ready to go. Michel slipped the Mercedes into gear and attempted to pull away up the hill. The wheels spun and the car never moved a centimetre.

"Just what I need" mumbled Michel under his breath.

"Are the wheels slipping?" enquired Mama as Michel persisted and tried to rock the car.

"Oui, Mama, but we'll get going in a moment" he replied. Well they did not do so and Henri got out of the Citroen and said he could not move either.

"We'll have to clear the snow from the wheels and try and get out into the middle of the road where passing vehicles have packed the snow down hard" said Michel and Henri nodded. With the shovel and the broom Henri and Frederik cleared the snow as best they could from in front of the rear wheels of the Mercedes and Michel managed to drive forward and out into the middle of the road. He and Frederik then did the same for Henri, and once he was stationed behind Michel they set off in convoy towards Grambois.

As Michel had predicted, the roads were clearer in town and they were soon heading out towards the autoroute in the light traffic. It was now almost midday, the temperature had risen and the slush by the roadside was beginning to melt in the faint sunshine as it occasionally appeared from behind the low, grey clouds. As Michel traced the familiar route towards his haven of peace at Grambois he closed his ears to the endless and mindless chatter from the four women in his car. He kept a watchful eye on cousin Henri in the rear view mirror as he did not want to loose them on the way.

Michel's mind was now humming as he examined the possibilities before him. He had decided to go to Le Touquet, but was unsure of two things, should he wait or go immediately after Christmas and should he go alone? He wrestled all the way to Grambois with his dilemma and when he swung the big car into his driveway he was still undecided.

"Here we are" announced Mama triumphantly as Michel stopped the car, slipped from behind the wheel, went up to the front door and unlocked it. Henri pulled in behind the Mercedes and soon everyone except Mama was out of the cars and breathing the crisp, cold air of Grambois. Some snow had fallen but it was light and patchy.

"What a lovely place" said Henri beaming at Michel as he returned to the car to retrieve Mama.

"We like it" replied Michel.

All the women went inside whilst Michel, Henri and Frederik eased Mama out of the Mercedes and shuffled her into the villa. They placed her in the armchair closest to the fire place and whilst Michel and Henri brought the bags in, Monique set alight the prepared open wood fire. With the heating on and the wood fire blazing the temperature in the villa soon rose dramatically.

As the women unpacked the food bags in the kitchen and Frederik stored some of the wine in the cellar, Michel said to Henri "let's have a drink on our own in the other room."

"Good idea."

Henri followed Michel into the spacious dining room where on the dark wood sideboard was a tray with scotch, cognac, martini and gin.

"Scotch?"

"A large one, please."

Michel poured two scotches and handed one to Henri.

"Salute."

"Here's to the future" replied Michel.

"You've a lovely place here, Michel, I'm sure you'll miss it if you come to Le Touquet."

"I'm sure I will, but I don't want to spend the rest of my life being a taxi driver round Marseille, I want to improve my income and have a better life, on your luxury boat for instance." Henri laughed at that.

"You know Henri, I'm ready for a change, I've spent years driving a bloody taxi and being chased around by the likes of Salvator and Gerrard, not to mention some of the customers. Mon Dieu!, there's a story or two I could tell."

"I'm sure" replied Henri.

"And there comes a time in every man's life when he has to

stop and think what he wants to do with the rest of it."

"I agree, I'm the same, I need to re think and start afresh, I'm tired of my business and tired of Jackie, we just sort of jog along, and I don't want that."

"Don't I know."

"I told you before, she's happy to retire to a cottage in Normandy and wait to die, I mean, how crazy can you get?"

"There's more to life than waiting for death" replied Michel.

"Exactly, that comes soon enough in any case."

"So true, look at old man Salvator, plunged off the Corniche to an instant death with millions in a Swiss Bank."

"A good example" agreed Henri.

"Another scotch?"

"Just a large one" replied Henri with a smile.

Michel poured the drinks and as he handed one to Henri he asked "how soon could your Aunt's old house be ready for me to live in?"

"It's liveable now, nothing wrong with it at all, but it's very old fashioned."

"Bon."

"Obviously the water and electricity have got to be reconnected, but it's all there and works perfectly."

"Bon."

"Thinking of coming to Le Touquet soon then?" asked Henri with a smile.

"Possibly, but I'm not sure."

"Do you plan to come alone?"

"I'm not sure about that either" replied Michel.

"Well here's to us" said Henri as he raised his glass.

"To us." They clinked glasses and took a sip as Monique came in.

"So there you are, secret drinkers, never asked all of us if we'd like one" she said firmly.

"We thought you were busy, ma petite, and wouldn't want to be disturbed."

"Really?" she asked with disbelief "well, mine's a scotch and you'd better ask everyone else what they want!"

A little while later they were all seated around the roaring wood fire drinking slowly and methodically. Frederik had set off with Angelique to walk her home and Michel was anxious to escape and see the lovely Nicole. He thought of various reasons for going out but dismissed them all. Then suddenly Hélène said "I think we should all go for a short walk before it gets too cold and dark."

"A good idea" said Michel.

"Mama will you be alright if we all go out?" asked Monique.

"Oui, don't worry about me being on my own, I'll be alright" she said dejectedly.

"Mama!"

"Non, you go, Monique, just leave me my tablets in case the pain gets too much." Michel raised his eyebrows at that and he noticed Henri did the same.

"OK, we won't be long."

"Possibly we could call in on Angelique's Mother and have a drink" mused Michel and Monique looked daggers and replied "we're just going for a short walk!"

"Oui, ma petite."

When they were all snugly wrapped up they set off to walk in the weak sunshine up into the medieval village. Henri and Jackie were enchanted with Grambois and its architecture, church and tiny cobbled streets. They were soon approaching Nicole's house and as they drew near, the door opened and Frederik stepped out. Michel called to his step son who turned and smiled just as Angelique joined him and then Nicole's lovely face appeared. Monique face fell as the walkers drew closer and Nicole called out "bonjour, bonjour, are you coming in for a drink?"

"Oui, merci" replied Michel before Monique could say anything.

"Bon, entre, entre" smiled Nicole and they all trooped in to her tiny, warm house. Michel did all the introductions as Monique put a brave face on the situation. With scotch's and cognac's in hand they all wished each other 'Bon Année '.

"What a wonderful house you have here" said Henri.

"Oui, merci" smiled Nicole.

"How old is it?" he asked.

"I've no idea, but it's very warm and cosy, ideal for just two people" she replied looking at Michel and Monique saw that.

"I'm sure, is it just you and Angelique?" asked Henri.

"Oui, unfortunately" she replied and both Jackie and Monique picked that one up.

Michel did not know how he could manage to see Nicole alone and his brain raced as the women chatted about Christmas and the new year. He could think of nothing and he gave up and left with his party of walkers. They passed Sophia's house and Michel looked up in the hope of seeing the nude artist but to no avail. Then crossing the square, Michel glanced across at the shop to see if Eleanor was about. Again no sign of life and he trooped back with the family to the villa. As they reached the front door and the women filed in, Michel said to Henri "I think it would be a good idea to put the cars away tonight in case we have a heavy fall of snow."

"Bon" nodded Henri and Michel opened the garage door and drove the Mercedes into the warm interior. Henri followed him in and parked next to the taxi in the spacious garage. As he got out he accidentally kicked one of the boxes containing the Romanian sandals and it fell open.

"What are these, Michel?"

"Ah, I meant to talk to you about those, they're high quality Romanian sandals" he replied. Henri was examining them closely and he said "they're not perfect, but they're quite good, ideal for the beach."

"Exactly what I thought" replied Michel.

"How many have you got?"

"I don't know, just that lot against the wall."

"D'you want to sell them?"

"Oui, I do."

"OK, I'll buy them, at the right price of course."

"Of course, but I must tell you, in each pair, one sandal is bigger than the other" said Michel.

"No matter, I can overcome that little problem."

"They're yours then."

"OK, how much?"

"Anything you want to give me."

Henri studied the rows of boxes and said "a thousand Francs be alright?"

"Perfect." They shook hands and left the garage. As they neared the front door Michel asked Henri "what's your address in

Le Touquet?"

"23, Rue Saint Jean, why?" asked Henri.

"Is that near you Aunt's old house?"

"Oui, that's in Rue de Londres, just off Rue Saint Jean."

"Why, Michel?"

"I just wanted to know where to find you, that's all."

"OK" smiled Henri and they went inside to the warm villa.

Monique had made a large pot of coffee and they sat around enjoying that whilst Henri and Jackie waxed lyrical about Grambois. It was late afternoon when Michel whispered across to Monique "I've got terrible indigestion, in fact, I feel quite bad with it."

"We've nothing here, ma petite, I left that sort of thing at Montelivet."

"Never mind, you can't think of everything, I'll just wander up to the store and see if they're open and what they've got."

"OK."

"Shan't be long."

He was out of the house in a flash and round to Nicole's within minutes. He pushed the sonnette and soon was in a firm embrace with his mistress.

"I can't stay long, ma petite" he whispered between kisses.

"Just stay for a moment, Michel, I need you, please."

"I haven't the time, I've come to tell you that I'm going away for a while......"

"Oh, Michel, non, you can't!" she interrupted.

"I must, look, I promise I'll contact you, but I must go!" Tears streamed down her lovely face and Michel felt deeply troubled.

"Au revoir, ma petite" and he kissed her passionately before he left her little house.

It was now much colder, the clouds appeared darker and the promised snow looked as if it was on its way.

Michel hurried along the street to Sophia's house and rang the sonnette. She was delighted to hear his voice and he was soon in her studio smothering her with kisses.

"A drink before you have me right here in front of the fire" she said with a smile.

"A scotch, ma petite, but I can only stay awhile" he replied.

"We'll make it quick, I promise" she replied as she poured a substantial amount of scotch into each glass followed by an ice cube. He watched her and admired her slim figure that was enhanced by a very tight fitting, low cut, red dress. She slumped down beside him on the settee and handed him his drink.

"Salute" said Michel as he raised his glass.

"Bonne année" she replied.

They drank and Michel said "I mean it Sophia, I have to go in a minute."

"Why, for God's sake?"

"I'm leaving Grambois."

"You've only just arrived, haven't you?" she queried.

"Oui, but I've decided to go back to Marseille."

"Have you forgotten something?"

"Non, I've remembered everything."

"Well then, you're not working are you?"

"Non, but I'm going back to Montelivet to pick up some things, then I'm leaving Marseille."

"What for?"

"I've been offered a business opportunity that I really can't refuse."

"Where?"

"In Le Touquet."

"Le Touquet?"

"Oui."

"You're leaving Marseille for Le Touquet? You must be mad!"

"Non, quite the opposite, I've suddenly become very sane" he replied.

"No time for a fuck then?"

"Non" he replied.

"But you will come back some time, won't you?"

"Oui, I expect so."

"Bon, well if you've no time to fuck, you'd better have a quick look at my painting" she said as she waved her hand towards the large canvas on its easel. Michel gazed at her masterpiece and was quite surprised. Sophia had painted in the snowy background and put more detail on the skiers. She had also painted a much larger figure on skis, in the foreground. The skier was a tanned, good looking man with his head slightly turned towards the skiers behind him. All in all, the painting was very good.

"It's not finished yet" she said.

"Maybe, but it looks good, I must say" replied Michel.

"D'you like my handsome ski instructor?" she asked.

"Oui, very much."

"Bon, I'm glad you approve."

"I do."

There was a pause whilst Michel sipped his scotch.

"Have you told Nicole you're going?" asked Sophia.

"Oui."

"And what did she say?"

"I've left her crying" he replied lamely.

"You're all such bastards" she said with feeling.

Michel nodded but made no reply.

"I have to go, thanks for the drink" he said as he stood up.

"Well, I wish you luck in whatever madcap scheme you're involved in" she said.

"Merci."

"In Le Touquet, of all places!"

They kissed passionately for some while and when they at last pulled away from each other, Michel noticed the tears in her eyes.

"Go now before I say something that I'll regret" she whispered.

"Au, revoir, ma petite."

Leaving Sophia he made his way through the arch, across the square to the village shop and was relieved to see lights inside the general emporium. He pushed open the door and was greeted by the smiling face of Eleanor.

"Oh, Michel, ça va?"

"Ça va."

"I didn't expect to see you yet."

"Oui, we came up after lunch."

"Bon, now then, we have some time alone, Jean has only just gone to the bar, so let's pop out the back."

"Non, Eleanor, I haven't got time."

"Come on, Michel, I have needs."

" I've come for some indigestion tablets and to say goodbye."

"Goodbye? Where are you going?"

"Away on business."

"Where to?"
"Le Touquet."
"Le Touquet?"
"Oui."
"What d'you want to go there for?"
"I just told you, business."
"What about your taxi business in Marseille?"
"I'm closing it down."
"Mon Dieu! Will you ever come back to Grambois?"
"Oui, of course."
"When?"
"I don't know yet, now, indigestion tablets please, the strongest you've got."

Eleanor turned to the packed shelves behind her and retrieved a small orange box and placed it on the counter.

"Twenty Francs, Monsieur" she said as the tears streamed down her face.

"Oh, please don't cry, ma petite" said Michel gently.

"I can't believe you're leaving" she replied between sobs.

Michel paused, put the money on the counter, leaned across and kissed her generous lips. She sobbed some more as he smiled and said "au, revoir, ma petite" and left the shop.

Michele hurried back to the villa as the snow began to fall and by the time he reached his front door it had already began to settle. Once inside he produced the orange box for his wife and family to see and went into the kitchen for a glass of water. Monique followed him and said "you were a long time."

"Madame Manton, wanted to chat" he replied as he swallowed two tablets.

"What about?"

"Oh, you know, Christmas, the usual things" he replied.

"Hmmm."

Michel looked hard at his wife and then said "I've got something in the garage for you, come and see." Her eyes brightened and she followed her husband out, slipping on a coat as she came. Michel opened the garage and unlocked the Mercedes.

"Get in" he said and Monique slipped into the front of the taxi and he joined her.

"Well?" she queried.

"I'm sorry, I've nothing to show you, but I have something to say to you." She looked anxious as he continued "I've given this a lot of thought and I want you to hear me out before you say anything." She nodded slightly and was fearful of what was coming.

"To begin with, I have to tell you that I do love you and Frederik in my own special way, and you both are, have been and always will be, a big part of my life." She looked even more anxious at that.

"But the time has come when I know that I need a fresh start in my life and you, ma petite, are very much part of the past that I must leave." She looked shattered.

"I well remember what you said to me here in August, when you told me that together we could look forward to a bright future, and we'd be very well off as Mama and Aunts died off and we would inherit everything they had, but I can't wait, I need a new life now, and I've decided to go to Le Touquet and join Henri in a business venture." The tears streamed down her face as she whispered "you must be mad, don't you know that I love you and I would put up with anything just to keep you with me?"

"I know, ma petite, I know."

"How could you do this to me?"

"Only after a lot of thought, I promise you."

"Is there a woman involved?"

"Non, ma petite."

"Not Josette Le Franc?"

"Non, ma petite."

"You're going alone?"

"Oui."

"When?"

"Now."

"Now?"

"Oui, I'm going back to Montelivet now and off to Le Touquet tomorrow."

"I can't believe this" she whispered as the tears flooded down her cheeks. She remained quiet and then asked "surely you can wait until tomorrow?"

"Non, ma petite, I've made up my mind, I'm going now."

"Spend one more night with me, please" she begged.
"Non, just kiss me and let me go."
"I kiss you now and let you go because I know that you'll come back to me someday soon."

She leaned across and they kissed passionately and Michel began to cry as well. With tears streaming down both their faces she turned and slipped out of the car and whispered "au, revoir."

Michel started the Mercedes and backed out of the garage into the cold, snow laden night. As he pulled forward and away Monique, pale faced, gave him a little wave. He swung the taxi out of the drive and drove swiftly down the hill to join the D road that would take him back to the auotroute and Marseille.

The snow began to fall more heavily and Michele began to wonder if he had done the right thing by not waiting until the morning. On the other hand, if there was a substantial fall of snow he would be cut off and stuck in Grambois with all the family. His headlights illuminated the myriad of large white flakes as they flashed towards the speeding Mercedes. Luckily the traffic was light and only a few mad motorists like himself attempted to drive in the deteriorating conditions. At last he reached the outskirts of Marseille and he deliberated whether to go up to Montelivet or drive straight to the Rue du Camas and Josette. He could not take the chance of getting stuck up the hill outside his flat, so he drove straight to his beloved. The snow was much lighter in Marseille and after parking in the cul de sac he let himself into the flat.

"Oh, Michel" she squealed as he walked through the door and flung his arms around his loved one.

"I thought you wouldn't come tonight, with all the snow" she said with a broad smile.

"Nothing would keep me away from you, ma petite" he replied as he kissed her passionately.

"Bon, now then, a drink?"
"Oui, a very large scotch."
"Bon, so are you staying tonight?"
"Oui, I am" he replied.

"Bon." And as he slumped onto the settee opposite the blazing gas fire, Josette poured the drinks.

"Here" she said as she handed him his glass "here's to us and may we have a wonderful year next year!"

"Here's to us" smiled Michel.

"Now then, tell me, have you spent your last Christmas without me?" she enquired as she cuddled up to him on the settee.

"Oui, I have" he replied.

"Bon, and now it's just us two."

"Oui" he replied quietly.

"You don't sound very sure about it" she complained.

"Forgive me, ma petite, I'm just very tired and a little emotional."

"I understand" she replied.

"I know you do" he said.

"Now then, have you eaten?"

"Non, I haven't."

"Bon, because I've plenty of food, so I'll start cooking while you relax, ma petite."

"Merci, my darling."

A little later Josette went out to the kitchen and started to prepare a light meal for them as Michel, now slightly overcome by events and aided by the amount of scotch he had consumed, slipped into a restful sleep in front of the fire.

An hour or so later, Josette awoke her Fiancé and whispered that the food was on the twinkling, candlelit table. She had prepared a light vegetable soup, followed by tender chicken breasts in wine with a selection of vegetables. A good variety of cheeses followed and then the meal was completed with vanilla ice cream. Cognac and mints rounded off a delicious dinner and Michel realised what a very lucky man he was.

Sitting by the fire they talked about the past year and the future, Josette was unsure as to whether Michel intended to marry her in the spring. He seemed distant somehow and she was concerned.

"Let's go to bed now, ma petite" he whispered and she nodded. He was quickly undressed and lay in the bed as he watched her slowly undress and slip into a beautiful lace baby doll top.

"Are you too tired, ma petite?" she asked.

"Never for you, but it will have to be slow and gentle" he replied.

She laughed as she slipped in beside him. They kissed for an age before he stroked her lovely breasts and then slid his hand down over her smooth stomach to her pubic hair. He touched and gently caressed her clitoris until she was moist and gasping gently. He rolled on top of her and slid with ease into her lovely firm body. His rhythm was gentle and putting his hands behind her back he lifted her slim body a few centimetres off the bed as she wrapped her legs around his waist. He increased his speed as she started to gasp more and more and at last, as he felt her tighten on him he thrust with all his might into her and released every drop he had in his body. They collapsed back on to the bed, panting and smiling with pleasure. When at last they had regained their composure he whispered "ma petite, I have to tell you something."

"What is it?"

"I know this is going to be a surprise….."

"Tell me, tell me!" she demanded, slightly afraid.

"Tomorrow…."

"Oui."

"Tomorrow, we're going to leave Marseille together and start a new life, and next year, sometime in the spring, we'll get married, because I love you so much and I know that I can't live my life without you."

"Oh, Michel, I love you so much."

"I love you too, ma petite, more than you'll ever know."

They kissed passionately for a while before falling asleep entwined in each other's arms and their dreams were as sweet as any lovers could ever be.

Follow Michel and Josette to Le Touquet and read what fate has in store for them in

'CATASTROPHE IN LE TOUQUET'

Printed in the United Kingdom
by Lightning Source UK Ltd.
107271UKS00001B/22-30